BEAUTY WAY

A Novel

BEAUTY WAY

A Novel

Bette Rush

SUNSTONE
PRESS

SANTA FE

Sunstone books may be purchased for educational, business, or sales promotional use.
For information please write: Special Markets Department, Sunstone Press,
P.O. Box 2321, Santa Fe, New Mexico 87504-2321.

Book and Cover design › Vicki Ahl
Body typeface › Laurentine Standard
Printed on acid-free paper

Library of Congress Cataloging-in-Publication Data

Rush, Bette, 1944-
 Beauty way : a novel / by Bette Rush.
    p. cm.
 ISBN 978-0-86534-868-4 (softcover : alk. paper)
 1. Navajo Indians--Fiction. 2. Women authors--Fiction. 3. Rock collectors--Fiction.
4. Vision quests--Fiction. 5. Indian magic--Fiction. 6. Man-woman relationships--Fiction.
7. Spiritual healing--Fiction. 8. Miami Beach (Fla.)--Fiction. 9. New Mexico--Fiction. I. Title.
 PS3618.U742B43 2012
 813'.6--dc22
                              2012002840

WWW.SUNSTONEPRESS.COM
SUNSTONE PRESS / POST OFFICE BOX 2321 / SANTA FE, NM 87504-2321 /USA
(505) 988-4418 / ORDERS ONLY (800) 243-5644 / FAX (505) 988-1025

For Hy, Geraldine, Mitch,
Brian, and Fifi
with a special thank you to
Alex Cigale

1

Nakai sat there waiting for her as he did every Monday, but the white woman was nowhere to be found. The air conditioning system at the library seemed like it was on the fritz, and the humidity this sunny, mid-June afternoon in Miami Beach was starting to sweat his neck under the jet black ponytail. But Nakai had patience. He would wait. Sooner or later she would show.

The Navajo's round dark brown eyes enhanced by his broad high cheekbones were well hidden behind the broad leaf spread of the Wall Street Journal. He knew though that his presence was visible nevertheless and he could feel the eyes of the regulars wondering whether this "dumb Injun" was just as capable as the white man of pissing away money on junk bonds and commodities.

Nakai the Navajo or Nakai the artist was used to getting second and third lingering glances and boy would they ever stare! Everyone that is who made up the SoBe crowd of wannabe starlets on rollerblades and the usual run of the mill New Agers who imagined that every Indian had something profound to say about anything, like he was on some perpetual "vision quest."

Although Nakai sneered at them, something pressed him to dress for the role, and now, sitting here on his slung back, navy blue cushioned seat, he knew very well that the fanciful clothing dressing up his six foot naturally tanned frame, had no resemblance to the cowboy shit worn by his relatives in the Four Corners Southwest. Hell, no standard issue jeans, Texas shirts, or straw panamas like his father wore would do here in South Beach. Shit! He was no bilagana rancher or some Apache wearing a bandana in some John Wayne movie, sitting here and waiting for some asshole to come up and call him "Chief."

No, my friend, he mused. Not only was he beads and buckles and buffalo nickels and painted war clothes. More important, he was a warrior well prepared for both the adoration and the fight!

"Hey, Nakai!" Tony the Cuban, with the title Librarian 2, smiled, passing by his chair.

Nakai nodded then swiftly moved his eyes back to the financial pages.

Sometime back a few years, Tony had asked him to sign a petition to keep the little refugee Cuban kid Elian in Miami. The big drama was that Elian's mother drowned at sea in a reckless, desperate attempt to escape Cuba on some raft with her six year old. The miracle from all that, they said, was that the kid, clinging to the raft, and some conjectured maybe even assisted by some dolphins, managed to hang in there until rescue found him. Once he was safe in Miami, everyone started to throw the political football around. Must they send him back to his father in Fidelland or should he stay here with some distant relatives? The shouting and protesting got out of hand and the plight of Elian Gonzalez made national headlines for days on end.

Nakai still had a mental picture of Tony's eyes, crying out about it, taking it really personal. Now, he tried to remember if he ever did put his signature on that petition but the only thing he could recall about that day was that he was either drunk or in one of his manicky states, or coming down from something he snorted the night before with that German bitch Hannelore. He must've signed the thing or Tony wouldn't always light up when he saw him. Hell, the kid had to go back to Fidel with his father. Bad ending, if you were a Cuban. But Tony was his friend now and maybe he could get some info from him. This was the second Monday the blond woman wasn't here and Tony would know why. He knew all the gossip.

Now, squeezing a silver squash blossom on the turquoise and heishi beads gracing his "buffalo-sized" chest, the Indian sighed loudly. It was too hot to read or pretend to be reading anyway, so he folded the newspaper. He would walk around a bit, scan the Native American section, maybe the magazines and videos and then approach Tony. It had to be done in a casual way, almost accidental, so no one would guess his intent, his purpose.

For instance, no one would ever guess that it bothered him that the blond white woman never gave him notice. Never chose to comment about his odd clothes or jewelry. Never cared to inquire why some full-blooded Southwestern Indian was living here in South Beach instead of on the rez. Instead, she would always be sitting at one of the computers, checking out websites. She was a writer, he knew, from the conversations eavesdropped between her and Jeannie, the other librarian. She wrote travel stories and some holistic stuff. Maybe even stories about Indian things.

Nakai now thought about the rings on the blond woman's fingers. They were large silver ones, with green turquoise raw stones which seemed to be rings of an unmarried woman, who was making an environmental statement as well, he supposed. He figured she had to be about his age or maybe a couple of years more. Maybe 38, but not 40. Though one thing was for sure. Despite her age, she did not have the worn, overly made up, played-out face like the crazy bitch Hannelore. She was fresh faced, almost naïve looking and somewhat vulnerable, and those were the very qualities that made Nakai want to know her.

Once he thought he caught her eyeing his Birkenstocks, particularly the intricate beading patterns he had worked into them about four Octobers ago, during the cleanup days after Hurricane Irene. While Hannelore spent hours, mopping up and fussing over her flood-stained drapes and rugs, Nakai found himself caught up in an exciting spate of creativity, resulting in these now worn out sandals that graced his calloused red-tanned feet.

The sandal on the left foot, the one Nakai thought of as "the feminine," was topped with a silver, black, gold and red beaded widow spider to honor the sacred Spider Woman who the Navajos believed taught them how to weave. The right sandal was topped with a beaded fat horny toad, Nakai's favorite protection symbol, in desert shades of turquoise, coral and sand.

For a fleeting moment on that particular day he considered approaching her as she started coming his way. Then, all at once, something remarkable happened that stopped him dead in his tracks. It was the clothing but not anything she was actually wearing, which he had noticed earlier was a pair of jeans and some T-shirt with "Colorado" printed across the bustline. It was the countenance that now gripped him and had him frozen, as he stumbled backward against the gray steel file cabinet.

Just like in some fantastic child's fairy tale, she came to him as an Indian princess in a blousy white shirt with flowing pink satin ribbons and a deep purple-velvet, ruffled, three-quarter length skirt, marvelously enhanced by an oversized old silver concha belt. Her hands were stretched out in his direction, calling him in, and they too sparkled with wide silver cuff bracelets, stamped with the wind and the sun and arrows moving in all four directions. And there was turquoise, that superb Sleeping Beauty, baby blue natural turquoise on her fingers and ears and in her hair.

Nakai felt dizzy just thinking now about that day, remembering how she presented herself to him as if in a three-dimensional dream. At the time, he wanted her completely -- a total possession of mind, body and soul. He swore to himself that he would be good to her, even during those unbalanced times he got possessed with demons. He would smother her with gifts that made her smile, and most of all, he would take her to the desert to his father, to the land of his people, his ancestors, to his Grandma Shima who passed on to the spiritual world. Nakai had been hugging the steel file cabinets when he finally came to his senses that day. He had wondered then as he wondered now. Did that really happen? Was I dreaming? Was it my mind playing tricks? Was I on acid? Maybe.

When Nakai walked out of the library that day of the dream, the answer presented itself in a familiar way. He had walked across the wide expanse of Collins Avenue to a grassy beachfront area shaded by the playfully swaying fat leaves of sea grape trees, where he sat down and prayed. At the time, he had been wearing a short-sleeved shirt, open to the chest, with two hand painted red and blue feathers and a yellow lightning arrow gracing the back. It was good protection because you never knew who could be coming at you.

The Navajo's prayer that day was to Shima, his grandmother, and it was in Dineh. Did he see what he thought he saw? Was his mind clear? He begged for an answer, for some sign. Then, miracle of miracles! Nakai felt a warm breeze kiss his cheeks, a kiss that reminded him of his dear grandmother. A few seconds after, looking over at his shirt sleeve, he saw the pretty red ladybug, riding up to his shoulder, happily telling him it was all for real.

Six months ago was when it all happened, right before Christmas. Six months had passed, Nakai now lamented, and he still had not made a move toward her. Worse still, maybe now she was gone forever.

Nakai proceeded to the checkout desk, carrying a DVD of Sherman Alexie's "Smoke Signals" and an audio self-help book by Marianne Williamson.

Tony seemed like the type to be interested in that New Age sort of thing. He waited patiently for Tony to finish helping some woman who had no library card and spoke only Hungarian.

"Hey, Nakai," Tony smiled, leaning over the desk. "That's a great Indian movie you got there. It's from that book about the Lone Ranger and Tonto, or something like that."

Nakai nodded, kind of surprised that Tony knew about anything Indian.

"That woman with the blond hair, that writer, once told me about it," he quipped. "I told her I'd read it and here it is right on the shelf!"

"So, Charlie recommended this one?" Tony grinned, running it through the scanner.

Nakai chuckled to himself. Charlie! What a funny name for a woman! He decided to keep his cool though, knowing that he less he said, the more Tony would offer. The bilagana, the white man was like that. White people had a hard time keeping their silence.

"She's still in Nevada," Tony said. "Jeannie had an email from her yesterday."

"Las Vegas, huh?" Nakai asked casually, as if to just make some conversation.

"No, not Vegas. She's out there doing some wilderness story. Hunting for minerals in the desert north of Reno." Tony handed Nakai the checked out material and all the info he needed. Her name is Charlie. She likes the desert. She likes desert stones. She's coming home.

Walking out of the library now, Nakai felt the oppressive wet heat penetrating straight into his nostrils. The deep purple wall cloud forming in the Everglades far to the west, would move his way soon enough and he could look forward to a drenching lightning storm by evening. It was always that way here in summertime. So different from the desert dryness and sudden strong summer winds of his childhood home in northern Arizona, in Chilchinbito.

Nakai was hearing his stomach growling and knew it was time to walk the six blocks south to his high rise apartment where Hannelore would be cooking dinner. It was fried chicken tonight because he saw her defrosting the chicken quarters that morning. Damn, he really hated chicken and that bitch knew it, which was why she cooked it at least twice a week out of spite. He wondered if she got that job she applied for yesterday at the nursing home because they needed money to meet the $1300 rent, since his silver work and art were not selling. The job was for a breakfast cook and Hannelore would be good at serving up some good French crepes for all the senile old people there and at least they wouldn't have to taste her fried chicken.

Opening the small leather purse he had been toting over his left shoulder, Nakai began to count out some bills and change amounting to about $11 that he had managed to swipe from Hannelore's handbag earlier in the day. He was in a good mood after finding out about the blond white woman, and even though he lied to Tony about knowing her, it did kind of feel like he and this Charlie were already friends. Now there was no way he was going to spoil this day by looking at Hannelore's witchy face across a plate of chicken legs!

An "S" bus was now headed toward him from the opposite direction, going north to Aventura and Nakai ran toward it, waving it down. Plunking in a bunch of quarters for the fare would still leave him enough cash for three beers at Johnny's Tavern on 65th Street. It would be sufficient to get him started before the ladies came in and made the usual fuss over Nakai the Navajo and Nakai the artist. Yes, it would be a good night after all. The ladies at the bar would buy him a hamburger or a roast beef on rye, and then they would give him anything else he wanted.

2

From her angle, some 25 feet from the massive gray-green clay banks of the Pinfire Opal Mine, Charlie Landers could see the fiery dark clouds and streaks of zig-zag lightning, now arriving as they did nearly every summer afternoon, way up here in Virgin Valley, Nevada.

Scary as those thunderstorms were, they seemed like comic relief from the mosquitoes and horseflies that busied themselves by stinging the miners and then sucking them up as they swung their six pound picks at the hard clay, hoping those rainbow-colored opal eyes would break loose before closing time.

Charlie, her shoulder length gold hair flowing with the north breeze, sat there, almost hidden in the high piles of tailings, those leftover shards from the miners of many yesterdays, who had come here with glorious dreams and then left exhausted, often dejected and mostly empty-handed.

At the Pinfire Mine today were Sander Miller, the University of Miami geology instructor, his cowboy cousin Doyle and his wife Kathy, all Charlie's traveling companions. Then there were the other opal miners, mostly familiar faces that turned up every summer in this forgotten corner of the earth. Mineral hunters, all of them were, seeking the prize that would surely come with earnest effort, a return on the 50 bucks they had plunked down to the mine owners for the privilege of being there.

All of them now, save for Charlie, were at it, pounding furiously into the clay. They went at it mercilessly, relentlessly, all the time checking for anything shiny, any black glass that might be opal and not obsidian, any fiery seam that could suddenly emerge from inside a 40-million-year-old petrified wood limb or some rotted chunk of log that could be the start of a fist-sized handful of brilliant pinfire opal. Virgin opal.

Charlie had her eye on Doyle now, as he climbed atop the clay bank, carrying a heavy lengthy steel pry bar. Almost on cue, she was prompted to zoom in on him with her Canon mini digital, kept secure in the upper pocket of her trail jacket, and Doyle, knowing and appreciating what was coming, tipped his leather black wide-brimmed hat in her direction, just before lifting the steel bar way over his head for effect.

It was the six foot two Texan's turn to perform the backbreaking job of clearing the accumulating overburden, which was now hanging menacingly above the miners' heads. Doyle's sarcastic name for it was "widowmaker" and Charlie was used to listening to his horror stories about all the body parts that could be instantly smashed should the weighty, rocky clay crack open and crash down on one of them.

Charlie sighed, snapping away, catching Doyle at his happiest. In a couple of short weeks she would be back in Miami, studying all these travel photos, remembering Doyle and how he enjoyed showing off his rugged smile, how his 40-year-old body still looked solidly packed in his Levi's, how sexy he looked, holding up that silvery pry bar to the heavens.

And then, there was Kathy, sitting there, all tightly wound up, with that world-weary expression on her lined face. Kathy never hid her dislike of the opal game, and Charlie let out an impulsive laugh, imagining all the arguments they must have had during the planning of this very unromantic vacation trip. Now, Kathy was taking something large and purplish from Sander, something he had just taken out from the clay, and Charlie could tell by the wild, contorted look on Sander's sunburned face that it was indeed precious opal.

The walk from the tailings to the bank was muddy with caking wet clay, a reminder of the recent snowy winter in northwestern Nevada.

"Hey, Sander!" Charlie yelled, making her way slowly through the mucky clay, watching her work boots turn orange from the mess. "Get that opal out of the sun before it cracks! I want a good picture!"

Cracking or crazing, as they called it, was common to much of the opal uncovered in Virgin Valley, due to its high water content, but that never stopped anyone from digging there. Ever since way back in 1919, when someone unearthed a pound of fiery opal, black as coal, that sold for $120,000, before finding its way to the Smithsonian, people came here hoping for a similar prize.

Sometimes, they would get a taste of those flashes of purple, green and red fire and just the year before, Charlie and her companions were witnesses to the thrill.

For 85 year old Big Ernie, it was never too late. Fifty summers, four days a week, two months at the mine was a gamble like playing the slots in Reno. No fancy tools for Big Ernie. No sirree. Every morning, the old farmer from Arkansas would plunk down his 50 dollars, and carry his special homemade tool down to the banks, not caring that the other miners would laugh at his hokey accent or the steel rod, hooked onto a doorknob, that he used to negotiate the tough clay bank. Then, nobody laughed that steaming hot day last year, when Big Ernie uncovered a jet black opal log so huge and full of fire that it took six local miners, working all afternoon and late into the night to help dig it all out. It was a spectacular find that easily made addicts out of all of them.

Anthony Newman, who was banking next to Sander, was already an addict when Big Ernie found the "glory hole." Newman spent all year saving up his salary from a factory job somewhere in Oregon to spend it all here at the Pinfire Mine. On Memorial Day weekend, when the Virgin Valley mines officially opened, the 30 year old Newman would be waiting in his classic outfit of camouflage parachute pants, with lots of pockets and leather holsters to hold all his mining tools. Newman's 1978 rusted brown Jeep was a regular at the mine's free campground, and it would be there every night from Memorial Day to the "last chance" Labor Day weekend three months later.

Sander laughed, checking out Charlie's clay packed boots, and held out the sparkling two by two piece of purplish opal, that was throwing out some green fire in two corners. He ran his fingers through his sandy brown pony tail, half hidden under a dusty layer of dried clay, and Charlie was happy to see he looked satisfied.

Banking opal this season had been pretty fruitless, and now, well into day five, Charlie calculated the total loss for all of them at $750. Pinfire made a profit no matter, even if the mine owners decided to open up banks that yielded next to nothing. Their claim was that the opal was virgin and whether you found it or not was really an unknown. She sighed, picturing Sander's lovely opal encased in a long glass vial filled with water, to be admired, and cherished forever.

Sander loved the area, which was the main reason they were all there. As a geologist he had a fascination with this desolate region, which was formed, he theorized, as a result of ancient volcanic actions that buried an entire forest. The trees, he and other experts said, drifted westward on a great lake bed, that was now dry, called Lake Lahontan. The tough clay that was all around and that now covered the rotting wood was formed as the result of the changes in the volcanic ash. As the wood rotted away, it was sometimes replaced by opal, which is why you could find opal logs and twigs and branches here.

So, while Sander clutched his find, looking like a happy kid in a toy store, Charlie saw it more realistically. Their sole find for the trip not only cost a hell of a lot of money, but also there would be no story to come out of the mine this year. No article for any of her magazines. She gave Sander a quick hug of praise and slowly made her way back to the tailings area, away from the diggers, the reality of failure slowly taking hold. Now, the memories of Big Ernie's famed opal that fired up the pages of so many human interest and travel magazines were but a grim reminder of life's vicissitudes. Last year's exciting destination could be this year's nowhereland.

The tears coming to Charlie's eyes this moment, though, had little to do with opal, or the magazine, and everything to do with Link. The sparkle of Sander's opal had brought it all back, the good times, when she would bring back that beautiful opal to her writing partner and he would ooh and aah about it, wishing he were well enough to do Virgin Valley.

Link had died of a heart attack a day before last Thanksgiving and Charlie was the one who found him all slumped over on the floor of his Miami Beach efficiency. One instant and his lifelong struggle with a bad heart was over. One instant and that mustachioed lunatic of a man who had joined her for coffee each morning at Jeffrey's on Lincoln was gone. Fourteen years they were together but then nothing lasts forever. The memories of that horrible morning and the lingering sadness that followed stayed with Charlie, day and night, a thick lump in the throat that would never go away.

For Charlie, the tears would well up at any moment, from a word, a picture, the sight of a shared friend or someone they didn't like, or even now, from Sander's happiness at finding an opal. It made no sense, that the tears would follow her everywhere, no matter how far she traveled, even to this remote corner of Nevada wilderness they called Virgin Valley.

3

The telephone rang twelve times before Shash Benally finally heard it and rushed to pick up the receiver. "Ya'ah'teeh!" the elder Navajo's voice boomed. They always called when he was in the bathroom, while he was taking a shower or while he was busy folding his long silver hair into the strip of white cloth, into the figure-eight type bun he called a "chongo."

A quick scan of the caller I.D. showed the familiar area code 305. Miami. It was Nakai, the youngest of his four sons, who liked to call real early, right after sunrise, like now. It was 7:30 Albuquerque time.

"Ya'ah'teeh, Shizhee!" His son's voice belted out. Nakai could hear some laughter in that sound, along with some excitement too, and the old man knew he would be in for some mainline "dola bichon" or like the bilagana called it, bullshit.

Not a week would pass that Shash did not receive some call from Nakai about some millionaire who thought his son was just the cat's meow. That someone was always going to bail them all out with all kinds of money so Shash could get away from Albuquerque forever and move back to his beloved birthplace in Chilchinbito. The problem was that it never happened. It was all talk.

"Pop," Nakai started off real slowly, "do you have a feeling today that something is about to happen?"

""Sure, I do," Shash laughed. "I studied the way the sun looked yesterday and the way the moon behaved last night and I'm sure the world is going to hell!"

Shash could hear Nakai's laughter with his good ear and it sounded a little too strong. It might have been cocaine talking or maybe what the bilagana doctors, the PhD's called the bi-polar thing. The split.

"Pop," Nakai's voice began to race so fast that Shash could hear the saliva rolling. "There is a yellow-haired woman with a man's name, and she can change into a spirit. I saw her do it like our holy Changing Woman. And, pop, she's a writer and she's going to tell everyone all about the government and big mining and what they are doing to the people's land. The uranium too," Nakai rambled on, "and the water, and all the stuff going on at Black Mesa with Peabody Coal!"

"That's good, son," Shash said quietly. "Make sure you tell her to write about that march they sent your grandfather on. Tell her it was no Navajo Long Walk like all the liars call it. It was a death march, my friend. Oh, and one more thing," Shash remembered. "Tell the woman with the yellow hair that we need money to build a good hogan out there. I want to tear down the old one. It's ugly, with all the old railroad ties we had to use to make it. It's too small to live in and it's not safe besides because it doesn't have a good foundation."

"I'll move on it fast," Nakai whispered. "We are going to have the best hogan. Tourists are gonna come from all around, from Europe. We'll charge them to stay there too. Hey, I know a guy who does solar panels and he can make the hogan self-contained besides."

"It all sounds good to me," Shash repeated with finality in his voice. "I'm looking forward to it. Now, I have to get going on the day, so hagoonee, Shi'yaazh," he said, ending the conversation.

Oh, well, Shash chuckled to himself, walking back into the bathroom. Maybe if you thought about these things long and hard enough, they could happen. Maybe some bilagana's article could catch on and get some attention. Then the government could get those BIA guys to figure a way out of the whole mess they created. After 50 years of this old house here in Albuquerque, with its peeling paint and falling plaster, Shash was more than ready to walk in real beauty.

Each morning at sunrise, the old man would go to the backyard, stand in the middle of the garden Bessie had created so long ago, hold out the blue flowered tratadine to Johona'ai, the Sun, and say in his own Dineh language, "Let me walk in beauty. Let me return to the land of my ancestors, where my birth cord lays buried out there in the sheep corral." Shash would then call in the sun, with cupped hands, feel the warmth and know that it all could be possible.

Soon, he would leave the garden and face the reality of what was. The door to his oldest son's room, his namesake's room, would be wide open, with his dirty underpants rolled in balls on the floor, the bed unmade, and with the all-around smell of something bad. It told him something. The only way he could get out of here was to sell out Shash Jr. and how did a Navajo do that? Could an old man throw his son in some white man's jail so he would stop stealing his silver? So he would stop snorting junk from a can at two in the morning? So you wouldn't have to listen to silence at the other end of a phone line and the caller I.D. saying "Anonymous"?

From the half-opened bathroom door, Shash now scanned the hallway for his 45-year-old junkie son and his alcoholic buddy, Johnny. Some reward, he shrugged, shaking his head in disbelief. All those years working his butt off as an electrician at Los Alamos, exposing himself to radiation and who knows what kind of chemicals, and being told to wear his hair cut short like the bilagana. And for what? So Bessie who passed to the spiritual world just four years ago would have the money to feed their five little ones, so they wouldn't have to depend on the crappy government handouts of block yellow cheese and powdered milk! So they could live here in Albuquerque and send the kids to public school and not some Catholic boarding school where the nuns used to beat the shit out of you for talking Dineh!

Shash knew it was all a mistake taking them off the reservation, but you couldn't turn back time. So many Dineh had all but forgotten the old ways. So, you wound up with a drug addict son and Nakai the manic something or other, and Jimmy who ran away 20 years ago and never came back and Sherman the drunk who only visited when he needed a handout. It was no surprise that his only daughter Lily moved far away to Montana just to forget about it all.

Now in his bedroom and satisfied that his son was out of the house, Shash carefully took down the watercolor painting of Monster Slayer, the Navajo warrior of the Creation Story. The picture that his Lily drew back in high school was positioned next to his clothes closet, and it concealed the fuse box underneath that served as Shash's hiding place for his Bank of America checkbook.

Slipping the checkbook into his jeans pocket, Shash walked out to the garage to check the mileage on his 1995 Ford pickup. The odometer read 132,035, which meant that Shash Jr. drove it less than a couple of miles just the night before.

"Central Avenue," Shash said to himself. "He bought his stash right close to here on Central." He thought for a few minutes about what piece of silver jewelry from the house his son might have pawned to get the junk. Then, slowly, dragging his left leg a bit, a habit of many years as a result of an old World War II injury, he climbed into the pickup. Yeah, that knee kicked up all the time, but it was nothing he couldn't live with and had never stopped him from getting on a horse in his young days.

Easing the old truck out of the driveway, he cautiously made his way around the other two rusted early 1980s Chevy sedans that kind of hugged each other on the overgrown grassy swale in front of the house. Just this week, he mused, the city sent him another notice to do something about those cars, calling them an eyesore to the neighborhood. But Shash was not about to part with Bessie's old Chevy and the other one was Jimmy's. He could come back for it one day. You never knew about those things. Besides, Shash let out a laugh, the city big shots had a nerve saying that about his cars when the whole neighborhood was an eyesore!

The elder Benally was headed to the Sandia Pueblo Casino for the breakfast buffet and also to carry on some personal business up top the mountain at Sandia Crest. It kind of depressed him to look out the window at Old Town these days and, since Shash Jr. was doing his business on Central, he had no use for the coffee houses there anymore. The motels probably housed a bunch of crack addicts these days because the cops seemed to be making raids now almost every night. Last week they closed some old motel and arrested everyone inside except for his son, who was able to slide his slim frame in the laundry closet and escape notice.

Catching a glimpse of himself in the car mirror made Shash smile. He liked the way he looked in his old Stetson. Even at his age, the men still envied him. His jet eyes were still as sharp as nails and the bones in his face were strong too. Yes, he still fit his name Shash, which is a bear in bilagana language, and he intended to stay that way until he reached 103, the age his own mother, his Shima, was when she passed on to the spiritual world.

The road to Sandia Mountain had special landmarks that withstood the test of time and development on the outskirts of Albuquerque. The purple mesas and clumps of desert wildflowers marked the distance for Shash and pointed him in the right direction. He pushed down hard on the gas pedal, bringing his speed up to 80 so he could get to the casino faster and not have to look at all the changes that marred his memories.

Slowly and deliberately, the fingers of his left hand traveled to that part of his neck where his silver hair folded neatly into the white cloth of the chongo, where in a stoned rage, Shash Jr. had tried to strangle him the night before. Then, neither changing expression nor blinking an eye, Shash the old warrior looked straight ahead and began to sing out loud, "Hay nay ahh ahh."

4

Lincoln Davis was 12 years old when he encountered his first UFO. It was noontime, or thereabouts, when he found himself walking through the double doors of the school cafeteria and onto the outdoor basketball courts where they lined up each morning for homeroom.

When a few years older, and investigating such phenomena became a career choice and obsession, Link would describe that UFO as a "classic, metallic, disk-shaped object that hovered some 20 feet above the steel fence that enclosed the schoolyard from the east side."

At the time of the encounter, however, Link just stood there, his pale blue eyes transfixed in adolescent awe, removing his glasses, then putting them back on again to be sure of himself and of the gun metal silvery craft that loomed as large as the schoolyard itself.

He was about to hustle back inside to report his discovery to Mrs. De Leo, the cafeteria aide, who might then forgive his transgression of cutting lunch period, when a glowing red light from the craft started blinking and the strange saucer took off at breakneck speed.

Ambling back now, in a somewhat dazed state, Link was relieved to see an empty cafeteria. So, everyone had returned to class without ever knowing what he did about the mystery craft, and the fact that he had somehow spirited himself in and out of the cafeteria unnoticed. It afforded him time to sit down on one of the long wooden benches and do some hard thinking.

What he had just witnessed was real, incredible and definitely from out of this world, or at least from out of the world that he knew. He was also keenly aware that in Jersey, especially in the part of Hoboken where he lived, you had to watch closely what came out of your mouth. The late sixties were a time of social change and old habits died hard. For Link, battles with rheumatic fever had kept him too weak to battle the muscled Italians, who sometimes mocked him because his named sounded "colored," and the Irish gangs who threatened him and called him "Jesus killer" because he was Jewish.

These vignettes from Link's life were coming to Charlie now in small bits, almost in beat with the slow steps of her moccasins that lightly kissed the cracked white sands of the Black Rock Desert. Her late partner's childhood had been one of illness much like her own, coupled with deprivation and poverty. Mostly, he had just spent a lot of time at his bedroom window, watching all the other kids play basketball or stickball or riding sleds in the cold Northeastern snows. She had an image of Link, a skinny kid, huddled in his bed, wrapped in a woolen itchy blanket, trying hard to keep out the dampness that would seep through the cracks of the old bedroom walls of the housing project.

Link's creative writing abilities stemmed from those early years, and became a lifeline starting at age ten, when his dad, Morty, a hard-working 35-year-old factory foreman, suffered a sudden fatal heart attack. At first scared and devastated by the loss, Link soon found comfort in the world of escapism. So, after school each day, while waiting for his mom to come home from her assembly line job at the doll factory, the ten-year-old would pass the time creating simple dramas and plot lines for his favorite actor Don Murray. Once he even wrote a song about finding love in a phone booth and sent it off to Perry Como to help revive his flagging career.

The sighting of the UFO a couple of years later served Link by sending a new urgency and direction for his writing abilities. In short, it was to be the opening act of Link's lifelong quest to seek out the paranormal and the unknown, and it was this mission that sent him across continents to a meeting with guru Sai Baba and Israeli metal bender Uri Geller. And it was on a plane, returning from Lima, Peru, and a talk with relatives of the "psychic surgeon of the rusty knife," Arigo, where Link met Charlie.

From her window seat next to this man who was at least ten years older than she was, Charlie elaborated on her unsuccessful experience trying to get color photos of the Nazca lines for the Miami Herald. At the time, she had been discouraged that her career was going neither here nor there and was impressed that Link seemed to know exactly what he wanted out of life.

Now, walking the desert, she thought about that serendipitous encounter that turned into a 14 year partnership. She and Link often talked about the fact that the meeting was probably no coincidence and that everything in life, provided you did not interfere too much, followed a certain pattern.

Charlie took a long swig of spring water from the half-gallon plastic jug she always carried along when she walked the high Nevada desert. The sun was way up there now and the temperature would likely top out at about 90. It had been awhile since she had last charted her surroundings and she carefully checked the four directions to make sure they were familiar ones. Deep stretches of purple plateaus and brushy high canyon came to her from the west, the narrow gravelly road zigzagged north, the craggy dark formation called Black Point was to the south and the clean vast flat sanded playa entered from the east.

It was easy to lose your bearings, walking about in this isolated, amorphous mass of grayish white sand, sage and rabbit brush. Get distracted for a moment by a prancing cottontail or the rattle of something potentially threatening and your familiar mesa might fade from view or decide to lose you behind a cloud. Then, thinking of Link and all the things that could have been was distracting enough.

Yes, 14 years was a marriage of sorts, she mused, and yet they had never even lived together or even known each other in the Biblical sense as the saying went. She loved him with all her being and he loved her as well, and the entire Miami Beach probably figured there was a whole lot going on with them. Charlie sighed, remembering. Link's heart could not handle the excitement of a sexual relationship and he had seemed almost grateful not to have that distraction. Then, Charlie had her story too, and she reluctantly admitted to Link that her desires had been killed a long time back by a predatory uncle who wounded her for life in a bedroom walk-in closet. Smiling sadly now, Charlie was nevertheless convinced that what she and Link had was a marriage of minds and hearts, and maybe that was marriage in the purest sense.

Now, resting on top of a small circular mound in the thick of the sagebrush, Charlie toyed with a piece of shiny orange and white spotted jasper. There were footsteps off in the distance. Probably Sander and Doyle, she surmised, looking for the larger jaspers that they could cut and polish and work into cabochon jewelry.

It was a desert of such stark beauty and power and she wished at that moment that Link could have made the trip here at least once. He would have seen right away that this was a place where anything could happen, and maybe last night, she was thinking, something did. Charlie shivered now, remembering.

The night before had been cool and clear and she had fallen asleep by a spring, close to the opal mine, where the stars sparkled like bright spirits on the tired rockhounds. Then, sometime, around two in the morning, Link came to her in a dream. Only it was not actually a dream but what Link would have called an "after death experience." Yes, it may well have been that, she thought, a psychic meeting of sorts with a loved one who had passed away.

That the ghost that came to her was Link didn't startle her as much as the way it happened. After all, Link had been in her thoughts for much of the afternoon at the mine and she was sure that he had been well embedded in her subconscious, so to speak. So, when she woke up shortly after the encounter, she immediately grabbed her journal, put a flashlight to it and began to scribble down what happened. She was not about to chance leaving it to memory for the following morning. Now, resting on the small rocky mound, she took out the journal from her trail vest pocket to look at her amazing entry:

"Somewhere in the middle of the night, Link called me on my cell phone. It rang twice, and then when I answered and heard his voice, I was startled for two reasons. First of all, the cell doesn't get any signal way out here in the middle of nowhere, and then, well, Link is dead. Yes, he is and yet he spoke loud and clear, asking me about my day, and if I found anything out of the ordinary to write about. He said something like 'I guess it will be awhile before we see each other again but I will find a way tomorrow to visit with you.' Then, his voice turned sad and he said he had to go. The thing is that I could see him very clearly, even though we were talking over the phone. He was his tall, lanky self, dressed in a beige shirt and matching slacks that I had never seen him wear before. His blue eyes were minus the glasses and his silly curly mustache and smile were disarming. The reality is that this was not a dream. It was something else. Of this I am sure."

The sky, as far as the eye could see, was a brilliant blue, with puffy bursts of clouds rising to the east of the playa, all giving it a slick sheen that blended earth and sky in one seeming continuous flow. The pattern had a discernable effect on the desert denizens that, to Charlie, seemed quiet and contemplative. A blue-striped lizard, poised on a silver-gray rock, kept the stillness. A cottontail, usually fearful of humans, sat gnawing contentedly at a yellow cactus flower, its long ears nearly within the grasp of Charlie's hand.

This special feeling, she thought, could be what Link often referred to as a universal understanding, something that she had never really grasped until now. As she sat there mesmerized by the changing patterns of the high clouds moving in the breeze, Charlie realized that you could not understand this in a million years, until the moment hit you, until it happened to you.

Letting out a long hard sigh, Charlie could now feel a hurt welling up in her throat. Somewhere along the way in this lifetime she had missed the boat. Now with Link gone, so was her only chance to experience real love. The moisture of tears felt weighty on her cheeks before she realized that she had been crying for some time. One day, she silently swore to herself, a good man will come to me again and this time I won't let him get away.

Charlie bowed her head now, and then looking between her moccasins, she saw something incredibly sparkly. There were two black obsidian arrowheads shining up at her from the cracked desert sand.

5

The old cedar tree jutted out precariously over the edge of some loose red boulders about 8000 feet up toward the crest of Sandia Mountain. Looking up at it from even just a few feet below, its branches resembling long arms that reached out to the city of Albuquerque, the tree appeared as if it were sucking up all the haze and pollution from way below.

In his younger years, Shash would get in his pickup and arrive at the visitor's center by six every morning and from there he would begin the hard upward climb to the top. So fearless was he then that often in the cold blackness of winter he would make that ascent dressed merely in sweatpants and a heavy sweatshirt despite the way below zero temperatures you would get high up in these mountains. Sometimes the earth would be covered in a foot or more of snow, but no matter, for Shash had always counted on making it to the old cedar tree for sunrise prayer. Then, once there, he would face to the east, to the sun, and with arms outstretched, he would call in the warm energy of Johona'ai Shiitra, my Father the Sun.

Now, with his elder years catching up on him, and the leg giving him some problems, he mostly had to settle for something far less majestic, like a sunrise prayer around the old neighborhood. So, instead of looking forward to the grand cedar tree, he had to settle for the little yucca at the corner of Daytonia in Old Town, a short couple of blocks from the house, and to boot, there were the dogs barking, breaking up the sound of silence and the pleasure of the wind at his back.

Sometimes he was able to quiet the dogs by shouting out their "secret names" in Dineh. The elders knew that every animal had a name that described who they were, just as he Shash was named for the bear because of his stamina and strength, and if you revealed that to the animal, they would know that you had no fear of them. This could be especially valuable knowledge if you happened to accidentally run into a bobcat or a rattlesnake. Knowing the secret name could get you out of trouble for sure.

"Ben ah shana hey, eeeeeeeh!! Shash now sang out the Shield Song, the prayer asking for the protection of the sacred horny toad. His steps were laborious as he made his way slowly up the mountain feeling the heat of late morning come up on him. In his jeans pocket, Shash carried a worn brain-tanned leather pouch that contained a small piece of black jet, a pearly abalone shell and a piece of coral that Nakai sent him from Miami Beach. Today, they were carried with one purpose in mind and that was to quiet the coyote.

The Navajo understood that the coyote and also the owl carry messages in the night and that those messages usually meant trouble. For Shash, four times the coyote had sent him warnings and today he was going to right things with the beast before they got out of hand. If getting away from his doped up son, if getting the new hogan in Chilchinbito, if getting pure water out there was going to be more than just wishful thinking, then he would need a brand new start. His son Nakai's empty promises meant nothing, but satisfying the coyote was the old way of doing things.

The episodes with the coyote went way back in time to a warm night in June, maybe ten years ago, when Shash had been planning to visit his niece Marjo in Wide Ruins for her high school graduation. The night before he was staying with his sister Rose just north of there, trying to get some sleep on an old Army cot, when sometime around midnight he had the urge to go.

The old outhouse was a few sandy yards from the old hogan, and as he walked in the emptiness of the stark scrub in the pitch black of night, he found himself chuckling at the sounds of chirping crickets and the field mice chewing on cactus. There was no moon to brighten the sky so Shash had no need to close his eyes to hear the sounds better. The old warrior was also listening for the familiar smooth howl of the coyote, that wily creature who kept watch while the two-legged creatures called man or Dineh were bedded down for the night.

But that night brought a disconcerting sound and a warning that kept Shash tossing in his cot until early dawn. Instead of the smooth howl, the coyote had a jerky barking sound. So what did it all mean? He wondered uneasily.

The terrible answer came to him the next morning when his arrival in Wide Ruins was greeted by the terrible wail of mourners. His cousin Bennie was there and he was speaking in a soft voice as he broke the news to Shash. His niece Marjo was done in by a sudden heart attack at 12:30 that morning.

Shash listened, with one question now roaming through his head. What time was it that he heard the coyote?

Then, a year later, almost to the date of Marjo's death, Shash was alarmed to hear that identical sound of the coyote, and this time, smack in his own neighborhood, right in the area of the yucca tree, of all places. Now, what could this mean? The old Navajo found out soon enough when, that very night, his old Army buddy Louis Tsotse, who had never been sick a day in his life, had a sudden stroke and passed away.

It was at this point, that Shash understood the power of his prayer and that he was being given messages, the kinds of messages his mother, a respected medicine woman, was able to interpret. No, he thought. It was not possible that he was given those same powers. For one thing, he did not know the words to all the many songs you needed to know to ward off bad things, to really help the people, but with the messages he was getting, he could surely warn the Dineh of impending disaster and maybe they could do something about it.

However, those years, despite the coyote warnings, seemed to bode well for the Benally family. They were so good, in fact, that the bark of the coyote slowly receded into the distance. Those were the years that they were blessed by the visitor from Alaska, the Inuit named Wolf who escorted his son Sherman back from the Indian bar in Gallup one cold January night, saving him from a drunken brawl with a couple of Chicanos. Sherman, a heavy drinker, would look to pick a fight and, in Gallup, it was always easy to find a taker.

The 19 year old Inuit had no reason to drag the Navajo with the ponytail out of there, except that they were both "cousins" and the guys were Mexican. For Sherman, it was his wakeup call, the start of a long "dry season" for which Shash and his wife Bessie were forever grateful. And so Wolf became a fast family favorite. Smiling and broad-faced, he would happily down Bessie's delicious frybread and mutton stew, and they would honor him by having him light the fire after dinner and eagerly listen to his stories of old Alaska.

For Bessie, who had long suffered the tribulations of her own sons, young Wolf was a breath of fresh air and the hopes of what could be possible. Now, climbing the mountain, Shash could once again picture the radiance of Bessie's face, the peaceful expression in her eyes during those wonderful years they were graced by Wolf's visits. Those were the years that Wolf was attending SIPI, the Indian college in Albuquerque. Yes, it was a demeanor that Shash had never before witnessed in his wife and he had prayed then that her new glow would last forever. And then, just like that, it all turned around again, as it always had.

The eve of the 50th wedding anniversary of Shash and Bessie saw a beautiful array of dressed-up children and grandchildren sitting around the antique mahogany dinner table, enjoying Bessie's famous mutton ribs and frybread. Wolf and Shash had been in a kind of playful competition, telling stories of the old ways and Shash, feeling secure in the love of his family, had forgotten to consider that he had let his guard down once again.

There was not a soul around that happy table that could have predicted that Wolf's life was in danger, that he would die that night of a heart attack, but he did. It was a sudden thing and since it occurred while he was sleeping, he probably never felt it, so said the paramedic. And Shash, who had felt so secure, content and fortunate that night, had just as quickly dismissed the vision he had experienced the previous night where the coyote had barked four times, mocking his complacency. Then, witnessing Bessie's grief in that early morning tragedy brought it straight home to him. If Shash had been vigilant, he would have found a way to satisfy that coyote and nothing more would have happened.

That coyote had to be somewhere close, Shash figured, and it was time to go after him and find him before any more damage was done. His Shima, his mother, the medicine woman had taught him how everything came in fours. There were four seasons, four directions, and the four elements of earth, wind, fire and water. And furthermore, if your home was where it should be in Dinehtah, then you lived inside the boundaries of the four sacred mountains. Now, the coyote had spoken three times and there had been three tragedies. Naturally, you could expect that fourth bark and the old Navajo had the terrible inkling that if he stayed put and did nothing it was going to happen real soon.

So, for a week, Shash walked the neighborhood, looking for a sign. Then one very early morning, just before dawn, it came to him. From somewhere around the old yucca tree he could hear the hooting of the white owl that prodded him to check the dirt around the area for coyote tracks. Sure enough, there they were. They were faded out but you could tell they were prints of that wily beast and that he had been there, maybe a day or so earlier.

Now, barely able to contain his excitement, Shash jogged back home as fast as his old, injured legs could carry him to share the news with his wife. He had found the culprit, all right, she would be comforted to know, and now that he knew where the coyote did his work, he could figure out how to satisfy the beast. Finally, Shash figured, he had come through for her.

Then the old warrior saw the fire rescue truck and it caused him to nearly double over in pain. The truck, pulled up at the front lawn between the two old Chevy sedans, was pointed straight at the open door to the Benally front porch, and there lying prone on the hardwood floor, he'd taken such pains to wax just the week before, was Bessie. Shash Jr. was sobbing and beating his hands on the wall, pleading with the paramedic to save her, but Shash knew by her gray color that her heart had stopped beating.

That was four years ago to this day, Shash remembered, as it was an anniversary of sorts. The thing was that during those four years he had not seen nor heard from that coyote and because of that, he took it to mean that the cycle was completed. But then, just the night before, he had a dream, an extraordinary one that really shook him up and made him realize that you could never be sure about anything.

In the dream there was a cedar tree with leaning branches and the sweet smell of berries and in between those branches, when he looked real close, he could see a set of clear dark brown eyes peering between the bristly greenery. There was no bark, but just a stare, just the eye contact with Shash.

So, at 2:30 that morning, when he awakened from that dream, Shash knew what he had to do. The plan was to have breakfast at the casino, and some biscuits and gravy sounded about right. He would need something fortifying to give him strength for the long upward climb to the top of the mountain. Then, as he climbed, he would go over all the words to the Shield Song to make sure he got them right. He would sing about the horny toad and its protective armor that could shield it and him from the lightning and thunder. He would sing out as he walked in slow sure steps all the way up to the outstretched arms of the cedar tree. If he really wanted that new hogan on the reservation, he would have to remove every obstacle and he would have to start by satisfying the coyote with the large brown eyes.

Sitting down now, close to some loose boulders a few feet from the tree, he could see the city of Albuquerque, its houses and buildings looking tiny and unimportant from so high up on the mountain. From 8000 feet, the city surely seemed less threatening than it did from I-40. He let his breathing quiet down for a few minutes and then he began his ritual. Taking the small worn leather pouch from his jeans pocket, he slowly unwound the skinny hand-cut leather strips which had been tied several times around the center of the pouch and carefully opened it. He removed the precious rocks one by one, setting them down on the ground under the cedar tree.

There, Shash would sit out the rest of the morning, the afternoon and nighttime and even until the next morning's sunrise if needed. He would wait for the coyote and make his offering, because he knew the same way his mother and all his ancestors before knew. If you could satisfy the coyote, your life could finally move on and everything could be possible.

6

Downing a third glass of imported Italian red wine at Enzio's did nothing to mellow Kathy and just taking note of the finger tapping and dour expression told Charlie all she needed to know about what was going on with Kathy and Doyle. While Doyle and Sander were engrossed in opal talk, just inches from them on the long wooden bench, Kathy looked like a rattler that would strike at just the right trigger word.

Charlie had been keeping her precious finds wrapped in tissue paper in a small zippered pocket in her backpack. Maybe, she figured, if she got to the Paiute trading post in Wadsworth, she could buy a piece of leather or a small medicine pouch to protect the arrowheads the way the Indians did. At this point, she really wanted to show them to Sander and tell him how she thought they were a gift from beyond, maybe from Link. But then, Sander would laugh at her the way he always did. He was after all just a science teacher, not a maven of the paranormal. Then, with all this tension coming from Kathy's way, this might not be a good time to bring it up anyway.

These so-called vacations to the outback were certainly not Kathy's choice of where to spend the summer months and the fact that Doyle, just this year, spent nearly $35,000 customizing their self-contained mobile camper just aggravated her even more. He had bragged to everyone at Austin Welders back home about his "traveling masterpiece," conveniently forgetting to tell them how it put Kathy and him in credit card debt for the rest of their lives.

Kathy hated this Charlie besides, and the fact that she always made such a big fuss over Doyle. Probably she would get him in bed real easy given half a chance. Of course, Doyle always had a sweet face for her. "Hey, come see the queen-size bed I built in here. It's got a ceiling porthole so you can look at the stars! Hey, Charlie, it's even got a flush toilet so you don't have to pee behind the sagebrush!" She hated it when Doyle would flirt to get her attention. In fact, these days, she hated just about everything Doyle did, especially these adventures he dragged her on, like to this horsefly infested Virgin Valley opal mine.

It was bad enough, his obsession with opals, but even worse were the constant investments in other mineral stuff. Right now, there were three weighty collections of opals, plume agate, blue fluorite and chrysocolla that Doyle somehow saw himself selling worldwide from a comfortable seat in front of the computer. There were boxes of rocks that cost thousands of dollars, but no matter, because Doyle said minerals were going to make them rich.

In the late 1990s, when selling on the internet started to become popular, Doyle had decided he would create a website that would be better than anyone else's. The goal was to earn some easy and fast money to pay for the new addition he had just built on their rustic, two-story cedar home in the Jollyville, Texas suburb. So, after an initial withdrawal of $12,345 from Kathy's retirement fund, he was able to afford the great minds of web design and all the available software to create the now defunct kathyskrystals.com.

Doyle always had the perfect comeback to Kathy's complaints. It really didn't matter, he would tell her, because sooner or later everyone was going to die anyway. To Doyle, the crystals were everything. The hunt for opals was everything, and if you had to spend a small fortune on a good camper to get out there to the desert you did it because that was everything. For Doyle knew, even if she, Kathy, did not, that if there truly was a God, it was in no church. God was right here, in the sagebrush, thistle and open sky of the northwestern Nevada wilderness.

Sander got up from the table and walked to the quarter slot machine at the front of Enzio's bar and plunked in two bills in change. Then Charlie decided to walk over just to check on his mood. "So, what's going on with them?" she prodded, turning her head in Kathy's direction. "If looks could kill, I say Doyle is a dead man."

Sander laughed out loud and then lowered his voice to a whisper. "It's the camper. It sunk in the playa quicksand somewheres near the Quinn River. Who the hell would ride near the Quinn River in a heavy camper this time of year? My cousin's a moron."

"So who got them out? Did he manage to get a signal to someone on the railroad?"

"I guess so. Or maybe someone here in Gerlach. I didn't ask him too much about it because he'd rather talk opals. Maybe the guy at the gas station got him towed out."

"Shit," Charlie grinned. "I thought you were with him today."

"No, I was walking the desert, actually looking for you. I saw Doyle pass by the Black Rock road on his way to the sinkhole and I figured you were with them."

"I got a ride out to the desert with some road crew going out to Soldier Meadows and then I hitched coming back."

"You always take stupid chances," Sander chided. "There could be all kinds of weirdos way out in that desert."

"Listen, Sander. There's something I want to talk to you about, but I need a Bloody Mary first. Do you think we can be anti-social and ditch the Texas duo for a little bit?"

"Sure," Sander nodded, running his hand through his unruly ponytail, having noticed Charlie's worried expression. Maybe, tonight would be the night she would want him. She sure seemed lonely enough. "Relax," he grinned. "Unlace the heavy boots and I'll get you a stiff one."

Enzio's was one of four bars in Gerlach, a town of 350 full time residents, and the only one that bordered the great Black Rock Desert. At one time in the distant past, a town named Sulphur dotted the area just south of the desert. Today, if one chanced the rocky, gravelly route between Gerlach and the city of Winnemucca and passed by Sulphur, the ghostlike remains of roofless log shacks would emerge, evoking images of the days when the discovery of gold silver and precious minerals made towns rise and fall like houses of cards.

Charlie surmised that she had found those arrowheads somewhere northwest of Sulphur. She had been trying to figure out a location point all day, just in case Sander wanted to know. She hated looking stupid in his eyes and he was good at asking questions, like the typical teacher he was. She set the points down on a small circular table, far enough away from the bar and even farther away from Doyle and Kathy. The arrowheads were lined up side by side, just as she had found them on the desert floor. As Sander set down the drinks in front of her, she geared herself for what she called his usual parochial observations, which was that there always had to be a logical explanation for everything.

Sander looked at the points and feigned a look of shock. "I'll be darned!" He shook his head, imitating Doyle's mannerisms. "Them sure looks like Clovis points to me!"

He took out a compact magnifying glass from the zippered pocket of his backpack to get a better look and as he moved the glass over the points, Charlie watched his face take on a more sober look. "Actually, he said, "they could be really ancient."

The two sparkling glassy black artifacts were almost identical, except that one was smaller and had a more rounded tip, maybe having hit its target and then smoothing out after riding the desert sands for thousands of years. Both were exquisitely knapped with the basal fluting characteristic of the projectiles of early Great Basin inhabitants. To Charlie, all she knew was that they came to her and that they were beautiful and even more than that, they were starting to take on an interesting larger-than-life meaning. She was feeling a masculine and feminine presence that somehow seemed to be tied into her early morning vision.

"Yes," Sander nodded, moving the magnifier across the "masculine" point. "These are definitely Clovis points."

Charlie took a long sip of her drink and decided that for lack of anything better to do at the moment, she would challenge him. Sander continually got on her nerves with his "in your face" way of throwing his intellect around. To her thinking, if they were Clovis points, then they could be more than 10,000 years old and it didn't really make sense that something so ancient could just be in the open all that time without being trampled to pieces by a wild horse or some other animal.

"Maybe," she said, "but how can you be so sure that some Paiute around here doesn't have that old striking tool right in his possession? Maybe one of the Indians at Summit Lake north of here or at Pyramid Lake still have a tool or two and know how to do that same exact kind of knapping. To me, these arrowheads seem hardly weathered."

Sander shook his head. "No, those guys have no reason to be sitting at the playa making points. The playa was once Lake Lahontan, not some dried up sand thing that it is now. In those days, there was game to kill. Hell, you even had mammoths around!"

Sander's face had the look of feigned exaggeration he normally reserved for some of his earth science students, the ones who couldn't seem to get their grades above a C minus.

"You see the fluting?" he went on. "You see the way it's chipped out across the center? The indigenous people made it this way so it would work better for the type of game they had to catch. They prayed on it to make food come for their families. They made this effort because they had to back then. "Charlie," he sighed, "you really don't get it, do you?"

Charlie fell silent. What did she gain by talking to this condescending creature? Of course, the early tribal peoples used carved pieces for prayer, and as with these arrowheads, each strike might be accompanied by a song, a prayer for the hunt for both food and the human enemy. But how in the world could you put a name on things? A Clovis point, for instance. Maybe so, but then again, maybe not. You really could never know about these things for sure. What made early man more special than contemporary tribes anyway?

Despite Sander's attitude, Charlie knew that she needed him for the rockhunting trips in the middle of nowhere. A woman alone could be in real danger in the back country, and much like Doyle, she needed to be here for the spiritual aspect of it all, not just for the minerals. So, whenever she got really pissed off at Sander, she would remind herself that not only was he her protection out here, but it was Sander who whet her appetite for the desert in the first place. Now, watching him get up from the table and fish in his pocket for two more quarters for Enzio's slots, she almost smiled, remembering the circumstances of how they met and how far they had come since then.

It was a rainy day in June, about ten years earlier, when the phone rang and the caller announced himself as "Sander Miller, the wannabe professor." He found out about her writing abilities from a mutual acquaintance and asked Charlie if she would like the job of proofreading his master's thesis entitled "Weak Repression of Rightward Transcription in Bacteriophage Lambda." That eclectic title made

Charlie wondered at the time, how a person could write a paper that sounded rather ambitious and yet have no idea how to write a declarative sentence.

Sander's mentor, at that time, a Dr. Roland Jameson, was an avid mineral collector whose displays of magnificent pyrite and galena specimens graced prestigious museums in California and in New Mexico. In an effort to impress Jameson, Sander encouraged Charlie to do a human interest story for one of her magazines about the professor and his noteworthy collection. Luckily for both Charlie and the professor, it all worked out well. Charlie, in fact, was even more impressed with Jameson, than the old geezer was with her. Just looking at his natural treasures, whet her desire to do her own searching, her own combing of the forests and deserts for the gems that lay hidden in the wilderness beyond.

For Sander, this was a grand opportunity to impress this young pretty writer whose only attachment was this Link Davis, a UFO writer whose heart problems did not lend to hiking 14,000 foot mountains or traversing the hot Southwestern deserts. This meant that Charlie would have to travel without her partner if she wanted to search for minerals or do a travel story, and who knows what good stuff could go on between the two of them? But then sadly for Sander, the good stuff he envisioned never happened. He would come to know Charlie for the workaholic she was, for the pretty woman who dressed to unimpress, in T-shirts and jeans, as guys looked longingly at her butt when she passed them by.

Now, he walked back to the table from the slot machine, hoping she would pick up the argument where they had left off. The trouble with Charlie was that she always gave up too soon. She had this faint smile of resignation on her face as she looked up at him. It was hard for her to totally dislike him, Sander knew, even when he sometimes sounded like a know-it-all jerk. He decided to sit down and give her a chance to say her piece, even if it sounded weird. You had to let women have their way once in awhile.

"I had a kind of dream last night, Sander," she started, "and please don't laugh until you hear this out totally. Okay?"

"I'm all ears," he said, placing both elbows on the table. "Tell me what's going on."

"I'm thinking that these arrowheads represent people, that they are symbols of Link and me, "Charlie blurted out. "That small one there with the broken rounded tip is me and the bigger one is Link and I think that he is telling me that he is watching over me."

Sander grinned. She was giving him her confidence as strange as the story was and he enjoyed watching her expand upon it all. "I hear you," he said. "Now tell me how you came to this startling revelation. Tell me about your dream."

"It wasn't an actual dream, Sander. He called me on the phone from a spirit world, I think." Charlie looked away from Sander. She could feel the negative energy directed at her. She and Sander were coming from two different places and there was no way he would get any of it.

"You know what I think, Charlie?" Sander's face had taken on a new look, something like that of a speaker at a lectern getting mentally prepared for a long drawn out and boring discourse. "I think, Charlie, that you really have to come down to clear reality or someday you will surely go nuts!" He banged his fist on the table for emphasis, causing the two arrowheads to jump.

Charlie felt the tears welling up inside. She could have kicked herself for revealing something so private to a man with such a parochial mind. So stupidly, she had let it all out, losing a sacred part of herself in the process. Link had been the only man to share her thoughts and carry her secrets and from now on she would return that trust by keeping any future connections she might have with him to herself and to herself only.

Wouldn't it be amazing, she thought, if somehow Link was now passing on information from some other dimension? She remembered the time she fell asleep in the crook of his arm at four in the morning the day after the World Trade Center explosion. She had been frightened, believing she had witnessed the beginning of the end of the world and could feel the heat of her tears rolling down her cheeks, just as they were doing now. But Link had been so calm then, as he usually was, reassuring her that it would all pass, that man's cruelty to man was just a transition to something greater.

So now, after a brief pause, his dying, it seemed like here he was again, back in her life once more. Charlie figured that, perhaps, that transition he spoke about was imminent, and as she sat there ignoring Sander's scornful talk and retreating to the safety of her own thoughts, it struck her that it was somehow important for her to get ready.

7

At 4:45 in the morning, Nakai staggered in the pitch dark up the stairs to his apartment. He knew that Hannelore was up and about, waiting for him, because he could hear her sharpening knives in the kitchen. Heading straight for the bedroom, he slammed the bedroom door in a grand gesture, as if daring her to follow. When he was drunk, he also got more pissed at her, and if she was smart, she would stay out of his sight for her own well-being.

Of course, he knew that the screaming would follow, as it always did, and in a way he welcomed it. It got all the tension out and the anger and he could handle anger much better than tears.

"Son of a bitch!" he could hear her cursing in that low sharp guttural voice some Germans had. Soon that voice would get louder until it would boom through every wall of the apartment. Nakai felt the sudden urge to retch, and Hannelore's silk white nightie with the Neiman-Marcus label slung over the side of the king-sized bed seemed to be the likely target for the vomit. She could wash it over and over and spray it with perfume, but she would never completely get the stench or stain out. He knew because he'd done it before.

He let it all out. The beers, two hamburgers, the pepperoni pizza, the whole ugly mess spurted, propelled out in large pink blobs that resembled tiny hills. Then, in a half-hearted measure of self-defense, Nakai hurled the foul smelling gown in her face, as she came at him, and then swiftly bolted out of the apartment into the night.

The dankness and smell of the beach and the solace of the waves would do him a lot of good and he could sleep off his drunk a whole lot better without that bitch. She could cry and call up everyone they both knew and tell them how the bastard left her to sleep all alone, but he didn't give one damn. She could never make a dent in this warrior.

Even when things were going pretty good between them, meaning she let him do whatever the hell he pleased without kicking up a fuss, he would still cringe every time she looked at him like some piece of primitive meat. But then most white women saw him that way, through eyes of lust. They told him they loved him but they really worshipped the Indian, and it was the worship that excited them.

The absence of a moon created an eerie semi-darkness on the night beach illuminated only by the occasional back light of a hotel or condo that projected fuzzy gold circles onto the sand. Nakai sat down inside one of those circles, pretending it was a special light that came for him, radiating his being out to those deserving of his night prayers. The problem, though, was that tonight, he felt no prayers. Instead, there was an inexplicable resentment and he knew that when this happened, the festering rage he carried inside would start gnawing at him

The rage was real yet unreal. He lived in this country that was his and yet he could never really belong with these Europeans who came here to colonize, rape, murder, pillage, to steal the Indian's soul. What was it that the Christian bastards used to say? "Kill the Indian and save the soul!" Today, they would call him a Native American, a term of guilt, if ever he heard one. Nakai preferred to be called Indian, pronounced Indun, or even Injun, because it told the story. It told about his father, Shash, who was taken off to a Catholic boarding school to have the shit beaten out of him for daring to speak in Dineh, his own language. They once made him walk shoeless in the snow, the nuns did.

Little by little, these Europeans speaking the enemy language, English, these bilagana, their ancestors and their descendents both, tore up the very fabric of tribal existence so you could assimilate into their goddamn melting pot. First they killed you with murder and disease, then they stole your sacred mesas and sent you on death marches, then they took your best sheep, your goats, then they kidnapped your children, and now you get their New Age children who come at you, smiling, to buy your silver and your symbols and a piece of your "Indian wisdom."

Well, Nakai would play the role of the Injun and give these "colonialists" what they wanted, and as long as they treated him like some spiritual "shaman" as they called it, he would dole out his attention sparingly and make sure they paid handsomely for it. Like tonight, with Hannelore doing her thing. She was lucky he let her off so easy without even one punch when he was drunk enough to smash her ugly puss to a pulp. But why bother? As long as he continued to excite her, she would come up with the money. Her father had a stash in Hamburg and he knew that if she kissed his fat German ass just the right way, he would wire it in.

If truth be told, Nakai had been swiping the money, a bit at a time, so Hannelore wouldn't miss it. A fifty here, a twenty-five there was the way he worked it. He figured that by now he had at least a couple of thousand stashed underneath a palm tree, four feet deep in the ground in a weeded area a few feet from the boardwalk at 31st. When he was ready to get the hell out of this place, maybe to see his father in Albuquerque, he would have enough for the grand escape. Nakai could see the time coming soon. He would wait patiently for the blond woman named Charlie to come back from her mineral hunt out West and then he would make his move.

Nakai now took the stretchy black elastic band off his ponytail and spread his lustrous black hair out to the wide night sky. He felt energy coming from the illuminated circle around him and he got up and began to dance and sing a two-step song he learned from his mother when he was four. He closed his eyes, feeling the heaviness of pre-rain humidity in the southwest winds. He imagined those winds carrying the tales of his ancestors in the blackness of the sky that reminded him of the precious black obsidian the Dineh called "baashineh."

He smiled now, feeling the tension in himself ease, and fingered the shiny obsidian arrowhead he was wearing in his left ear. At that moment, he knew exactly what he was going to do. When morning came, he would take the arrowhead and fashion from it an earring for the blond woman with it. He would make an eagle out of silver, with its claws holding the arrow in its embrace. If he concentrated on this creation hard enough, then he would not have to make the first move when she showed up, because she would come to him. His prayers and concentration could make that happen, he was sure.

When morning came, Hannelore was certain to calm down and pretend nothing had happened because there was no percentage in starting an argument and getting him going all over again. She would see him and want him to make love to her and as much as it pained him to do that, Nakai thought he might give her a poke if she made him a good breakfast. Scrambled eggs, some ham and hot French bread sounded good right now, and he was imagining the aroma of it all, especially the strong coffee, coming from the kitchen of his apartment.

Nakai was still standing in the circle of light when the hotel lights went off and the first birds of dawn began chirping all around him. Then, a flight of small green parrots made landfall on the roof of the hotel behind him, screeching silly sounds that made Nakai crack up laughing.

The obsidian arrowhead earring in the palm of his hand felt warm and beautiful. When you were a Dineh artist named Nakai you had the gifts to create the beauty that could draw all kinds of people your way. He could hear a chuckle under his breath and the saliva rolling down in his throat and that felt good. He decided to laugh out as loud as he could so it would resound from end to end, from corner to corner, without frames, in a powerful flow of energy forever outward and upward to infinity, to the whole universe.

8

At 11,000 feet, the north wind whistled out a warning that life was not about to get any easier if you kept on climbing.

"Hey, are you guys cool with things?" Doyle Miller was checking as he always did for signs of altitude sickness here, high up in the Colorado Rockies, on the high slopes of Mount Antero. "Don't be afraid to say so, Charlie, if you got a headache or dizziness or whatever."

Charlie did feel some shortness of breath but nothing too major. Besides, she figured, Doyle had just about every first aid remedy there was if she did get into trouble. He was never one to throw caution to the wind. He always carried the extra half-gallon of water in his backpack and made sure that Kathy had a whistle in case of danger and he made sure that both he and Kathy had their very own snake bite kits besides. Charlie laughed to herself, knowing that the snakebite kits were of little use on top of the mountain, where the only sign of life was an occasional coney scampering about, seeking out crystals to line its deep dirt holes.

They had two thousand more feet to climb along the narrow trail that criss-crossed from Mount Antero to neighboring Mount White, and it was still a hard climb to make before you could even smell an aquamarine. Maybe a thousand feet up from there before you could dig for the really good, transparent blue.

Charlie found herself stopping every five minutes or so to catch her breath and to take in the amazing view from so close to the top of the mountain. It was awesome. No other word for it. There were mountains of purple and gold and sweet, sheer, deep blue sky, that pure blue you got when the air was thin. But she was starting to feel weak and disoriented now and soon it would be hard to hide it from the guys, especially Doyle. She needed Doyle and Sander to even get started on these trips and the steep drop beneath her was a stark reminder of how she could never venture alone, apart from them, in these hills.

She had a vivid memory of a hike a few years back on Topaz Mountain in the Thomas Range of northwestern Utah, a terrible moment when she and Sander lost each other. The uphill climb had been more difficult than usual because the knoll that produced beautiful honey-colored topaz had been undermined by dynamite blasting. The earth felt shaky under her feet and she felt herself slipping. Calling out to Sander just produced an echo of her own voice into the 500 foot deep canyon she was about to drop into. Grasping a handful of branches of a Mormon tea plant, she began to mentally prepare herself for the fall. If she positioned herself flat on her back, with her hands at her side and her head turned upward, she could probably survive the sheer slope with some broken bones and bruises.

Then suddenly, as if in a B movie the voice of a stranger rang out. "Do you need a hand?"

Charlie grabbed onto the large fingers of a heavy set, curly haired, thirtyish, rugged-looking type who just happened to be at this out-of-the-way knoll at the exact moment she needed him. A miracle? Perhaps, she thought for the moment. But even as he pulled her to safety, Charlie smelled something funny and she had the uncomfortable feeling that this man had been watching her, knowing that this part of the knoll was impossible to pass.

Merle Jones was the name, he said, and she later found out that he had indeed been watching. In fact he was an ex-con in the habit of scaring females in deserted spots like Topaz Mountain. For more than an hour he kept Charlie company, entertaining himself by telling her scary stories about his lengthy prison stays for rape and manslaughter. The wild look in his eyes told Charlie he had plans for her, but she had been there and done that and this time she would know what to do. She understood the minds of warped men, just as she had understood her uncle Jake and his plans for her when she was only 13. No man would ever take her by force again as long as she lived, even if she had to kill him.

Feigning a dramatic calmness, she listened to Merle's story, even throwing him a sympathetic glance every now and then. "Hey, Merle. Your past is your past. You have to move on. Right now, we have topaz to dig for and I need you to help me." Where did she learn how to act like that? Merle sat down close to her with his hammer and chisel to help her loosen the hard gray topaz-bearing rhyolite. When the time was right she would ask for the hammer so she could assist and then she would go for his eyes.

Fortunately, that moment never came to pass. There was Sander coming down the mountain to the knoll, looking for her, and right in the middle of Merle's goriest story, the one about how he killed his best friend's wife. "I never knew that there was so much blood in the human body," Merle sighed. Charlie shrugged and let out a low sigh, pointing to the muscular guy coming down the mountain.

"My husband, Merle. I'll introduce you, but don't stand up too fast, because he's an avid hunter. Always looking for critters. Once went for what he thought was a grizzly and shot another hunter by mistake."

Charlie's face brightened now, registering her bravado at that crucial moment, and she took pride in the fact that it never kept her from climbing in these remote mountains, the chance you could meet a crazy. The formidable weather conditions alone, the tearing winds and sudden lightning storms, the treacherous switchbacks and road cuts laden with boulders, were enough to scare away all but the diehard mineral hunters. Still, this hike was worth it, and if you had the guts to 4-wheel all the boulders and switchbacks at least part of the way and then climb the remainder to the top of this Colorado fourteener, you were in for some world class mining country.

It happened every year at around the same time in late June or early July, when the snow melted just enough to tackle this supremely rugged terrain. The season would start, perhaps when an old Jeep four-wheeler managed to make its treacherous way along the barely serviced road cut up and around the switchbacks to a golden, grassy knoll about 11,000 feet up the mountain dubbed the "parking area." The intrepid rockhound withstood the shaking, and swerving, and dips in two-foot streams as the old Jeep, put in low gear, battled valiantly to get him to the aquas, and fluorite, and phenakites and smokies, and just about anything else that glittered up there.

Today's adventure in Sander's old Jeep had been a real stress for Charlie and her body felt fairly shaken up at this point. He had been driving at five miles an hour or less up the downward tilting roadcut when at one point he cut it too close and the rear wheel narrowly missed the edge on a 180 degree switchback. Then, there was the problem of a couple of stubborn snowdrifts that required some manual labor with the heavy shovel Doyle toted for just such an occasion.

Charlie could see Sander and Doyle in the distance now, hugging their heavy ski parkas up to their throats, and for a moment she laughed out loud, thinking about the hot summer weather she and Sander left far behind in Miami just a few short weeks ago. She would let them walk, even lose them, and it wouldn't matter because she knew they would always keep her in sight from way above. She decided to take a rest on a large boulder and read her journal entry from yesterday. There was so much she needed to remember from this trip and the events of yesterday were going to take on some meaning even if she had no idea why. Charlie started reading her own scrawl:

"A Navajo named Dennis was heading to the July 4th song and dance festival in Window Rock, Arizona. We found him somewhere near Shiprock, New Mexico, where he was standing next to a stalled smoking pick-up. We had just about enough water to cool the truck down, but he insisted that he had to get to his mother's home somewhere on the reservation, just south of there in the Chuska Mountains. 'Doyle went on to get us a motel room in Salida because it's the kind of town that can fill up fast on a weekend, especially around the 4th of July. Sander and I, well, we decided we needed to get Dennis back.

'Our Jeep was all junked up, top and bottom heavy with well-worn suitcases, plenty of rocks and assorted camping junk. The bed of it was down to accommodate all the junk until we could unload it somewhere to make the Jeep lighter for the Antero trip. 'Dennis is up front with Sander. I'm on all the clutter in the back and the trunk is open to give me air. I'm maneuvering, changing positions as we make the steep climb up the Chuskas. I'm most comfortable with my feet dangling in the dust. 'Halfway there, we see some New Mexico State Troopers sizing up the wreckage of a doomed Ford pickup that dropped 700 feet into the forested wilderness. Who was I to complain about my feet dangling in the dust?

'We get to Dennis's mother's old hogan. She comes to greet him, along with three goats and a herding dog. I think that Dennis is maybe 50 but his mother is ancient. She could be 100. She is deaf but she understands when we pull up that she's going to miss the song and dance because her son has no transportation. Then, I think that maybe they will stand here on this road and wait and someone will come by and take them there. It was all possible. Maybe even, we could take them.

'There is poverty all over. The old hogan is made of railroad ties. Ironic. The coming of the railroads drove the Indians out and now the hogans are made with the unholiest of materials. This hogan should be made with the finest of cedar. It should be a holy place but instead it is made from discarded railroad ties. There is no running water on this land. It's been spoiled by Peabody Coal, by uranium mines and whatever is left that is good, Dennis says, is all siphoned to Las Vegas for the rich people. He wants to say the rich "white" people but he doesn't because we are white and he doesn't want to offend us.

'There is an outhouse fifty feet from the hogan, so this old woman has to trudge out in the middle of the night in the wintry snows to relieve herself. Or maybe, she keeps a bucket near her bedside and stays inside to keep warm, in the hogan that is heated with butane on the coldest nights.

'She has lived this way so long because she expects no different from a government that forgets the elderly, especially the tribal elderly. But like the rest of tribal America, she is not going away. She will not be a vanishing race and the white people, the bilagana in the government here, better learn to live with it."

Charlie closed her journal, got up slowly from the boulder and continued her slow steady climb. Doyle and Sander were way up there now, and walking at a pretty good pace considering all the artillery they were hauling. There were eight-pound sledge hammers for excavating hard rock, large pry bars and four-pound rock hammers. The equipment weighed them down but was absolutely necessary to move big boulders, to dig on permafrost to expose pockets of blue and gold crystals, to find the precious hidden virgin aquamarine.

For Charlie, her tools were the minimum, those she could attach in some way to her trail vest. The most useful one was a small aluminum rake-like utensil she picked up at Safeway to comb through the soil but she also carried a standard Estwing hammer and a small chisel for cracking rock. For capturing any great story that might come her way, she had a good Pentax mini camera securely zipped inside her top pocket. The key was to travel lightly and she did but she always carried enough water if she needed a quick oxygen fix to get her through the thin air of such high altitude.

Hikers familiar with Mount Antero's terrain know that there is a low trail and a high one, the low one being easier but much longer to climb. To save time today, they had all taken the high road. Somewhere at about 13,000 feet where the high and low meet there is a trickle of water that forms little puddles every few feet as it streams down the mountain. The earth here is of a fine gray crystal, with tiny patches of green, the only plant life that still dares to grow so high above tree level.

It is here that Charlie would stop to be alone, on her own. She would sit down awhile, drink some water, eat some trail mix and wait until she recovered her strength enough to explore a bit. Maybe she would see how her arrowheads looked in the morning sun. Maybe, if she got lucky, an aquamarine might roll down the mountain and she could reach out and snatch it. Up on Mount Antero any miracle was possible.

9

"He has excited domestic insurrections amongst us and has endeavored to bring on the inhabitants of our frontiers, the merciless Indian savages whose known rule of warfare is an undistinguished destruction of all ages, sexes and conditions." (Excerpt from the "Declaration of Independence.")

Edythe Yazzie was standing, her right hand placed solidly across her heart as the fourth grader with the long purplish-black braids and plump face recited the Pledge of Allegiance in Dineh. Next to her, Shash Benally remained seated on the long wooden bench on the top tier of the amphitheatre, half-listening and half-studying the worn out print of the old school textbook. The "Declaration" was highlighted in yellow and the part about the savages had a large black circle around it.

The opening ceremonies for the Navajo Nation's July 4th Song and Dance were now underway and as much as Shash enjoyed all the festivities and contests, this kind of patriotism for the "enemy people" always irritated the hell out of him. Even worse was that from his vantage point way up top, he could see the panorama of much of the fairgrounds and what he saw displeased him. A Ferris wheel moved to the beat of "Under the Boardwalk," bilagana rock and roll music, and the concessions were hawking snow cones, hot dogs, hip-hop music and cheap imitation Indian jewelry imported from China.

The big shot tribal council members and their families were up there on the stage, setting up mikes for the "dola bichon" speeches, and then there were the singers, who would compete for prizes all dressed in store-bought western shirts and bolo ties made of nickel silver and cheap stabilized turquoise. One of the big shots was putting the finishing touches on the navy blue crepe paper drape trimmed with red and white streamers and balloons.

"Imagine," he nudged Edythe, "tribal people celebrating the white man's independence day. We ought to be ashamed of ourselves."

Edythe smiled at Shash. She was overjoyed to be seated next to this good-looking proud warrior who seemed destined to be her dance partner for the next three days. She kept silent so he would go on.

"We were code talkers, putting our lives on the line in World War II, and for what? So, we could come back and watch these bastards take our land, our sheep? They just keep on doing it. So, who the hell are you pledging to? The Bureau of Indian Affairs?"

Despite Shash's complaints, Edythe watched his face go soft as the dancers started to take the field. The men were dressed much like Shash, in tribal patterned hand-made and store-bought shirts and colorful velours, jeans, boots or traditional high moccasins, straw panamas and lots of turquoise jewelry. But Shash was really taken back by the women, dazzled by the swirl of deep purple velvet ruffled skirts, cinched at the waist by silver conchas resting on sashes of colorful woven yarn. It was enough to bring back memories of his Shima and the times when Indians dressed like Indians. Here at the festival even the tiniest tots were ready to parade around in their white broad buckskin, beaded moccasins.

Edythe Yazzie had stitched her own clothing and that made Shash happy. He was proud that she was considered to be one of the finest seamstresses in Navajo Nation. Her heavy Sleeping Beauty turquoise and silver Zuni style necklace fell just right on her white cotton ribbon blouse and her deep purple velvet skirt partially obscured her broad boots that were dressed with white strips of broadcloth. She was aware that Shash was giving her the once over. Earlier he had commented about how he liked her grayish-black mass of hair tied back with heavy threads of white yarn that stuck out from the back of her bun like a broomstick.

In fact, when Edythe put together her outfit, including her turquoise and coral earrings shaped to look like thunderbirds, she surmised that Shash, who rarely missed a ceremony, would be there. It was a full year now since her beloved Henry had passed on to the spiritual world leaving Edythe, his wife of 43 years, with a three bedroom adobe home set on five acres of reservation land in Tohatchi, New Mexico. She was alone and she was a good catch and she knew it.

Yes, she was a bit overweight. Maybe fat. Maybe she needed to lose fifty pounds. But she was still a good catch. She could cook up a good stew and make great fry bread and she knew that Shash missed having all that, but what gave her really good encouragement was that she found out that Shash, the best dancer, the best looking and one of the finest spiritual elders around was interested.

In his early years, Shash would be riding the bucking bronco at the Indian rodeo. He even still had the ruby encrusted silver belt buckle he won so long ago for staying atop a bull for a full sixty seconds. Edythe also heard from a reliable source that Shash had been cast in some of the fifties western movies, even once with the notorious John Wayne who was known to do the impossible-- kill six Indians with one bullet!

Yes, Edythe could feel the electricity still emanating from this man sitting next to her and she knew it was he, not she who could still turn heads at this festival. Moreover, she wasn't fooled as to why Shash had an interest. The talk around was that he wanted to return to the land, to the Dineh people, to speaking his own language, not the enemy language as English was called around the reservation. In short, he needed a place to live and Edythe knew she was his meal ticket.

She had arrived here early in the morning, before the summer desert heat could wilt her and went right over to him and asked him if he wanted to be her dance partner. Edythe Yazzie was never shy, not one day in her life, and this was no time to fool around. She knew they would never win any contest the way things were set up but it really didn't matter.

Twenty singers would be up there, maybe. There would be some solos, and a few groups and they would each get a chance to belt out three songs. While they sang and were judged, the dancers, dancing to the music, would be judged at the same time. Doing the skip dance, the Navajo favorite, they would have to keep time with the drum. The judges were picked by the tribal council members and they would walk the circle of dancers, scoring points on costume, gracefulness and so forth. Edythe figured that there would be at least 60 songs today to dance to and Shash had some years on her. Anyhow, she thought, it was a beginning for them.

"I suppose it's good that at least for a few days every year the Navajo women can put away their blue jeans and sneakers," Shash griped. "The way these young women dress just like the bilagana is a darn shame!"

"I agree," Edythe nodded.

Shash got up now to walk to the field to greet the other dancers, his competition, with Edythe following a few steps behind. After a round of soft hand clasps and "yahtees," the dancers all took their positions in the circle. If truth be told, Shash was a little embarrassed to be in the company of this fat woman, and he also knew that she was a liar besides. She kept telling everyone that her late husband had been killed by lightning and Shash knew that lightning never struck a Navajo. That's what the horny toad prayer could tell you. He figured that Henry got a heart attack or something from being fat like his wife.

Today, Shash figured they would all dance the skip dance and tomorrow the two-step. Edythe was unaware that Shash did not enter the singing contest this year, which he often won, so that he would be able to dance with her. At his age, the old legs could never win any prizes, but just last year, he'd won big singing "Hiroshima," the Navajo code talkers' song about the agony of World War II. What a joy it was to beat the small hand drum, singing out "Iwo, Iwo, Iwo," and making some of the dancers get so carried away that they just stopped in their tracks to listen.

So, just this morning, Shash had made up his mind that he was going to enjoy listening to all the other singers and would not give in to jealousy. The songs were all beautiful, after all. They were all about the sunrise, the mountains, the grinding of the corn. Here in this great corner of the universe you didn't have to listen to some country singer with a guitar yakking about drinking beer or some Mexican serenading some senorita.

Shash turned his head back to the stands for a moment to make sure the old small history book with the "Declaration of Independence" was still there. Maybe he would not be singing for prizes today, but Shash had other ideas to impress Edythe, and also the rest of the crowd who would be talking about him and Edythe all week. After the opening ceremonies, he was going to convince a couple of tribal big shots to let him get up and talk and then he would let loose everything he knew about this document of complaints the colonists had voiced to the British so long ago.

The Declaration was made more than 250 years ago, but that did not matter to Shash. As far as he was concerned a tribal person had no business celebrating the white man's holiday of pledging to his flag. Let them hear first hand that paragraph about the "Indian savages" and how they killed all the white women and children. Let these folks hear all those lies so they would know exactly how this "life, liberty and the pursuit of happiness" hadn't worked out, even to this day, for the Dineh.

Having Edythe Yazzie right by his side gave Shash the needed clout, the wherewithal to shoot that arrow straight through that darned flag. Alone, those two honchos sitting up there, could refuse him the opportunity to speak, but Edythe, with her wealth and prestige, was just the bow he needed. For Shash was not only determined to make his way back to the reservation, he would make it as a voice, a voice in the decision-making of a new Navajo people. Yes, that hand in his on that sandy dance floor was the ticket to his future, and he knew it, so he gave Edythe his most charming smile, and together they made their way up toward the stage as the tribal members were about to take their seats in front of the patriotic colored crepe paper banners.

10

On his fourteenth birthday, Lincoln Davis had an experience that he thought was almost as extraordinary as his earlier encounter with the UFO.

It came to him in a very strange and unexpected way, while he was cramming for a Spanish conversation exam. On question number two, Pablo asked Maria Elena, "Como esta usted, hoy?" There were five questions with answers to be recited aloud with total perfection and already Link was stuck on number two.

For Link, who was a good if not great student in every other subject, world history, English lit, you name it, this course in conversational Spanish really threw him for a loop. Conjugating verbs left him cold and if he had to recite orally even the simplest infinitive, say, "hablar" which translates to "speak," Link was in trouble. He would invariably put the accent on the wrong syllable or mess up the past and present tense. Every exam was a bear, a hurdle on a long road to nowhere.

So, on his fourteenth birthday, Link sat there in the living room on the green and yellow flowered couch with matching boulder shaped pillows, which also served as his bed, in the one bedroom apartment his mother now rented in the Park Slope section of Brooklyn, trying to figure out the answer to question number two. He knew the question translated to, "How are you today?" and the answer Maria Elena was supposed to give was "I am fine." The translation for that was on page 54 but Link decided that for once he was not going to give in to that. Instead, he would stare at the page and keep saying, "I am fine, thank you," and maybe the answer would come to him. The "thank you" was easy. "Gracias." Everyone knew that. So what if he pronounced it like it had a "z" in the middle instead of a "c". The Italians in his neighborhood did much the same thing.

"I am fine. I am fine. I am fine," Link kept repeating for a good quarter of an hour. Then, just as he was about to throw in the towel and turn to page 54, something remarkable happened. A tiny light in the shape of a blue dot, probably no more than half an inch all around, popped up in front of his reading glasses. It was an instantaneous event, something like the light bulb that appears above a cartoon character's head when he has a sudden idea, and much like that shiny light bulb, that blue dot connected Link to the answer to question two.

"Estoy bien. Estoy bien, gracias," he found himself uttering softly, trying to get a grasp on the thing, to physically touch the blue light that flickered on and off, on and off until it finally died.

That morning, Link ran through the page of questions and every time he got stumped, which was just about every time, the blue light would appear like a magic fairy godmother carrying the answer. I wonder, he thought if it'll be this way in class tomorrow.

The next day, Link had the answers to the questions asked by the Spanish teacher, Ms Faber, and the best part was that no blue light was necessary. He came to the conclusion that somehow the blue light had correctly implanted the answers the day before and they would now live inside his brain for always.

For the next decade of Link's life, the tiny blue light would return from time to time, whenever he found himself up a brick wall in his search for life's answers and with all the confusion going on, it was comforting to be able to sort through it in such an interesting "out of this world" way. So, despite all the hardships he had faced with poverty, bad health and losing his father so suddenly at a young age, Link felt supremely blessed. He felt connected and at peace and ready to accept any challenge that living or dying had to offer.

Charlie placed her daypack between two gray boulder rocks on a low hill, a couple of feet from the narrow creek more than 13,000 feet up Mount Antero. It was tough going for her this morning, after camping out here all night at such a high altitude.

Usually, by the time they'd gotten to Colorado, she had built up a certain "getting used to" level for the high Rockies. You came from Miami, which was dead flat and then by the time you got to Mount Ida, Arkansas for the quartz, you were already at 800 feet. After you rockhounded Nevada and Utah, you had about seven or eight thousand feet climbed and usually that was enough to bolster Charlie for Antero. But this year it was not, and with the wind coming at her face and chest this morning, it was difficult to hike even a short distance without hearing her own heavy breathing.

Charlie made the decision to stay put for awhile instead of walking down and losing 500 feet which is what Doyle might recommend. In a little bit the sun would come out and it would warm up somewhat, and hopefully it would blow off the clouds that were now starting to build. Normally the thunderstorms held off till afternoon, and Charlie hoped they would for awhile, at least until she found an aquamarine.

Too tired to hike, she scanned the terrain swiftly with her eyes. This was day two and none of them had found any prizes yet. Charlie discovered a trick awhile back that seemed to help find minerals when the terrain featured so much sameness of earth or sand. She learned that if you sit for awhile, everything becomes more distinguishable, that the nuances in color become more outstanding and the sparkling things come up clearer. The method always helped her out in the jasper fields around Escalante in Utah, and she decided to try it here on Antero. She smiled now, reminiscing about Link's blue lights. Maybe they were really aquamarines, she mused. Maybe if she thought up a really tough question, the lights in the form of blue glass would magically appear.

From her rocky, grassy spot at the narrow creek, Charlie could hear Doyle and Sander hammering about 500 feet up the mountain. The wind brought their laughter her way and she envisioned the two overgrown kids breaking boulders, playing in the dirt, seeking out vugs of crystals of aquas and smokies. If only she was a guy and strong today, or maybe keep her sex but be twenty years younger. Then again, she'd seen women of seventy hike up these mountains and she was jealous of them also. These were women with muscle who could soar with the breeze, with no fear of their hearts stopping, with no fear of the unknown.

Charlie had a small steel claw in her trail vest and she decided it was a good time to use it. The claw worked like a rake and it could move the top layers of soil so you could spot a stray stone or two that might be hidden underneath. It was the one thing you could do if you were forced to rest awhile. Sometimes a fragment of blue could show up, and if you moved slightly upwards, you might discover a small pocket somewhere that could contain the real treasure. Sander did that all the time. He would find a piece of something and then circle uphill. Once he and Doyle tapped into an area of permafrost that way which they managed to cut a block out of. It was a warm enough day that it melted somewhat and they found a pretty purple fluorite inside.

As Charlie raked and her eyes became more accustomed to the nuances of color all around her, she noticed that there was a hint of blue several yards away to her right. Moving slightly over, she could see sparkles that indicated it could very well be a beryl. She would wait a few minutes and if her breathing allowed, maybe she could get over there. What was that saying? So near and yet so far? Who was she kidding? Not a chance in hell she could make her way over there. A bitter tear now rolled down her cheek and she held back the urge to curse out. Instead, she took out her camera to record the beauty of this purple and green paradise that mineral hunters called "the premier rockhounding site in America." Would the readers of her magazine even guess from this camera shot that Charlie was forever stuck in one spot up this gorgeous mountain?

Sometimes when things were starting to get out of control, Charlie would find herself uttering the Hebrew morning prayer as her mother had taught her. "Modeh ahni lefonechah melech chai vekayam...." Charlie now heard the words coming out and, without thinking, she pressed her hand to the breast pocket of her trail vest where her two arrowheads now sat, enclosed in a small leather pouch she had picked up at the thrift store in Salida. She shut her eyes tightly as the wind did its fierce dance around her. In a minute she would have to remove her woolen hat and parka despite the weather so she could breathe easier.

By now Charlie had made a decision about the arrowheads. There would be no more mention of them to Sander or anyone until she got back to Miami. There was an Indian there, she remembered. He was kind of a strange character, dressed in costume, who often came into the library. There was one time, in fact, that she was sure she noticed a black arrowhead dangling from his ear. Maybe if she approached him, she could talk to him about it all and he wouldn't laugh at her. Of course, he might not even want to talk to her. A lot of Indians thought white people asked stupid questions and they were probably right. She remembered someone once asking him why he didn't live on a reservation.

Charlie's thoughts were broken by a sudden flash of lightning and as she looked across the mountain, she could see the heavy puffy clouds starting to gather, closing in on Antero. It was time to make her way down to the Jeep before she got fried and maybe it was just as well. She placed her right palm on the stony ground to gain leverage and felt something suddenly roll down the small hill right into it. Checking it out, she was fascinated to see a small clear, pencil like aqua crystal. Her heart beating rapidly now, she looked up into the heavens for an instant wondering how and why. Then, she kissed the little crystal, opened her little leather pouch and placed it carefully between the two obsidian arrowheads.

11

Nakai fixed his eyes on the ant nest rising like a pyramid from the mess of wild sea oats near the boardwalk at 21st Street beach. He enjoyed being out here at dawn, when it was empty, before the tourists came out with their cameras. The ant nest reminded him of a time back when he was three or four years-old. He was shaking a sacred rattle outside his grandmother's hogan on the reservation when she caught him in the act.

"It's not a toy," she scolded, taking his hand and leading him to the edge of the broad canyon. "See, Shi'yaazh," she said, pointing to an ant's nest. "What you see?"

"It's round," Nakai had said. It was the first thing that came to his head.

"What else is round?" She asked, pointing to a hawk flying high above them.

"The bird's nest is round. The hole in the ground the snake makes is round too."

"The hogan we the people live in is round," she said, "but the bilagana, the white people in Albuquerque, they make square houses. This is why, Shi'yaazh, why your poppa, your shizhee, must come back home to Chilchinbito."

The tan sand felt warm and damp under Nakai's bare feet as he took slow, deliberate steps toward the wide expanse of green and turquoise that was Miami Beach's parcel of the Atlantic Ocean. His tranquility was broken only by the occasional nuisance of a jet ski roaring by, making some waves in otherwise calm seas. Out here, there were no thoughts of Hannelore, the kommandant who ruled his apartment, de-germing it all the time with lemon air fresheners, French perfume scents and cedar incense. Her father had wired over five grand just yesterday, with the full knowledge that it was going to some Navajo Indian, but it was a small price to pay to keep his angry miserable daughter away from Hamburg for the short run.

60

Yeah, Hannelore and her father shared one hell of a brutal history, he mused, and the bitch enjoyed recounting every year of her pathetic existence to anyone willing to listen to such stories. Old Franz Hermann was the respected doctor who treated his wife and daughter Hannelore like branded cattle, or sheep, or prisoners, or slaves and Hannelore carried the scars to prove it. Then, there was that one day, when he got sick of screaming at his wife and had some men, dressed in white, come for her to take her away to a sanitarium, a crazy house. She wasn't crazy, Hannelore cried out, but nobody believed her or nobody chose to believe her because her father had too many connections in Hamburg. For that outburst though, her father had left her gagged in the closet for two days.

No doubt, that whole experience had a lot to do with why Hannelore was so cold-blooded and nasty. Well, Nakai did not give one damn about that. He wasn't about to feel sorry for some white rich bitch from a demented family. Could these European assholes ever even guess what it was like to be really poor? To be Indian poor on some rez? No water to drink. No electric. No toilets. No hope. No, they just went on with their idiot notions of what a Native hyphen American was, maybe as some spiritual being who just prayed all day and could tell your future with a crystal and go up on the mountain and have some vision at any Goddamn time. They could never imagine you might live out of a pickup truck or in some tar paper shack at the edge of some border town right near a liquor store set up to get you drunk so the Mexican gangs could beat the shit outta you!

Nakai kicked the sand sprinkling it like sawdust in the air as he pictured his father now, sitting in his old chair in front of that chicken-shit house in Albuquerque. What a big deal it was back then to build a house off the rez in the big city and Shash was just the man for the task. Yeah, there he was, Shash working for some bilagana, earning less than everyone else because he was an Indian back then, not a Native-American. There he was, 150 miles from the reservation, trying not to piss away too much of his salary on whiskey and Skoal so Bessie could buy enough Bluebird flour for the fry bread, so the kids could have something better for breakfast than government commodity powdered milk and those junk bars of processed cheddar. So, there he was, Shash working in the bilagana world so his kids could go to public school instead of some damn church school run by nuns. It worked out really super 'cause the kids all got the chicanos and the bilaganas beating up on them instead. And, there was Shash managing to give the kids an allowance so they could discover how to lose their spirit to beer, cocaine, speed, heroin, meth. So they could get so stoned that they would be ashamed of their grandma and of that sacred hogan back in a place called Chilchinbito.

Nakai took off his beaded Birkenstocks and walked to the edge of the shore where the ocean water immediately rushed up to form tiny bubbles around his feet. The water was warm, about 86 degrees, and soothing. By now, he had worked himself into a near frenzy just thinking about Shash, and the current coming at him kind of brought it all home. He had come to the beach to forget all the crap and just to concentrate on a future with Charlie, but now the way he was feeling he was getting bad vibes about her too. He ground his foot deep into the wet sand and kicked out, creating a cascade of dark brown sand globules and spurts of seawater.

What was this Charlie doing out there in the desert anyway? Did she care anything about the tribal elders living out there on the rez with no clean water to bathe in or to drink? Or was she shooting pictures of some touristy New Age gallery in Santa Fe or Sedona? Would she be interviewing the old forgotten warriors like Shash or was she just making small talk with some Pueblos hawking plastic bear claws outside the Governor's Palace?

Tony at the library said she looked for minerals and that was what his grandmother did, that bent old lady with the velvet skirt who saved her smile for her few goats and sheep. She always looked for the little red stones in the ant nests outside her hogan. He wondered if she were alive today, would she still live the old way with no electric in a hogan or would she be in one of those HUD houses that were spread all across Navajo Nation?

Nakai smiled now, thinking about his grandma picking up those stones.

"The ants understand the earth, our Mother," she would say, picking up some red ones and some clear ones and occasionally one that was light green, but first she would make sure that the ants were done there, that there were none still working. "They use these stones to build their house," she would explain, sometimes placing them in the palm of her grandson's hand. Then, she would study the area uphill from the nest to see if there were the bigger stones, the bright red garnets. She loved telling Nakai the stories about how the ants built their homes like the Dineh did, from all the elements around them.

Nakai observed carefully everything his grandmother did. He may have been only three or four but even at that age, he knew it was important. There came a day when she placed several clear round stones in his hand and her eyes met his and she offered a statement that was so profound that to this day, it made Nakai shiver to think about it.

"Shi'yaazh," she said, these clear stones will be for the medicine rattle. We will put it together with pieces of the skins and blood of our people."

Nakai's feet were ankle deep in the surf now and he was watching a school of mullet run past him swiftly and away, feeling the rushing memories of the long ago past. He felt calmer now. The sea always seemed to have that effect, ushering in the memories that counted and pulling the bad stuff far away into the nothingness.

Thoughts of Charlie gave him hope, and he mused a bit, wondering if she knew how to search for garnets or peridots in an ant nest, if she knew like the ant knows, just how sacred those minerals are. Many people who looked for beauty in the stones knew. They were observers and the plants, the trees and the animals often talked to them.

Nakai was sure that he could feel his grandmother's hand in his and in the early morning light he bent over to pick up an olive shell. He would hold it until Johona'ai the sun would rise up toward him. Then he would toss the shell way out, as far as he could throw, to the ocean's edge on the other side, to eternity.

12

If you placed a bottle of penicillin capsules or a plate of cheddar cheese or hamburger in any environment with a temperature above 72 degrees, it would spoil pretty fast, you would figure. This alone, reasoned Sander Miller, could be proof enough of what happened to the human body every July, August and September in Miami Beach.

Sander called his home "Sweat City" and at this time of the year he sometimes felt as though his body was one big mold filled with all kinds of fungi, and he could feel those fungal itches on his ankles, on his chest, on his balls, between his toes and even stretching the imagination somewhat, on his brain also.

On the beach itself, the ocean seemed to get caught up in it also. You could take a dip in the Atlantic way down SoBe or at Key Biscayne and go home with stinging welts caused by the tiniest of jellyfish or sand fleas. The minuscule-sized creatures would rub into you as you bathed and attach themselves inside your swimsuit, with nowhere to go but inside your skin, and those creepy crawlies were everywhere in South Florida. To Sander, none of this was surprising. After all, the South Florida of the new millennium was the perfect host.

The ocean, the sand, the palms and the air itself were all compromised by the recent spate of 40-story condo monstrosities that blocked out sea breezes and spewed out wastewater and even frequent leaks of raw sewage from the antiquated undersea pipes that could not handle the volume. Then there were the cruise ships, coming in and out of the Port of Miami and Port Everglades up in Lauderdale, that sometimes dumped their own garbage overboard or leaked oil into the sea, and those tiny menaces called jet skis that raised noise pollution on the waters to new levels of inanity.

Miami Beach had been Sander Miller's home for more than three decades and for him it was time enough to have witnessed the extinction of most of the natural coral reefs, sea grasses and other life support systems. It was more than enough time to have hopelessly watched the slow poisoning of the Everglades that he loved by the industry they called "Big Sugar." He had loved to take his canoe along the Turner River and listen to the night sounds of the frogs and observe the day beauty of majestic flamingoes and so many other gorgeous species of bird life and now, suddenly, it had mostly vanished. Then, even worse, was the parasitic encroachment of the human beings who came with new housing developments and parking lots that kept expanding farther and farther west into Everglades territory.

Sander was just a kid when he was transplanted to South Florida from Ozone Park, Queens, New York and at that time he had no idea that he would become part of the State's population boom and, therefore, part of the cause of its environmental decline. Charlie was also a New York transplant, and so was that weird dead writing partner of hers, Link, that Charlie couldn't seem to shake off.

Sander had hoped that this rockhounding jaunt would get him closer with Charlie, but the way she was acting, like Link was still alive and kicking, made the whole trip a wash. Toward the end, she was really acting distant and weird and he would see this strange expression in her eyes when she didn't know anyone was watching. He wondered what the heck she was writing in that diary all the time because she surely had no social or sex life that he knew about. Maybe she wrote stuff about a dead writing partner coming back as a Clovis point!

Sander grimaced, thinking about Charlie's possible past history, and realized that she probably knew very little about him also, except for what she saw on the surface, which was a cynical know-it all who more often than not went out of his way to upset her. She had no idea where he came from. She just knew what she saw and didn't find it too impressive. Sander scratched his cheek, thinking about it all, and how he never really came to grips with his own history and all the rights and wrongs of it.

His mother had called his father "some piece of work" and the courts called him a "deadbeat dad" because he never sent any money after the divorce. But then, his dad took him fishing all the time in Sheepshead Bay and he had always an easy smile, the same one Sander saw when he looked in the mirror. Of course, if his father had sent the money, then they could have paid off the mortgage on that old house with the fake brick siding and he and his mother would not have wound up living with Aunt Kate here in Miami Beach.

Sander, as luck or misfortune would have it, still lived in the same two bedroom walkup on Michigan Avenue that his mother had rented more than 30 years ago. The semi-furnished place still looked much the same as it did then, when Ava Miller walked each morning to her job as secretary at a law firm just four blocks down on Lincoln Road. The daybed in the living room, had undergone several reupholsteries but it still had a green cover and flowered boulder pillows, similar to the style from the mid 70s, and Sander slept there whenever he was between marriages, low on funds or simply just plain lonely. When his mother died, it was natural to take the place over and then, when it was offered as a condominium a few years later, it seemed the right thing to buy it. For Sander, the place appeared destined to be his forever.

There were two ex-wives in Sander's life, both forgettable, and both coincidentally named Diane. The first Diane was 40 to his 25, and was an English teacher at Beach High at the time she claimed that Sander was the father of her unborn. Too young and naïve to ask questions, Sander believed her all the way to the altar, having no idea that it was Diane's "biological clock" and nothing more that told her she was pregnant. Diane rushed to put a payment down on a three bedroom home in the Gables and they moved in a month later to await the bundle of joy that never would be. Nine months passed and then Sander was a free man who walked as fast as any 25 year-old would, given the circumstances. When Diane cried out that her whole "dream went under," Sander could only wonder how he could have been a part of any woman's dream.

Second Diane came five years later on American flight 1453 to Las Vegas. She was Ms. Nebraska looking for fun, and sharing a night of mind-blowing sex and drugs at a cheap motel near the Strip convinced Sander that they should have a life together. A week after the Las Vegas chapel ceremony, the reality that they had nothing in common set in, and the parting was mutual and amicable.

To Sander, seated now at the old antique roll-down desk, all this was like a distant past life. The present reality was to get through the six week's worth of mail that had accumulated while he was out west playing with rocks. On his first day back home, the compressor in the living room air conditioner bummed out. A fine greeting when you go from desert dry to 100 percent humidity! A brown lizard was peeking out at him from an empty vase. The critter looked skinny, like he'd been trapped in the house for weeks and Sander opened the window to let it out. He watched intently as the lizard skimmed across a large quartz crystal he'd uncovered two years earlier in the Quachita Mountains, in Mount Ida, Arkansas.

Sander's apartment was host to all kinds of critters who found entrance by way of a window crack or open door, and quickly settled into the comfortable habitats that Sander's rock collections afforded. The coral rocks and opal wood, Tampa agate bubblies and assortments of red and yellow jaspers were everywhere the eye could see. Specimen pieces lined the floors, bookshelves, cupboards and kitchen counters. Some placements were purposeful and were meant to decorate a desk or end table and other minerals were dropped in an empty spot or corner somewhere just because they had nowhere else to go. In any event, any one of the large specimens could provide just the right cover for the South Florida special, the super-sized hairy, shiny dark brown roach called the palmetto bug.

The sounds of the familiar strains of "Fur Elise" emanating from the cell phone intruded upon Sander's enjoyment of his own thoughts and for a moment he considered just letting it ring until it went to voice mail. He glanced at the ID and saw it was from Austin. Doyle, he thought. He's back home in Texas.

"Hey," he called into the phone. "What's up?"

The voice at the other end sounded strange and kept breaking up. It sounded like Kathy, not Doyle, but he couldn't make out what she was saying. It took a few minutes more before he realized that there was nothing wrong with the phone but definitely something wrong at Kathy's end.

"We got back to Texas on Tuesday," she said, her voice cracking. "Then he was gone again on Thursday morning and so was the camper."

The Colorado State Trooper had called just two hours before to give her the bad news. A loose boulder, high on a rock wall along I-70 East, slipped down, crashing in on Doyle's windshield. The pickup, with the top-heavy camper attached, skidded off the road into the face of a huge cliff somewhere around the city of Rifle. The contents of the pickup, which included jasper from Battle

Mountain, thunder eggs from somewhere in southeastern Oregon, mahogany obsidian from Davis Creek, California and amazonite from Lake George, Colorado all spilled out onto the roadway causing two other minor accidents.

His cousin Doyle was dead and that was the main gist of it. For the life of him, Sander was amazed that in this whole story, only one thought came to his mind. From where they found the smashup and the body it was obvious that his son-of-a gun cousin had been obsessed. Doyle Miller had gone back home with his wife, then decided to leave his wife and had been heading back again to Northern Nevada. Doyle had snuck out of his house like a teenage runaway and was schlepping back to Virgin Valley for more opals!

13

"We can't use these, Charlie," said Laura Rivera, the art editor of "Travel Unusual" magazine, shaking her head. "Maybe it's your new Canon but those photos of the Black Rock Range aren't clean. Too much haze in the background."

Charlie's eyes fixed on the ghost-like image that appeared to be rising above the greenish-brown mountains like a puff of white smoke. The smoke seemed to be molded in the shape of a man on a horse, a translucent white horse, and the sight of it was at once surreal, a bit eerie and yet easy to mistake for just smoke or haze.

Laura was sitting across from Charlie at a rectangular blond mica table in an outer office normally reserved for the magazine's archive of articles, photos and assorted artwork. There were 24 medium sized 5x7 photographs spread in no particular order across the table and Charlie also had the corresponding transparencies with her in a small black folder which she knew would offer no greater clarity.

Ghosts? How could she explain to Laura about these spirits that were now coming to her? Nothing in Charlie's background had prepared her for this. Her mother and father lived and then they died. Link lived and then he died the same way but somehow his death started all this. When those you love pass on, you talk about cherished memories. You say the Kaddish, the prayer of mourning, and then you are supposed to move on with your life. No ghosts. Just memories. Do Jews even believe in ghosts?

Laura went back to her office to take a call from the magazine's managing editor, Michelle. They were talking about doing a story on a museum for covered wagons in Gillette, Wyoming. Michelle needed dynamic, colorful slides from the museum, even for something like an old dusty wagon. It was the way things were done in the competitive world of travel magazines, and the glossy covers and page layouts decorating the walls of Laura's office told the story of this five-year old Miami-based journal's fascination with far-out places. In this magazine you would never find a story about Vegas, New York or Paris, but "Travel Unusual" would transport the reader to those hidden treasures – the caves, the outback, little known galleries and museums and occasionally a ship or hotel purported to house ghosts.

Charlie looked at her photos and let out a soft sigh. This magazine, like most contemporary magazines generally sought out the middle ground and in this case, it meant they could write about "safe ghosts" but not Charlie's ghosts. Those ghosts that made doors open and close, that caused rattling and lights to flicker on and off like you saw in the movies were the safe ghosts. They were the ghosts you might find aboard the Queen Mary or inside the old Biltmore Hotel here in Coral Gables.

It was going to be a tough sell but Charlie decided she would go for it. Not easy, she thought but not impossible either. She knew that the magazine's readership had gone from a small circulation of about 25,000 readers to a whopping 134,000 in the last two years and it was no secret to Laura and Michelle that Charlie's stories about the West were a main attraction for their readership.

Charlie picked up a loupe with 3x magnification from a small collection of glass loupes lined up on a navy blue cloth in the midst of all the photographic material. Laura used these loupes to examine the quality of the slides and transparencies sent to her from syndicates and freelance photographers and if she could find nothing to her satisfaction, she would use art from the stacks of CDs or computer generated photography that lined two giant bookshelves. Charlie was waving the loupe in a circle when Laura came back in.

"This stuff on the Black Rock Desert, Laura, you really have to examine more closely," Charlie said, handing her the loupe. "You think it's all haze but you're wrong. Just look at the photo really close and tell me what you see."

Laura noticed Charlie's eyebrows knitting together in a worrisome frown and she also saw that she was breathing a bit deeper. A flash of Link Davis's face came to mind and Laura could almost visualize that look Link had when he set out a batch of UFO slides to demonstrate the purpose of the UFO Museum in Roswell, New Mexico or Area 51 in Rachel, Nevada. Sometimes Link would be

70

breathing so heavily that all the veins in his neck would stand out.

"Hey, what's going on with you, kid?" she asked, touching Charlie's shoulder lightly as she placed the loupe squarely on the ghost-like image. Sometimes Charlie got too much into New Age weirdness and that worried Laura, because she really liked her. She often thought that if Charlie were less of a puzzle they might even be friends.

Laura moved the loupe around the photo and then Charlie handed her the matching slide to study it. "What do you see, Laura?" she prodded. "Tell me what you see!"

"Okay, Charlie," Laura whispered, "but calm down." A look of disbelief started to register on her face. "I see a spirit coming out of that rock! I see a fucking spirit coming out of that rock!"

Charlie nodded now, satisfied that she made her point. "I had them developed at Jerry's."

Jerry's Tropical Photo Studio was the big one in South Beach, the one the models used to compile and update their portfolios.

"When I first saw that, I had Jerry check the emulsion himself to see if there was some damage to the film or the camera. He told me that he's never seen anything like this."

Laura shrugged, but her eyes stayed glued to the ghost of a rider and his horse. "I know already what Michelle's gonna say," she grimaced. "She'll say that the readers will suspect a hoax. That you doctored up the photo to create Johnny Whitehorse."

Charlie laughed, letting off some tension. "Well," she said, cupping her chin in her hands, "we started out looking to do a feature on the beauty of the great Black Rock Desert, not on a ghost, and nobody except me really goes there anyway, except maybe to see the Burning Man festival in September."

"So, what are you saying? That the ghost adds some unplanned intrigue to the experience?" Laura was getting interested. "You mean like we don't have to say that's Johnny Whitehorse up there, but just set that photo of the desert there and let the readers use their own imaginations?"

"Kind of," Charlie chuckled. "You've got three or four photos of the playa and the rock formations and one of them has the rider on the horse but I don't put that as a caption at all. The reader looks at the picture and says, 'Hey I got to write a letter to the editor, Max, there's a ghost in that picture and nobody at that magazine caught it!'"

Laura smiled, thinking of the possibilities. "Could you really see a bunch of tourists out in the Nevada desert searching for a ghost?"

"Sure," Charlie nodded. "Everyone wants to be scared a little. Of course, if they really met up with Johnny Whitehorse they would totally freak out."

Charlie opened up another manila envelope with more desert pictures and handed them to Laura. "Same Black Rock Desert with much more clarity, only they're last year's pictures."

Laura studied them carefully, looking for a hint of ghosts but there were none.

"These are really good", she noted, "and we could use them to complement the ghost one, but like you said, they're last year's pictures."

Charlie broke out in laughter again. "Laura, the Black Rock Desert has looked the same for the last 400 years! It's wilderness for God's sake!"

Laura sighed as she always did when Charlie's reasoning won out. Besides, all the stories that they ever did on Nevada seemed to go over well. There was the article on Area 51 and the one on the ghost town Rhyolite and the powwow in Stewart awhile back. Then, Charlie always had the imagination to make the story more intriguing and this ghost, if the readers noticed it, could be really sensational. For a moment she almost forgot that Charlie herself truly believed in this ghost and that the staff at the magazine jokingly referred to her as the disciple of the weird Link Davis.

"Okay, Charlie," she said, nodding her head. "We'll push for September so you can get the Burning Man thing in also. We've got a week to closing here, so you've got to get it to me pronto."

"I'll write it like the ghost isn't there."

"Exactly, Charlie," Laura agreed. "But we'll plant Johnny Whitehorse so strategically that he can't be missed. "We want to make sure we get lots of comments in the letter box."

Charlie's face took on a more somber look now. "You know, Laura, that ghost was really there."

Laura tapped her finger on the table. Somehow she should have figured there was something Charlie hadn't told her because in the world of Charlie nothing ever seemed to happen the way it did with normal folks.

"So, what you're saying is that you actually saw Johnny Whitehorse out there?"

"No, Laura. I didn't." Charlie hunched over the table a bit as if she were trying to hide her eyes. "What I'm saying is that ghost will not appear for any of those tourists but I know for sure it was there for me even though I didn't know it and I first discovered it when I saw the photos."

Laura was about to ask the obvious question of "Why you?" when Rosario, the editorial coordinator, a small raven-haired woman, entered the room holding two tiny cups of a strong murky sweet concoction known simply as Cuban coffee.

"Gracias, Rosario," Laura smiled gratefully, handing a cup to Charlie.

For a few moments the two just sat there in silence savoring both the taste and the interlude this coffee break afforded them. Laura finally broke the silence.

"So, off the record, can you tell me about this?"

"Maybe I don't even know what there is to tell," Charlie kidded, but Laura wasn't fooled. She could tell that something happened to Charlie out there in the desert that was out of the ordinary, something that made it easier for her to accept that the ghost picture was real. For Charlie though, the moment of telling had passed. Sander didn't believe her and neither would Laura so what was the point of getting into it?

"Hey," she joked. "Maybe my time is coming and the guy on the white horse was coming to take me into the sunset! Or maybe Johnny Whitehorse is an Anasazi ancestor who returned to take a look at this lost planet of the 21st century. Judging by what's going on in the west with the strip miners, the loggers and those coal companies crapping on sacred mesas you can't fault the ghosts for returning to try to right some wrongs."

Charlie got up from her seat, in a gesture that meant she was ending the discussion but added a thought to let Laura know there was definitely more going on than met the eye.

"You know," she said, "If I'd known that ghost was out there watching, I probably would have made an offering. Then again, maybe he was making an offering to me. I found an ancient treasure in that desert, Laura, and someday, not now but someday, I'll share it with you."

Charlie's eyes were tearing up and Laura decided not to probe further. She got up from her seat and embraced her as she always did when they ended an editorial meeting. Charlie always liked the hugging that Cubans got into because it personalized the whole relationship and made it more than just a professional hookup. Maybe someday she and Laura could have a real friendship, but right now the timing didn't feel right for it.

Walking out into the strong sunlight from the air-conditioned office made Charlie dizzy. She decided to grab a sandwich and some coffee at the food court at Bayside Marketplace, the open air mall across the way.

Perhaps, she thought, she should have imparted the whole desert adventure to the art director, but what would Laura have gotten out of knowing about her arrowheads and the dream about Link? She was even intimating that the readers would think the ghost picture was a hoax. Maybe Laura was projecting her own thoughts. Maybe *she* thought it was a hoax. After all, why did she give the ghost the fictional name Johnny Whitehorse?

Whatever. Charlie realized that she was starting to take all of this too personally without really knowing if any of it had any meaning. But then Link always said that everything had a meaning and that it would all fall into place if you opened up and allowed it to flow in. He used to talk about the synchronicity of life's events and how simultaneous events had a meaning beyond mere coincidence.

The horn from a silvery gray Lexus SUV honked at Charlie and she realized that she was about to get killed crossing Biscayne Boulevard on a yellow light. That's what you got for thinking too hard in the great caring city of Miami. It was infinitely easier to think about what she was in the mood for at the food court, a slice of pizza or maybe Greek salad. The rest, she decided, she would leave to the fates. After all, the way things were going, it was just as likely that she had no choice in the matter.

14

"One morning, First Man took a walk right at the sunrise and he saw that the mountain he called Ch'ool'ii was topped with fog. He thought he would climb up it and then walk down from all four directions beginning with the east, then the south, the west, the north and then back to the east. From the east he then climbed all the ways up to the top and that was when he saw a newborn baby girl lying on the sand. Thinking maybe it was all in his imagination, First Man did the climb one more time from all the directions to be sure. Yes, he saw that the baby girl was still there and nobody to this day knows her father or her mother.

First Man and First Woman raised her and some say it took the girl only four days, some others say four years, to grow up into a beautiful young lady. She became known as White Shell Woman but then later on she took on the name of Changing Woman or Azdzaa Nadleehe, the mother of the Dineh clans."

Shash Benally was telling his six-year old grandson Shash III, the son of Shash Jr. and his second ex-wife, a Chicana named Rosalie, the Navajo creation story about the beginnings of time. Shash and Shash III were sitting close together on a patch of hard sand outside the small hogan that Shash Benally had fashioned out of discarded railroad ties about 50 years back, a time when for Shash, life still held some hope and promise.

It was a temporary shack back then, and the big hogan made of cedar was going to be built for all the ceremonies. Shash had thought about just where he would place Bessie's wedding basket for the medicine ceremony. He would teach all his children's children about how you made the hogan sacred for yei bichei and he would take them to all the song and dance festivals and the squaw dance too, even though he hated that name and the way it was used by the bilagana.

Boy, time sure passed by fast. Fifty years at least and still no cedar hogan. Just this patched up mess that reminded one of all the bad times, the coming of the railroad and the clearing out of all the tribes. Just looking at those railroad ties was a reminder of the persecutions, the harassments and confinements of the Navajos and all the other tribes to parcels of undesired lands they came to call reservations. Yeah, in time his little grandson would learn about it all, but for now, Shash would make sure he learned only the good things. Maybe that way, he would avoid the mistakes of his father. Maybe he would marry a good tribal girl, stay away from drugs and alcohol and learn to walk the Beauty Way. You had to be positive and always look ahead. It was the trick to the survival of his people.

Still, early that morning, something happened in the darkness of the old hogan that had made both the elder Navajo and his grandson shiver and shake. This was the reason that now at 8 AM, they were sitting here, outside of the hogan, too timid to go back inside.

"Grandpa," Shash III asked softly, running his hand through his blue-black bangs, "are those voices going to come back again?"

His grandfather did not respond and Shash III was getting the feeling that he was both stumped and afraid. It was the reason that he was telling stories this morning, the boy knew. It seemed like whenever his grandfather worried about something, he would sing "Hozhoni" the "Beauty Way" or tell a story from the beginning of time or about the old ways. Sometimes that could help you forget and move on, he always said.

Somewhere around midnight it all started. Shash had wanted his grandson to "sleep traditional," he said, so he went to get some sheepskin from his cousin Mary in Wide Ruins to make a soft bed for the little one. When the voices started, Shash III was asleep in the skins and Shash's thoughts had started to wander.

Miami, he was thinking. What a hell of a place for his son Nakai to wind up in and with that strange bilagana German lady who had a mouth like a rattlesnake! Once Nakai was as innocent as his six year-old grandson, before he let the bilagana get to him and fill him with so much rage, and before his mind split into the crazy mishmash that controlled him.

Shash was thinking about all of that when the voices first started coming at him. They started softly, so softly that he could not make out if they were talking or if they were praying. He recognized the language all right. It was Dineh. Now, Nakai always spoke about hearing the voices and Shash just figured his son was mental, but here he was thinking about his son and here come the voices!

So, not knowing if it was just his imagination at work, Shash did the only thing he could think of to prove his sanity. He decided to do just like First Man would do. He first walked out of the hogan and then walked back in, approaching the door which faced east from all four directions. He would find out this way if he was just an old man losing his marbles. If the voices stopped when he walked out the door then they were coming from the inside of the hogan. If he still heard the voices outside, then he was in big mental trouble because the voices would be tracking him.

Fortunately, Shash noticed that each time he walked out the door, the voices ceased. Then, no matter from which direction he approached the hogan, those voices would start back up the minute he went inside the door. That meant that he was not crazy, but Shash shivered anyway, because those voices could be something else.

The "chindi" were spirits of the dead and Shash worried that for whatever reason they might be coming back to haunt him. Why? He had no idea. As far as knew, no one had ever died inside that hogan because if they had, he would not be there and he probably would have taken down the hogan or burned it. What's more, he had just completed the offerings at Sandia Mountain and he was sure all of this nonsense was over.

A friendlier possibility was that the voices could be ancestral holy people singing out for Shash and his grandson but how to know which? He thought to wake up his grandson who was in the deepest of sleeps, but then decided to do nothing and wait for morning. He sat down on an old mattress next to the young boy and eventually dozed off, falling into a deep dream.

In the dream, there was a ceremony, a kinaalda, the holy puberty ritual held for a young lady when she first starts to menstruate. Shash could see First Man and First Woman and all the "yeis" or holy people celebrating Changing Woman's arrival into womanhood in songs and dances of prayer. It was a beautiful dream and when Shash awoke, he took it as a sign that the earlier voices he heard were good, but he could not be sure.

There, in the early morning darkness, he thought about calling up his son Nakai to talk about it and picked up the cell phone from the dresser. Maybe he could reach him before he went out for sunrise prayer so he could learn more about the voices.

"Grandpa," Shash III called out to him, just as Shash realized the phone was low on battery, "I had a really funny dream last night about grandma."

"About grandma, huh?" Shash looked at his grandson quizzically.

"I had a dream that grandma came back and she was singing to me. Only she looked prettier and more skinny and she had yellow hair."

"Yellow hair, you say? That is not possible little boy," Shash said, now a bit shaken and confused.

So many thoughts were running through his head now. There were those voices that his son Nakai talked about and then the last time he talked about some bilagana woman in Miami who was going to change things. Maybe she was the one that his grandson saw in that dream.

Whatever the story, Shash was certain of one thing. Until he could figure out to his satisfaction the mystery of those voices, he and his grandson would have to keep out of the hogan, and they could do that all day if need be, because Shash had enough stories to keep Shash III happy for an eternity.

15

It is illegal to collect ancient artifacts on federal, state and public land. Tony the librarian just said so and Charlie verified it on a reliable BLM website.

Charlie let out a sarcastic laugh. So her great desert find could actually land her in jail! How ironic it all seemed. Yet here she was, yellow legal pad to one side of the desk, laptop plugged into the library's terminal on the other side, taking notes about what kinds of stiff fines the penal system could impose for the crime of picking up two arrowheads. Now wasn't this the same government that spent 500 years killing the same Indians who crafted these beautiful points? Besides, if she had not found them and some cow trampled them instead would they then arrest the cow?

She had come here this morning half-hoping to talk to that fancy looking Indian with the shiny long hair. Well, he was here, all right, but now she was getting cold feet. He was sitting in front of the magazine racks reading, of all things, the Wall Street Journal. Maybe it was a good thing though that he got into all the economic bullshit of the country. If he was less traditional, he might not look upon her as some thoughtless white woman who callously collected Indian artifacts. She would never dig up a gravesite or desecrate a mound, but still, how would he know that?

What propelled Charlie to approach this rather sullen seeming man was no doubt what Link Davis used to call "the need to know." It was always a reasonable justification for requesting classified UFO government papers through the Freedom of Information Act. Her need to know about the two obsidian arrowheads was reason enough to initiate a conversation and hope he would be open to it.

Nakai was able to keep his eye on Charlie by lifting and then lowering his eyes quickly as he scanned the pages of the newspaper. She was fidgeting nervously and her face seemed a bit drawn since he had last seen her before her long western trip. Her pale facial color told him that she had a weak heart and probably the mountain climbing made her feel weaker. She was wearing thick socks and sneakers on a day that was close to 90 degrees and with a humidity that probably brought the heat index up somewhere around 105. It was a good moment for her to come over to meet him and he began to concentrate in that direction.

He did not seem too unapproachable to Charlie. He was wearing jeans and some kind of open vest and his hair, which was usually down around his shoulders, was tied back in a ponytail today. Not his usual array of jewelry either and she suspected that it was because of the hot weather out there. He had on a small necklace with some heishi shells and turquoise instead of the heavy squash blossom she was accustomed to seeing and she could see only one earring which looked oddly enough like a dangling black obsidian point. She closed her laptop, picked up her legal pads and walked over to him, standing about a yard and a half away. When he looked up from the newspaper, she would go for it.

"My name is Charlie," she announced in a voice that came out softer than she had planned. "If you would be so kind, when you have a free moment, I would like to talk to you."

He enjoyed her modesty and slight nervousness. That was a wonderful start.

"I am Nakai," he said, looking up, his eyes meeting hers for the first time.

Charlie noted the pronunciation of his name, with the emphasis on the first syllable. It sounded Navajo, but she also recognized some Apache in him. It was his expression that was at once sullen yet intense. He got up from his chair, placed the newspaper back on the reference desk, and then motioned for Charlie to follow him out of the double glass doors to the street.

They crossed Collins Avenue to a small patch of crabgrass and palms and Nakai was thankful for a brisk westerly breeze that was coming strong at the moment, keeping it from getting too sweaty. He was keeping his cool but was quietly pissed at his choice of clothes for the day. The morning felt like rain and he didn't think that Charlie had returned from the trip yet. If he had known in advance of this turn of events he would have at least worn the white shirt with the four beaded feathers on the right pocket. So much for intuition!

Charlie's watch read 10:45, which to Nakai meant that Hannelore would be heading out of the apartment shortly to her new job at the Hebrew Retirement Center in North Miami. For a brief moment he could imagine her spitting in some senile woman's soup, she was that mean. He motioned for Charlie to sit down next to him under a medium sized sea grape tree that could offer some degree of shade anyway. She watched him flick a red ant from his big toe, and smiled. "It's why I wear sneakers around here."

"Yeah," he grinned. "I left my desert home for the red ant way."

Nakai surprised himself. It was a rare moment that he wanted to make a white person feel any comfort. Here he was trying to break the ice when normally he enjoyed watching people, especially white people, squirm. He quickly focused his eyes ahead, purposely trying to lose any sense of familiarity.

"So," he said, "you talk and I listen"

"Well," she said, patting the bed of crab grass beneath her, "I found two arrowheads out in the Nevada desert." Her voice was shaky and hoarse, not the way she meant for it to sound.

"I don't know where they came from. One minute they were not there and the next minute they were right in front of my feet."

Nakai said nothing, waiting for her to continue. So far there was nothing spectacular about what she was saying. People all the time saw things in the desert that seemed to be there and then weren't. Sometimes it was the way the sun fell or the way that all the desert rocks might look the same at first glance. So Nakai waited, but Charlie got quiet. She was clamming up the way people sometimes did when they thought you would see them as a nut case. That told him something about her. The fact was that most of the nut cases just babbled on about nothing, especially the New Age ones. They would brag to you how they put out white light or attracted angels.

"Maybe those arrowheads found you," Nakai finally offered. "Sometimes when you ask for help, the ancestors come to guide you."

He watched her move her hand to her jeans pocket and take out a deerskin pouch with a leather drawstring and felt his excitement start to build. He could not believe his luck that this Charlie carried these ancestors wrapped in leather instead of in her laptop bag. He would have to work hard to keep his voice and gaze as stoic as white people expected, a game that most of the time he enjoyed playing.

She handed the glassy, precious arrowheads cautiously to Nakai, hoping he would not tell her it was against the law for her to have them.

"How did you know to wrap these points in leather?" he asked, holding out the points to the sunlight and avoiding her gaze.

"Oh," she said. "Everyone protects precious things from breaking."

He smiled at her innocence in thinking that she was explaining to him, Nakai, something he didn't know, but at the same time he was marveling at the ancient treasures he was holding in the palm of his hand. Nakai knew these arrowheads well. They were the kind that the Anasazi, the earliest medicine people used, their "footprints" that could be seen in the deserts of the Southwest. They might have been 10,000 years old or more, yet they were as beautiful and precious as the day they first touched that sand.

"So, you have two here, a tall masculine point and a shorter fatter feminine one," Nakai commented, looking for a reaction.

"Yes, I know," Charlie nodded, making Nakai feel slightly miffed.

She had come to him for some answers but now it seemed she was aware of everything he was telling her. He would have to catch her on something here to keep control of all this, to lead her in the right direction, in the direction of Chilchinbito and his father.

"So, tell me now," he asked, touching her arm lightly, "tell me the direction these footprints were facing when you found them."

Footprints. Charlie had heard that reference before somewhere, maybe in a book, about artifacts being footprints of the past. But no, she had never thought about which way they were facing when she discovered them. It all happened so fast.

"I have no sense of the directions out in the Black Rock Desert" she sighed. "I mean, I know that desert enough to find my way back to the Jeep, but that's about all."

"And how do you find the Jeep?" he prodded.

"I kind of look to the playa which is flat and gray or white, depending on the weather, and then to the familiar rock formations on the opposite side."

She looked perplexed for a moment but then came back with a statement that threw Nakai off center and left him feeling once again that he was losing control of this meeting.

"My guess is that the playa is to the east and the mesas to the west but then the desert all winds around when you walk a quarter of a mile one way or the other so it's hard to say. It just goes on and on for miles and miles."

"I gather you don't carry a compass?" Nakai felt his voice rising and the last thing he wanted was to show this Charlie he was indignant. It just made no sense to him because all the bilagana, the white people, and especially a white woman would carry a compass in the wilderness.

"No," she said, shaking her head, and seeming more confident. "I know the Black Rock Desert. I even walked across it once, from mountain to mountain. I don't need a compass there to find my way."

Nakai finally turned his head to face her, and the intensity of his black eyes went right through her. When he did this, he usually commanded attention and sometimes even reverence and fear with white people.

"Listen to me now," he said, "because this is imperative. It is important to know the direction of these arrowheads. When you come upon this kind of ancient treasure, you must observe everything."

Charlie nodded, unshaken by his new demanding tone. She was thinking suddenly about Sander and what he would think of this conversation. It was funny in a way, because Nakai was making the same kind of blanket statements that Sander often did, like he had the market cornered on this kind of knowledge. Of course, in this case, there was no percentage in challenging Nakai when she was seeking any information she could get. She would tell him whatever she knew.

"These arrowheads," she said, taking them from Nakai's palm, "were parallel to eachother like this." She placed them next to each other on the grass, with the points at the same level so that the taller of the two seemed that much taller. The sun was out strong so they were very sparkly."

"What else do you remember?" Nakai was happy that she had at least some kind of memory.

"Well, okay," Charlie said, slowly recalling something. "They were pointing right at me."

Nakai let out a loud disappointed sigh. This was the kind of statement he would expect to hear in some well-packaged New Age novel. He didn't know why he expected to hear something better from this Charlie, but he did and he was starting to lose patience.

"So, the ancestors were looking right at you, eh?" He had an edge to his voice now and Charlie could feel it. If he was going to mock her, so be it, she thought. He wouldn't be the first guy to throw her a curve.

"Yes, as a matter of fact they were," she said, putting more confidence into her voice. I'm also sure that they were not there when I first sat down. The sun was out strong and there were no shadows and I pretty much know what I saw. And maybe," she added, "this is more important than whether they were facing east or west or pointing at me or away from me."

Nakai mused a bit, listening to this white woman who presumed to know as much as an Indian about these matters. She could get to him and make him really angry but what was the use? Besides, he was enjoying the back and forth more than he thought he would. So, what was the harm in taunting her a bit? After all, it was she who finally came to him for some answers.

"Why do you suppose these ancestors wanted to find you? Nakai asked, raising his eyebrows a bit.

"How would I know!" Charlie shot back. "You're the one who decided that these are ancestors who came to help me! Listen," she said now, lowering her voice, "I'm sorry I am so out of sorts. When I was out there, I was having a hard time getting over the death of my writing partner, Link Davis. My mind was not in a state where I was studying everything.

Link Davis. The name struck a chord with Nakai, and for the moment, he fell silent. He remembered him vaguely as a tall guy with a mustache and a crooked kind of smile. The New Agers used to talk about him all the time. He would hear his name mentioned from the kinds of people who confused the occult with tribal ceremony, like the reiki crystal healers and the guys who sold you rose quartz to heal your broken heart. But what they didn't know was that Link Davis was of a different, far more dangerous breed, because he got into metal bending and UFO's and entering into other dimensions. Those guys could get into worlds that mortal man could not dream about. They had been there and they knew, and Nakai knew also because he had been there too, many times.

"Link Davis was connected," Nakai stated, looking up at her. He had no idea that she had been such close friends with that man, although, he might have seen them together a couple of times at the coffee house.

"Have you heard from him?" he found himself asking. He knew at once that the question was shocking and unexpected. He also knew by these two arrowheads that found their way to her that she had.

Charlie started to speak but found herself stammering. She was totally taken aback by the question. She had no idea that Nakai had heard about Link, but then again, he was fairly well known in his field.

"I was thinking about him...I mean...I was at the opal mine in Virgin Valley with my friends Sander and Doyle...and...yes, it happened."

Nakai could not resist the temptation to interrupt and he hated himself for it, but he had to know.

"This Sander and Doyle, are they boyfriends?"

Charlie stiffened. "Doyle was killed on I-70 a few days ago. I'm a writer and I travel a lot, looking for stories. I don't complicate my life with boyfriends."

She hated this line of questioning and all men got into it. You would talk for a few minutes and it was always something like, "So, do you live with your family here?" when what they really wanted to know was do you have a husband, boyfriend or current lover?

"Let's go on then," Nakai said, trying to act as matter-of-factly as he could when that piece of information was thrilling him to no end. "So, you were at this mine that was near the Black Rock Desert?"

"Correct," she said, picking up the thread, "that was where I had the dream or where, maybe as you say, he came to me. It was a phone conversation that happened when I was sleeping."

"Or when you thought you were sleeping," Nakai interjected.

Charlie proceeded to carefully relate the story in its entirety, trying not to leave out any detail that could be important. At least he was listening and not mocking her, the way Sander had. In fact, he seemed to be listening very intently.

He waited until she was done so he could be reasonably sure that what he told her made sense.

"Those arrowheads then came right after the phone call?" he asked.

"The very next day in the desert as I told you."

"Well," he said, "So, what do you think?"

"I think that the big arrowhead is Link and the small one is me and that means we will be together for always."

Nakai grinned. "No, that can't be it because the arrowheads are ancestors. "They are likely your mother and your father who came to comfort you."

Charlie was stunned. What he was saying actually made sense. It also made her remember something else. She opened her purse and pulled out a small photo album. Her hands were shaking as she opened the page to the photo of the ghostlike image emerging from the mountains, the vision that Laura dubbed Johnny Whitehorse.

"I took this photo in the desert very close to the time I found the arrowheads," she said.

Nakai removed the photo from its holder and stared at it in fascination. It looked like the ghost of a man riding a horse over the mountain.

"This is a chindi," he said, the pitch of his voice rising a bit.

"A what?"

"A chindi. A spirit rising from the spiritual world. It's him. Your friend Link Davis.

Nakai stood up and took her hand to let her know the meeting was over. She could not help but notice that his hand seemed to be trembling a bit.

"But why did his ghost come to me?" She had a need to know.

The Indian wrapped his arm around her in a kind of half embrace.

"I think he came to tell you that you will soon be taking a journey."

"A journey?" Charlie asked. "But I just returned from one."

Nakai smiled at her and patted her shoulder.

"In beauty," he smiled, and started to walk off toward the pavement. Then turning around, he saw her still standing there watching him.

"Don't worry," he shouted, waving his arm. "I'll come back for you. I'm going to take you there, I promise!"

16

The low hills of grayish brown dirt left standing from the once active phosphate mine hid fossil treasures and Sander Miller was determined to find them. He had parked his Jeep discreetly behind an abandoned orange grove, a short distance from the "NO TRESPASSING" sign that was supposed to bar access to the hills of the old Central Florida mine.

The narrow two-lane roads that led into and out of the city of Barstow, revealed several once operational phosphate mines that were touted as treasure troves of ancient shark teeth, dugong bones and possibly a tooth of two from an ancient four-legged creature. Sander had visited every one of the mines at one time or another in this area, appropriately called "Bone Valley."

His last visit had been in April and he had come with Charlie and a couple of students from the university. Charlie complained then about the nests of fire ants and stickers in the weeds. The thing was that while she always kvetched about something, she was always the first to uncover something really special, just like those Clovis points she found out in the desert. That sunny April afternoon was no different and she had picked up a two inch shark tooth that had mineralized over the years to a pearly olive green shade. It was damn exquisite and she knew Sander coveted it for his collection. Then she did what Sander would never do. She gave it to him as a birthday present right before they left for the west.

He was thinking about all that and it seemed like it was no fun anymore doing these trips solo, now climbing up the machine made hills, stepping between the high grass and weeds that were starting to grow back in the fertile soil.

He had called Charlie about a week ago, leaving the message about Doyle's accidental death and was surprised when there was no return call. He tried a few more times, still coming up empty and then he called again two days ago and left word on her voice mail that he was coming up here today, but still no response. True, Charlie always complained about these phosphate mines polluting the waters and earth, but in spite of her ranting, she still liked to see what she could uncover once the mines closed down. He never knew a time she was not ready for some treasure hunting.

So the question was, where was she? He must have called at least a dozen times but her cell was always turned off and her voice mail at home always on. Maybe she was still pissed at him over that arrowhead thing

The sun was beating down fairly hard now and Sander knew his face would get a really bad burn. He had that fair skin that required a good straw panama and lotion with a high sunscreen but he had neither. Even more bothersome were the gnats swarming around the man-made, stagnant, smelly stream left over by the mining operation. The closer you got to it, the more you got eaten alive and Sander, of course, had forgotten the repellent also. It was natural, because he had always counted on Charlie to remember the details.

Charlie. He could not seem to get his mind off her, which was odd for him. Just a weird feeling that something wasn't right. He could drop by her place tonight and talk to her. See if he could make peace. For as long as he had known her he never thought of her as someone who held a grudge for very long and if she really thought that wacko space cadet Link Davis was contacting her through some Clovis points, well, whatever!

The sun was outlining something long and black on the opposite hill and Sander walked right through a thorny bush to locate it, scratching his arm from his elbow to his wrist with the effort. You had to make the move without hesitation because often the sun would peek in and out of the clouds, and when that happened, a brown or black fossil would just blend back into the sand and be lost. Sander's prize, a black inch and a half ancient alligator tooth made the scratch well worth it. It was a beauty and completely intact. Charlie would love it because she loved alligators.

Sander held the tooth in his hand as he made his way down the hill. He thought about giving it to Charlie as a kind of truce offering. Then again, maybe he wouldn't, because he had never found one like this before, so sparkling and clean. It would be a perfect addition to his Florida fossil collection. He wrapped it carefully in some tissue paper he carried to prevent any breakage and put it inside the pocket of his trail vest for safekeeping.

Should he give it to Charlie or not? These kinds of decisions always bothered him and he hated the selfish streak that tended to rule his choices in life. He walked toward the Jeep, still thinking about it and decided he would go to her door and see what happened. If she opened the door and smiled at him, she got it. If she told him to get lost, it was his. It was kind of like playing heads or tails. Potluck. Putting your hand in the grab bag. It's what his whole damned life was about anyway.

17

The earliest memory Charlie had recorded in her diary, years back when she was much younger, was of dark red splotches of blood on her white pillow and the blasting sirens of an ambulance approaching the house. On the bedroom ceiling, the dancing shadows of the oak tree limbs were transformed into shapeless monsters that changed shape to the rhythm of the flickering of a street light down below.

Since she had been aware of the ambulance sound and the ghoulish ceiling figures, Charlie figured she must have been about four years old, but then recalling it now, that faded red brick house in Queens and the old oak tree, she also remembered looking out from a yellow crib and that would have put it at around three or even closer to two. Then there was something else tied into that event. A long narrow room with drab green walls and rows of beds with bars that slid up and down with clangy noises, and children crying. A nurse gave her a needle and lied about it saying, "It will hurt only a little bit," and then the next thing she knew it was morning and her uncle Manny was sitting across from her smiling and promising her a toy merry-go-round.

The old brick house, like many of the properties on the narrow streets of working class Queens, was attached on both sides by similar houses, all two stories and adequate enough to shelter nuclear families like Charlie's. In her earliest days, it wasn't just her parents living there, but her maternal grandparents, her uncles Manny and Jake and her sister Raye. Then, little by little, that family began to move away, and by the time Charlie was eight and Raye 10, it was just the two of them, their parents and Uncle Jake. The house now seemed so much larger and she and Raye loved to use their imaginations, and the empty bedrooms, to play pretend games. Sometimes they were high society ladies having tea and gossiping about their friends and sometimes they were teenagers having a party with their favorite movies stars. They decorated the rooms in crepe paper, swatches of material and colorful drawings to suit the theme of the day.

Considering it all now, Charlie figured that growing up could have been a lot worse. She might have even enjoyed it in spite of her fragile health had it not been for her hostile uncle Jake who held dominion over the household. For it was Jake who had property title to the house, who set the rules for who did what under his roof and who decided which one of his subjects to torment. His usual choice would be the weakest and so Charlie was always fair game.

Charlie's dad, Jonah Landers, labored hard to support his family, often ten or more hours a day as a welder at a small shop in Astoria, not far from their home. Jonah arrived at Ellis Island as a teenager two and a half months before the Nazi's surrounded his family's small village in Poland. He never saw his parents, grandparents, four sisters and two brothers ever again. There was never to be any discussion of the holocaust in the Landers house however, because Jonah said that they had to move ahead. But Charlie would often notice her father switching stations on the TV set late at night, searching for any documentary about the war. He would sit there, shaking his head or pounding the coffee table, as if he were searching for some kind of meaning in the catastrophe.

It was middle-class America of the 70s, and the life of the Landers family must have seemed uneventful from the outside. Jonah worked and Anna, her mother, took care of the house, frying hamburgers on the gas stove and sewing clothes from Butterick patterns for the girls on her old-fashioned treadle sewing machine. There were candles lit for Shabbat every Friday evening and Passover seders shared with family and friends around the big, round, lace- covered mahogany dining room table. They kept a kosher home, with separate dishes for meat and dairy, and there were rules to follow regarding what you were not permitted to do on the Shabbat. The rules seemed tiresome and inconvenient and often out of step with the times for Charlie and Raye, but still they seemed to make you feel more secure, especially during the worst of times.

Anna was weak, suffering from osteoporosis, arthritis and a host of respiratory ailments and Charlie inherited her genetic makeup. On the good days, she was able to play hide and seek and tag and all the backyard games with the kids, but on the bad days, the least effort would result in a fall, a fracture, a bleed somewhere, or a bad asthma attack. Her earliest memories were of doctors coming up the stairs to her room, in the days when they still made house calls for emergencies, and of the ever-present sight of a thermometer ready to be stuck somewhere unappealing. Charlie didn't recall what happened to her the night of the blood-splotched pillow, but once, when she and Raye were teenagers, Raye remembered that it was Uncle Jake's fault. He had punched Charlie in the mouth, Raye said, because Charlie would not eat the chicken liver at dinner.

It was a past life of sorts to Charlie now, as she rested her head in a kind of half sleep in the back of Nakai's Chevy van. They were all gone now to the spiritual world, even Raye who crashed her silver Olds into a tree, killing herself and Jonah almost instantly when Charlie was only 18. Then, a couple of years after that, uncle Jake had a fatal heart attack, leaving Charlie alone to take care of her mother Anna, until her mother died of staph pneumonia on Charlie's twenty-first birthday. It was a dizzying time of both loss and growth. There was furniture and a house to sell and college to finish. And there were decisions to make about her future as a writer that she would have to make alone, and alone she seemed destined to be for a very long time. That was until Link came along.

"Hey, you okay back there?" Nakai was checking her out from the driver's seat. He had been singing something repetitious in Dineh that she figured was meant to put her to sleep. It didn't work though and she was getting restless and uneasy on this third and hopefully final day of this trip to Chilchinbito in Arizona.

He told her that they were going to visit his father, Shash Benally, who was a medicine man and that he could help her settle a few things in her mind with the arrowheads. It seemed like a good idea at the time, going to visit someone with knowledge of these things, but now it seemed like a big mistake. Here she was alone with this guy who seemed a bit strange, in a van he stole from his girlfriend back in Miami, visiting an elder who might not even care to see a blonde white lady.

She should have told Sander where she was headed, she thought, but then he would have just laughed at her as always. Even more likely than that, he would have tried to stop her with scare tactics about "rez" Indians. Maybe, when they got to Gallup, she would leave a message on his voice mail. Charlie closed her eyes, trying to get into sleep, but she was overtired. Nakai had insisted on driving straight through, just taking cat naps along the way, either in the van or at a rest stop. They were now somewhere on I-40 around Grants, New Mexico when he came to a sudden stop.

"Hey, do you ever find rocks up there?" He was pointing to a mountain about a mile away.

Charlie got up slowly from her crouched position to look out of the window. "Mount Taylor," she said, recognizing the peak. "No, I've never climbed that one."

Nakai grimaced. "You white people call it Mount Taylor. We call it Turquoise Mountain or Tsoodzil. It's one of the four."

"The four sacred mountains," Charlie said softly. "I heard about them."

Nakai nodded. "There is the east mountain called Sis Naajini. The white people call that one Blanca Peak. The west one, the one you call San Francisco Peak is Dook'o'oostiid. Then there is the one in Colorado to the north, the La Plata, that we call Dibe Nitsaa.

"Then Tsoodzil is the south mountain," Charlie offered.

Nakai fell silent. He was secretly thrilled that she pronounced the Dineh name so well. He opened the door of the van and stepped out to get a better look at the mountain. It would be dark in a couple of hours and Charlie figured they would be in Chilchinbito soon after that, maybe about 9:30 or so.

"Time is of no importance out here," Nakai said, as if reading her mind. "It's not like writing for a magazine. There are no deadlines and no places you have to be." He opened the rear door to help her out onto the red sand of western New Mexico. Together they began to walk toward Tzoodzil and Charlie, feeling more secure now, was thinking she had made a good decision to come here.

"Do you know about Asdzaa Nadleehe, the Changing Woman?" Nakai asked.

"She is from the Navajo creation story. Right?"

Nakai took Charlie's hand in his, smiling. "Yes, we Dineh have our own story about how it all got started. We don't do Adam and Eve." He laughed and shook his head. The story says that she opened up to the sun, who we call Johona'ai, and from this she had twin sons."

Charlie grinned. "That makes about as much sense as Eve being created from Adam's rib"

Nakai squeezed her hand in a playful way. "You know, Pop says we have to believe these stories to keep the Dineh alive. What do you think?"

"I think so too," Charlie agreed. "Stories keep people focused and together. It was like Link and me writing about the things we believed in."

Nakai said nothing. Link was gone and no threat to his future. No need to dwell on it.

"What about the twins?" Charlie asked.

He noticed that she was standing still and her breathing was a bit labored. They were less than a quarter mile from the sacred mountain and Nakai guessed that the walk was going to be too much for her. It was getting near nightfall and he decided he had better not pursue it this time or she might not make it in one piece to his father. He found himself feeling sad that she was not a strong woman.

"Yes, the twins," he said, pointing to a low solid rock for her to sit on. "There is a story about the twins but you will think it is a fairy tale."

Charlie grinned, happy that Nakai was not going to push the long hike. "My life often feels like a fairy tale."

He turned away from her because sometimes these stories brought tears to his eyes and he did not know why. Maybe because he'd heard them over and over from his grandmother and then his mother and they were both gone now to the spiritual world.

"The twins were the Sun's children but the Sun wouldn't own up to it. Instead he went off and found himself a new wife."

"Did the twins know he was their father? Did Changing Woman ever tell them?"

"No," Nakai shook his head. "Changing Woman wouldn't tell them because the Sun was violent and she thought he might kill them. But then, somehow, I don't remember exactly how, they found out anyway."

Nakai, still standing, looked down at Charlie now, sitting with her hands folded like a first grader wanting to be a good student. He made up his mind then and there that he would tell the story as you told it to another Dineh and he would forget that she was a white women. After all, she trusted him enough to have come this far when he was a total stranger and she had no idea just how wild and dangerous he could be. She had taken her chances and now so would he.

"At the time we are talking about," Nakai cleared his throat, "maybe millions of years ago, there were so many monsters roaming this land. One of the Twins, the one we call Monster Slayer, wanted to get rid of these monsters so the human race could grow in peace."

"What was the other twin called?" Charlie found herself intrigued by how well Nakai could relate this ancient story.

"The other twin was known as Child of the Water. Well, both twins were conceived near a beautiful waterfall."

Charlie's questions were interrupting Nakai's train of thought but oddly enough, it wasn't bothering him. She was a writer, after all and it was probably her nature to probe.

"Anyhow," he went on, "the boys decided that they needed to go to their father the Sun so they could get weapons to kill the monsters. The Sun was sure to have bows and arrows made of thunder and lightning which was exactly what they needed.'

Nakai paused to catch his breath because this story always excited him. Here they were, two young boys out on an adventure to kill monsters. It was every young Dineh boy's dream to be Monster Slayer and it was still Nakai's dream even as a grown man.

"Do you know about Spider Woman?" he asked Charlie.

Charlie nodded. "She teaches the young ladies how to weave."

"Now, that's good!" Nakai cleared his throat, trying to hold back his excitement. "Well, when the boys took off on their adventure, they came upon Spider Woman's home, deep inside a cave in the ground. When they went in the cave, they saw that the walls were decorated with feathers of every description and color.'

Spider Woman knew who their father was and warned them of all the dangers they would encounter in trying to get to their destination. She gave them corn meal and fed them a small piece of turquoise and a bit of white shell which she said would make their hearts strong and give them courage. She also taught them prayers to recite and gave them feathers that would help them when they got into trouble."

"What kinds of trouble?" Charlie looked up at Nakai. He seemed agitated now and his eyes were squinting.

"Oh, the usual," he said, kicking a small stone in the direction of a souvenir shop that was now blocking part of the view of Tsoodzil. "There were sharp reeds that could kill you, moving sand that could bury you if you fell in it, canyons that could crush you."

Nakai was laughing now but in a mocking way. "You see the Indian or as the white people say, the Native American, has always had obstacles to face and get through." He pointed to the souvenir shop. "You see that despicable place? The white tourists go there to buy a piece of us. It's an obstacle but someday we will get rid of it. We won't be Indians anymore. We don't come from India. We are Dineh, the People."

Charlie nodded in agreement. "I hate those shops too. They are faceless and sell cheap junk. If tourists want to buy Indian crafts, they should buy directly from the people, the ones who sell at the fairs, on the streets and at the flea markets."

Nakai felt his anger dissipating. This woman seemed to get what he was talking about.

"So," he continued, "the twins, after going through all kinds of terrible obstacles like I mentioned, finally reached their father. But that turned out to be another hell for them, because he had a new wife and refused to admit they were his children. He even tried to kill them by giving them poison tobacco and also by putting them in a scalding sweat house."

"And they survived?" Charlie asked.

"Yes they did." Nakai looked grim. "They did survive it all and when Johona'ai, the Sun saw they were so strong, he admitted they were his sons. He gave them the weapons they needed to fight the monsters."

Charlie laughed at the irony of it. "So, after going through all that, they now first had their real work cut out for them!"

Nakai smiled at her. He found himself enjoying her biting comments.

"When we saw this sacred mountain from the car, I thought about that story and I'm glad I told it to you. You see, every time we tell the story, we remember it like it was told to us. Like when I told you the names of the sacred mountains, back then maybe millions of years ago, the Sun asked his two sons to name them also.'

"And the sons named them exactly as you did?"

"Exactly the same."

Nakai extended his hand for Charlie to grasp. It was nightfall and the air smelled damp. It was possible that they might get some needed rain. It was time now to continue on to the reservation, to bring this spiritual white woman named Charlie to the old Hogan in Chilchinbito, where pop would be waiting."

18

From the narrow doorway of the old Hogan, Shash Benally stood watching Edythe Yazzie drive off in her shiny, deep green, Jeep Grand Cherokee. They had enjoyed spending much of the afternoon baking fry bread in the old stone oven which peeked out from two sagebrush bushes in back of the Hogan. Now, darkness was starting to creep in and Edythe, who was afraid to drive at night, decided to leave by sunset.

It was one week to the day that Shash had dreamed about the strange spirit but he decided that he would rather stay put in Chinchilbito at the hogan than return to Albuquerque. Living here for awhile in this very modestly furnished eight-sided home of molded railroad ties wasn't the worst thing you could do in summertime. For the time being, there were no worries about chopping down wood for fire to make it through the 10 degree nights or getting some butane tank started to heat the place. Besides, it also afforded Shash the time to be able to court the well-to-do Edythe and now to see if his half-crazy son Nakai would actually make good on his promise to visit.

Shash was sure that coming to Chilchinbito could only be a good thing for his son, much like coming home to his grandmother, to his ancestors, to the sweet smell of the desert by night, to the voices of field rats chomping on cactus, to the horny toad stretching on the stone, to the midnight howl of the coyote, to the hushed monotone of Dineh prayer at sunrise. Coming here would heal his son and put him in balance. Make him whole again. It would bring him hozho, the beauty that is what being Dineh is all about.

The old hogan had a coal stove inside as well as a foldout table and a box spring and mattress, covered with a southwest tribal patterned quilt from the I-40 trading post. Then there was also the army cot Shash could set up if needed, if Nakai really brought along this "spirit" blonde lady as he said he would.

The elder Navajo laughed to himself, as he took a seat on the small white wicker rocker parked outside near the door. The aroma of the night sagebrush filled his nostrils and he would sit and enjoy it for awhile. So many changes he'd witnessed in his lifetime, and none of them good, but the sagebrush smell, well that was forever. He was smiling at the thought of Nakai convincing some white woman to come out here. Now, why in the world would any woman with half a brain want to travel anywhere with Nakai? Couldn't she guess he hated the bilagana by every word that came out of his mouth? Sure there was that witch of a German lady who hung all over him but she was one really nasty rattlesnake! His son was mental and the average woman should be scared to hell of him!

How Nakai would make the trip was a question that popped into Shash's head as he sat there rocking in rhythm with the soft evening breeze. His son probably stole the witch lady's vehicle, he figured, because there was no way you could escort a white lady across country by Greyhound bus! Then, two headlights way in the distance caught his eye and he could see the desert sand swirling, creating tiny dust devils up the dirt road. Since nobody else ever came this way it had to be either Edythe returning for some reason, maybe car trouble, or his son Nakai. More likely it was Nakai coming up the road about a mile away now, giving Shash just enough time to retrieve the ceremonial necklace of turquoise stones from the closet to give his son a proper greeting.

It was important for Shash to do everything right, to follow the old ways, and, besides, he felt good about himself when he wore turquoise. Fortunately for him, he was dressed just right, with his newest blue pin striped shirt and jeans he just purchased a couple of weeks ago at the Gallup flea market. All that to impress Edythe. So now all he needed was to put the necklace on carefully, so not to mess up his chongo or the white cotton cloth that tied his hair so neatly in the back.

The necklace was made up of about two dozen raw turquoise stones and in the center it carried a drop of four circles of heishi beads in coral and turquoise. It tied behind the neck the old fashioned way, with braided yarn instead of a metal clasp. Shash enjoyed looking at it as it sat hanging from a purple velour pullover. Now, outside he could hear the car driving up the dirt road to his hogan, so he quickly lifted the necklace over the hanger and set it around his neck. Then he checked himself in the mirror, gave himself a wink and a smile and stepped out to meet his son and the woman with the man's name who came to visit all the way from Miami.

19

"I don't give a damn what you're saying," Kathy Miller lashed out. "It's your fault Doyle is dead. You had to know he was going back there. You and your precious Charlie knew all about it but you didn't dare tell me!"

Sander was not having a great morning and this line of conversation with his cousin's wife was just adding to his angst. Yes, Doyle was dead and nothing he could do now about it but Kathy needed someone to sound off on and chose him. Hadn't she considered all the possibilities of what could happen to anyone whose passion was to climb mountains and walk deserts in search of the unknown?

"So, don't believe me!" He barked back. "I was as surprised as you. I knew Doyle was bugged with opals but I was sure we were all done for this summer. I certainly was."

"Well, I'm not yet ready to believe you," she continued, "and if it is like you say, then why is Charlie not answering her phone? I've been calling day and night for the last four days and no answer, and these days everyone has caller I.D."

"I don't know why she isn't answering," Sander said, getting a bit worried. "She was as upset as I was when I told her about the I-70 rockslide," he lied.

"You can't believe all the bills he left me with," Kathy said, in a softer tone.

"And all the rocks," Sander could not help adding.

"Yeah, the minerals. I've been thinking of selling them to pay off the credit card bills. Maybe, you and Charlie want to buy some of his opals or fluorite or something."

Sander started to let out a laugh but caught himself. "No, Kathy. The glory for me is in the finding, the discovery. There's no thrill in buying."

An incoming call on Kathy's line saved Sander who waited for her to put him on hold before he disconnected. Life was so simple these days. You could be saved by "call waiting" or an email you forgot to answer. All kinds of tricks to free you up for what really mattered and what did matter right now for Sander was finding Charlie.

Last night, he checked at the condo but the problem was that Charlie never told him she was the only one there who spoke English. He had always known she was a private person, which was the likely reason she chose a Cuban setting to live in. He also realized when he got there that in all the years he knew Charlie, he had never been invited inside her apartment. So, after a few "Buenas" greetings, he asked a group of old timers if they had seen Charlie Landers.

"Who he?" and "I no know" kind of capped it off for Sander, giving him a restless night. He vowed to pursue it at Charlie's morning haunt, the library, which was only four blocks from her building.

Despite the heat, which had already set in by 9 AM, Sander opted to walk on the beach, something he rarely did these days. Used to be he'd walk barefoot at the shore all the time, collecting the olive shells and oolite coral common to the area, but with so much erosion in recent years and with all the subsequent dredging, it was hard to find anything worthwhile anymore. The sand was warm and inviting and, even though it was mid-summer, you had until about noon before the sand would really burn up under your soles and make walking barefoot unbearable.

Newly constructed 40-story high rises now loomed in the distance, causing Sander to grimace. "Megastrocities," he mumbled to no one in particular. He hated the idea that these condos were worth a million or more to some wealthy South Americans who didn't give a shit that they effectively blocked out the sun, the view of the beach and shut off the breezes for everyone else. For a moment, he felt a twinge of jealousy that Charlie could probably afford to rent in one of those monumental structures if she wanted to, that she was good enough as a writer and photographer to actually earn a real living at it while his earnings as a teacher kept him in that old apartment in that much less desirable section of the Beach.

It was low tide and Sander spotted a lone cowry shell that rode in on a soft sudsy wave. He had not seen one of those in a long while and it gave him the brief urge to bring out the old snorkeling equipment. A lot of residents liked to snorkel or jog the beach or take a morning swim. Charlie said she often swam early, but somehow he knew that this morning she would be nowhere around. He decided to walk off the beach and head straight for the library before he got too depressed thinking about things.

There was a long low coral rock where Sander rested for a few minutes to put his sandals back on. Now, he had to consider what to do with his small collection of oolite, olive shells and the cowry and made a quick decision to leave the stuff under a sprawling sea grape tree to be retrieved later. It was certainly nothing any thief would ever want, he was thinking, and that was one of the beautiful things about being a rockhound.

The name that popped into Sander's head was Tony. There were a few other library people Charlie talked about from time to time but he could not recall their names, so Tony was the guy to look for. Just in time, he thought, as he reached the library at the same time a loud thunderbolt came close by him. The sky had suddenly turned a deep purplish black, signaling the onset of a classic Miami Beach summer downpour. It was the first thing all morning that gave him a real laugh. The crazy, unpredictable summer storms were just about the only thing he really liked about living in South Florida. Within minutes, the blinding rain would clean all the streets and water all the vegetation to a deep green color.

The guy at the reference desk looked young and decent looking and Sander guessed that he was Tony.

"What can I do for you, Sir?" he asked, looking up from his computer.

Sir, shit. Sander despised it when they called him that. It made him feel like an old geezer.

"Have you seen Charlie yet this morning? She is supposed to meet me here."

Nothing like putting it directly, Sander figured. When you ask that way, there's no time to concoct any phony responses. It was the way he taught his classes. The way he did everything.

"If you mean Charlie the writer, no I can't say I have," Tony smiled.

"Well, if you do," Sander added, "please tell her to contact Sander because there is an emergency in her family."

"And you are a relative?"

"Yeah, I'm her brother," Sander nodded.

Tony looked interested now. "Wow," he said. "She never told me she had a brother. I thought she was an only."

"Well, I'm it. You have any idea when she was here last? She's not at home." Sander's hands fiddled in his pockets. He seemed to be getting nowhere fast.

"Actually, now that I think of it," Tony said, scratching his cheek, I haven't seen her here for awhile. The last time was maybe four or five days ago, when she was hanging out with Nakai."

"Nakai?"

"Yeah, the cool Indian. I'm sure you know him. Everyone does around here. He's an Apache or Navajo, a silversmith."

"Oh sure," Sander nodded not having the faintest idea who this Nakai was. He was starting to get an uneasy feeling nevertheless, remembering Charlie's obsession with those two arrowheads.

"Where is Nakai at?" he decided to ask. He had nothing to lose if Tony didn't know or didn't want to tell him. If there was an Apache living here in South Beach he would find out soon enough where he was located.

"They say he's at the Carlton," Tony offered, "but today is Saturday, so he's probably selling his crafts at the farmer's market."

Sander grinned. "Then, I'll head toward Lincoln, I guess. I can always use an organic pina colada."

"They've got big ripe tomatoes," Tony grinned, "and just last week, Jen got a gorgeous orchid plant for only thirty bucks."

Tony pointed to the tall pretty brunette who was seated at a computer, helping an elderly guy retrieve his email. She smiled at Tony and it was obvious the two of them had something going on. Sander felt a twinge of envy.

"He's going to the farmers market to look for Nakai," Tony shouted across the room.

"He won't find him," Jen laughed. "That certified nut case he lives with was in here screaming that he stole her van and just took off somewhere!"

"Wow! I missed all that!" Tony grimaced. "When did all that take place?"

Sander quickly excused himself and made his way to the door. The facts were now getting clearer. Both Charlie and Nakai were missing shortly after they were seen together, no doubt discussing the arrowheads. At this point, he did not know anything else to do but head to the farmers markets and look for this woman Jen called "the nut case."

Why all this bothered him, Sander really could not say. Charlie was a grown woman and she was entitled to do as she pleased and if she wanted to run away with some Indian, that was her business. Or was it? Shit, he thought. I hope to crap I'm not in love!

20

Shash Benally was a big guy, a strong looking man whose face and demeanor belied his many years, but Charlie observed that father and son had more differences than similarities. For while Nakai was also powerful looking, his strength was mainly in his broad chest and generous biceps while his dad's was distributed more equally in long muscular forearms and legs of a wily cowboy. Shash reminded Charlie of posters she had seen of bull riders at western rodeos.

If you put Shash and Nakai side by side, Charlie noted, they might even seem to belong to different tribes. Nakai was shorter and his face was darker and rounder, more Apache looking, where Shash, with his lean face and more prominent nose, resembled the old black and white photos of Lakota warriors. Her guess was that Nakai resembled his mother and took after her as well. His father was much more reserved and calm, which was a welcome relief from the excitable Nakai with the mood swings and personality quirks she had been attempting to accommodate for the last couple of days.

They were seated outside now on beach chairs in the dark stillness of the summer desert night. Nakai and Shash were in conversation or rather, it seemed to Charlie, it was mostly Nakai chattering and Shash listening. She sat there politely saying nothing, just observing. It was their time as father and son and who knew how long it had been since they had last seen each other? Probably a fair amount of time, she surmised by the topics and relatives they were talking about.

So many of the sentences were punctuated with the word "bilagana" which Charlie knew meant "whitey." But she knew they were not discussing her but more likely the country's politics. Every now and then, Shash looked her way and smiled in a kind way. His hands were folded in his lap and he seemed at peace with himself. When Nakai asked questions about the children of those elders who still lived humble lives here in Chilchinbito, Shash's reply was always the same. "They lost the old ways. They drank and stole from their parents and grandparents and from each other because they lost the old ways."

Shash liked to nod his head and say "Aoo" which Charlie understood as meaning "yes" in Dineh. His voice was soft, monotonous and soothing and it sounded good to Charlie after the long arduous ride and that, along with the sweet smell of desert sage, made her happy that she was here. Then, Nakai finally looked her way, throwing her a bit off course.

"Charlie," he motioned with his hand, "show my father the arrowheads."

"Oh," she said, fidgeting with her hands nervously, realizing that she was having some guilt feelings about picking up those artifacts. What if Shash Benally was judgmental about it? They were both facing her now, waiting. No one had said anything to her up until then, and in fact, seemed to ignore her.

Nakai had never formally introduced her to his father either. She was unsure if that was on purpose or just because he became forgetful in the joy of seeing his father.

Feeling as if she were performing for an audience, Charlie opened the small leather pouch and removed the two arrowheads, whose gleam was barely visible in the dimness of the evening. Nakai had carried out a lantern from the hogan but the small circle of light could not match the power of the sun for showing them off and without the shine, they did not seem so special to Charlie.

"Give them over to my father," Nakai said in a somewhat commanding tone.

Well, if he was ordering her to hand the artifacts over to a Navajo elder, she supposed it was a moral decision. Nakai held the lantern close to shash's hand as she placed them carefully in his palm.

With his free hand, Shash opened the buttons on his shirt and then took the arrowheads one at a time from his palm and rubbed them on his chest, saying "nizhoni, nizhoni." He then gave them back to Charlie and repeated the word, "nizhoni," then adding, "That's beautiful, honey. Very beautiful."

Charlie watched as Shash rose slowly from his seat, the way the elderly often did.

"I guess you guys are hungry," he smiled.

They followed him into the hogan and Charlie could see the look of disappointment on Nakai's face, that his father had said nothing more about those arrowheads. He saw a smile on his father's face though and wondered what that was all about. He would not have imagined that Shash was thinking about the fry bread he now had an excuse to finish. There were three pieces left from his baking venture with Edythe and he had, in fact, thought that Nakai might be coming which is why he baked extra. And it came out real good because Edythe did things the old ways. She knew how to stretch that old Bluebird flour and she used hot grease just the way Shash liked.

Shash opened one of the cabinets and took out a half-filled jar of honey and some strawberry jelly packets he had taken home from Denny's when he had breakfast there the other morning. Not exactly dinner but it would take care of the hunger anyway. He had endured in his life on a lot worse. Then, the next morning, he decided he would treat them both to breakfast at one of the tortilla joints in Window Rock. Maybe get a good plate of eggs and some corn mush. His son always liked that.

The important thing for Shash was to appear nonchalant and he put on the Indian stoic look as he loaded the plates with the huge mounds of fry bread. Maybe though the frown lines at his age were a bit hard to conceal, he wondered, even behind a pair of tinted reading glasses.

He was worried, and his son Nakai was the reason. He looked out of kilter, even more so than he remembered and he hoped that he was not headed for a nervous breakdown. He was also concerned about this pretty bilagana lady that his son thought was a spirit.

It was true that the mind could play tricks on you, Shash was thinking. Here, he had that vision just the other night and it sure scared the hell out of him and then, his son saying the blonde lady was a spirit. Well, maybe she was, but it wasn't for any reason his son had in mind. The fact that Nakai thought she was a spiritual creature because she had found some arrowheads was totally wacko, a bunch of dola bichon! Now, he wondered what kind of story he gave her to get her to come all the way out here. So many times, the ladies fell for Nakai because they wanted a bad boy. This one though, she looked at him different, like he was onto something. Maybe, Shash thought, he ought to have a word with her.

"Thank you," Charlie smiled, as Shash placed the dish with the fry bread in front of her. She was really hungry but had not realized it until now. This last leg of the trip had really been trying, with Nakai acting really antsy. He was probably nervous about seeing his father. A lot of men had issues with their fathers and she could see that Nakai was doing his best, for whatever reason, to try to impress Shash. She recalled that the last time they had any food was about five in the morning at some IHop in Amarillo. After that, Nakai had just kept on driving.

"You must be tired young lady," Shash said with a kind smile.

Charlie nodded. "That I am. It will be good to sleep somewhere other than in a van."

Shash turned toward his son. "I think we're going to give her the box spring over here and you can take the cot. Me, I'll sleep outdoors and enjoy the desert air."

"Oh, no, Pop," Nakai said. "I've been away too long. It's me who needs the desert air!"

Shash nodded, even though he felt somewhat uncomfortable sleeping in the same room with this pretty bilagana woman. He hoped that no one from the area would find out and tell Edythe.

"Hey, Pop," Nakai grinned, "do you remember the last time we were together in this old House?"

Shash shook his head. "I can't say that I recall."

"Shima boiled us that Mormon tea and we sat on pillows on the floor singing riding songs."

"Riding songs, huh? Ah, yes, I do remember." Shash let out a laugh. "You probably were no more than 17 years old."

"Hei and aho and a heya!" Nakai's voice boomed out an old familiar song.

"Well, I guess, I'll see if I can get this old stove to workin' and make us some tea," Shash beamed. "Now, you just keep going with that song, son."

"Hei heya ho ho heya heya heya..." Nakai sang out, now remembering the words.

Shash took down two pillows from the bed for Charlie and Nakai and a small blanket for himself, never losing the rhythm of the song. Charlie sat down beside him and looked on as father and son proceeded to make a small fire in an old abalone shell filled with cedar and began to sing together.

"Hei and aho and a hei heya...."

It seemed to Charlie as night fell, the small fire burned and the smell of the sage tea they called ts'ah filled the air of the hogan, that there was nothing as important in the world as the sound of that song.

21

Sander Miller spotted the crazy lady at the farmers' market within minutes of his arrival there. Easy enough to do, because her face looked like one of those photos from a botched plastic surgery lawsuit, and the faded blond hair with the gray roots had not had a serious touch up in months. She sat between two huge planters filled with impatiens and periwinkle flowers at a small table displaying silver and turquoise jewelry.

It was a clever idea, Sander thought, sneaking in the Indian jewelry between the plants. He knew the rules of the farmers' markets and that was to sell fruits, vegetables, plants and anything derivative, which could include smoothies or even blueberry muffins. So she was crazy, maybe, but she wasn't dumb.

He was about to approach her when a couple of South Beach regulars beat him to it and asked her about Nakai. They were young, female and pretty and one of them was wearing a large bracelet that seemed similar to what was displayed on the table. Sander figured it would be easier to back off, and just hang around and listen. This crazy lady looked like she could burst out in rage at any trigger word and if he didn't have to be the target of the venom, that was all to the better. Let this duo take the hit.

"So, you don't know where he is?" Hannelore grimaced at the two women. "Well, guess what? I don't either."

The woman who was not wearing the bracelet, pointed to a silver and turquoise ring on the table. "He was supposed to have my ring ready today. I gave him forty dollars last weekend."

"Oh, I see," Hannelore laughed now a little too loudly. "He was going to make you a beautiful ring and instead he took the money and ran away with my van. You will be waiting for your ring for a very long time, I think."

The two women stepped back away from the crazy lady, intimidated by her harsh laugh and words, but some other shoppers apparently were not. Sander ran his fingers through his ponytail and watched with interest as a heavy-set Latino in a tribal printed shirt came at her with a pointing finger.

"My wife Ana paid a hundred bucks up front for a silver and coral bracelet last week and if it isn't here I want the money back!"

"Then, show me the receipt because I don't believe you!" Hannelore did not flinch.

"You ugly bitch! You were right here when Ana paid you and you never gave us any receipt. You know my wife bought all kinds of stuff from the Indian and you. She always trusted you."

"Oh, well," Hannelore said, now shaking her head wistfully. "Next time be more careful who you trust because he ran away. He took all my money and the van and he's gone."

Then, suddenly, Hannelore burst into tears, grabbing for her purse and spilling more silver jewelry out all over the table.

"Go ahead!" she cried out. "Take whatever you want! Take a different piece that's worth more money if you want! Just don't care anything about me, that I'm left here all alone while he runs off to the desert with some blonde bimbo!"

It took all of a second for that outburst to register in Sander's mind and another for it all to come together for him. The disappearance of his rock buddy had everything to do with two magic arrowheads and an Apache that had a crazy as his woman. And now, Charlie was headed out to the desert with this Apache, no doubt, way out in New Mexico or Arizona, in the vast thousands of acres of reservation land, acres of vast nothingness.

Hannelore was in grief when Sander dared to approach. Any normal person would ask him his name and who he was and what he wanted but she was all screwy now and wasn't about to give it much thought, Sander surmised.

"Nakai," he asked, looking her in the eye. "Do you think he is dangerous? Do you think he will rape that blonde bimbo?"

Hannelore looked up, her eyes now half shut with tears and mascara flowing freely down her cheeks. She did not know who this character with the ponytail was, but she was ready to assail Nakai to the heavens and did not care who was listening.

"Oh no," he won't rape her!" she lashed out. "Indians don't rape women, you know. He will probably kill her!"

22

The metallic disc had a fiery orange glow to it, almost as if it were trying to warm the leafless, naked branches of the old sycamore tree as it hovered by.

Link Davis was desperately trying to steady the old trusty Leica in his trembling hands, when a flurry of red and green lights suddenly appeared above a low hill a few yards away. Then, almost as if on cue the lights began to spin in a clockwise direction, floodlighting the clear midnight sky in a dazzling, Christmas-like display.

Link got up the nerve to come to Pine Bush, New York, at the urging of other field investigators for UFOA, the Unidentified Flying Object Association. The group had gotten word of numerous sightings from police and air traffic controllers in the general area of Middletown and especially in Pine Bush. It was a cold January in the early 1980s.

At first, this woodsy area seemed quiet and uneventful and Link was wondering how long he would have to withstand such frigid conditions before something happened. He kept his guard up though, because the townspeople he had spoken to in the last few days told him they witnessed these lights off and on for at least 15 years. Link knew that the calm façade could change in the blink of an eye, having had similar experiences himself.

Photos taken by curious and frightened locals had been analyzed by a notable physicist who attempted to explain away the oscillations, whorls and vectors of the objects, calling them multiple exposure star trails. As Link found himself smack in the presence of these strange lights, shivering despite his heavy shearling jacket, he fearfully recalled the words of one believer who warned him that "when you are within three feet of those lights, they can pick you up in seconds, put you back down an hour later and you won't remember a thing!"

So, Link knew he had to run, because if what that man said was true and he allowed himself to be "taken up" in the craft, he might forever be a slave to these extra-terrestrials. From this time on, into the future, they could call him out, give a command, and much like someone under the spell of a hypnotist, Link would obediently follow it to the letter, never even remembering that it ever occurred. He dashed now across the field in the opposite direction, praying that those lights would not give chase, and, in a flash, he understood why the U.S. Air Force downplayed reports of these aerial phenomena. They were scared shitless because there was no explanation! If you don't understand something, you hide it. You cover it up, because if you admit you don't know, then the whole country, the whole world goes haywire!

The aroma of sage hanging sweetly in the stillness of the summer night air was calming to Charlie. She sucked it in through her nostrils, trying to make sense of why she had awakened to find herself here in the dead of the night. The sound of field rats chomping on cactus and the croaking of the frogs and singing crickets told her that this was a healthful place to be in, but she had no idea how she got here or how far it was from Shash's hogan. The sameness of sagebrush that was illuminated by moonlight gave her the impression that somehow she had lost her way. By morning, she might have to dig under the cactus for some water to drink.

Looking at the moonlight and a few clustered odd green lights in the distance, reminded Charlie of Link's obsession with UFOs. Maybe, she thought, those green lights had been closer to her at some point, and perhaps part of a craft like the one Link had witnessed at Pine Bush. Maybe she was experiencing that phenomenon the UFO investigators called "missing time." Link often talked about how unsuspecting ordinary folks could suddenly be approached by a craft or a light and then, against their will, be taken up for experimentation by aliens. Then they would awake in some strange place, maybe an open field, hours or even days later and not have any idea what happened or how much time had elapsed.

Sitting down with her back resting against some rabbit brush, feeling the sensation of fear starting to knot up her throat, she closed her eyes and tried to remember just what happened and how she got here.

The last thing she remembered was a hot sunny afternoon in Gallup, walking alone and visiting some of the many trading posts that dotted the old railroad town. It was her second day with Shash and Nakai and the two men were planning on passing the day preparing for a "sweat" that night. They were going to gather some stones and cedar when a middle-aged Navajo man named Les Tsotse came by, at Shash's suggestion, to drive her into Gallup so she could enjoy the town and do some shopping. She recalled that later in the day they met up again at the appointed spot, the Thunderbird silver supply store, for the drive back to Shash's hogan where Nakai was preparing stew.

Charlie had been confused because she assumed that you were supposed to fast before the sweat but she sat and had dinner with them, attempting to join in a conversation that was now largely in Dineh and it seemed almost as if the men decided to exclude her on purpose. The talk continued until past 10 PM, when it was too late to go to a sweat or anywhere. This kind of thing was not uncommon among the Navajo, she understood. You could make plans to do something but then those plans could change at a moment's notice if the feeling was somehow not right.

At any rate, feeling very much like a fifth wheel, Charlie had gone over to rest on the cot, moving it to a far corner of the small hogan. She tried to pretend that all this really did not matter. After all, she was just an outsider and they were going about their usual business of being Dineh. She thought about calling someone, maybe Sander, but there were no telephones out here in the desert and a cell phone would not pick up out here either, not even on roaming.

So, here she was, all alone out here with her thoughts, just the far off sound of a coyote's howl breaking the silence, trying to figure out just how she got here. She wiped the dampness from her face and realized that her eyes were welling up with tears and she was silently crying. That was when she heard the sound of footsteps coming toward her.

23

Nakai would not sleep tonight even though the old sheepskin and straw bed he put together did fine. He had been standing silently in the darkness, listening to the desert song spinning in his ears, smelling the sweetness of the sage and watching Charlie a short distance away, all huddled up against the brush. It was a good thing there hadn't been any rain, Nakai mused, or she would be covered in ticks by now. He had not realized just how hungry he was for this land until he got here and, more so, how much he had missed his father, his Shizhee.

It was a rough trip just getting out to the southwest, with Charlie constantly distracting him by taking notes all the time and hardly saying a word. Boy, she was sure an odd one. She wasn't even aware that he was putting on his Injun stoic routine or she didn't really care about it. The truth was though that he badly needed some speed or a drink to keep him high energy and focused on seeing his father and the land. Now, the old familiar sounds were doing a great calming job and not to mention that pop looked strong as a bull, not bent and old looking as he had feared after being away for so long. He wondered when had he last seen him anyway?

Yes, Nakai marveled. Sure, his father's face had a few deep furrows here and there but he was as tough and stubborn as Nakai remembered. More than that, Shash still had a way of seeing right through him, and Nakai knew that his Shizhee didn't trust him worth a shit. He hoped that a few days out here with him, the good earth under their feet and the raw power of the mountains, could change things. He would walk with pop, call in the Sun and Air People and get back to the old ways.

A coyote's cry in the far off distance, reminded Nakai of the old stories about the skinwalkers who covered themselves in coyote skin and roamed the mountainsides in the early morning, scaring the shit out of their enemies. Yes,

Nakai nodded, as he walked slowly toward Charlie, and noticed she was shaking at the sound of the footsteps. This was all the good stuff he had come for, the stuff that could make him whole again.

Charlie let out a soft cry as he approached, and Nakai saw she was frightened, and with good reason. She had awakened in the hogan from a nightmare of sorts and had been screaming so loud, that he could have sworn the hogan was shaking. Then, she quickly fell back to sleep, still shaking as if she was possessed by something. Nakai decided that he had better carry her outside and away from pop and he did. She was probably no more than 20 yards from the hogan but in the darkness, he knew she was feeling quite lost.

Both fascinated and oddly disturbed by Charlie's behavior, Nakai stood in her path, feeling also surprised that he felt no joy in her obvious state of confusion as was the usual case when he saw white people suffer. Under any ordinary circumstances, Nakai's first instinct would be to leave a person like this in pain and off-balance, maybe scared and cold all night long. Hell, he was hard-wired like that, and he might have even considered doing some skinwalking routine to really terrify her. He was good at animals' night sounds and could do a pretty good grizzly, but then again, Charlie was bright enough to know she was far from grizzly country. No bears at all in this desert wasteland.

"Nakai!" Her scream broke the silence, and he could see her shaking again, no doubt startled by the shrieking sound of her own voice upon recognizing him. Yet, Nakai could feel the sense of relief in her hard breaths. She had been scared, all right, but it was not about him or this place Chilchinbito. There were bad spirits about her, possessing her, eating her alive, and Nakai had to protect her. He opened his arms to her and her limp body fell into him, her blonde hair falling over his chest.

Nakai would sit with her just like that with his strong arms locked around her, until the shaking and sobbing stopped and she was all right again. A cool breeze began to filter into the stillness of night and Nakai listened attentively to it for a message, as he always did. The old Simon and Garfunkel "Sounds of Silence" came to mind. The desert was really the only place you found this kind of silence. No distractions like trees to break the monotony of the scrub and brush, and at the moment not even a frog croaking or a cricket's song. He would wait just like this for something profound to happen, for dark secrets to be spilled, and they would, because it always happened that way.

This Charlie, he knew, had some deep secrets, which was why she was who she was, one of those hands-off kinds of women. For Nakai, it was kind of interesting because he was so used to female attention. All those South Beach girlie girls, walked around him with those hiked up skirts, just hoping, but this blonde lady, who could have her pick of bedmates, did not seem interested in sex at all, and that was what made her seem so spiritual, probably, just like the Virgin Mary.

A gut instinct told Nakai there was violence in her history. She seemed cautious around him and maybe around all men, except for that dead friend who was a psychic or a psycho or maybe both, Nakai mused. Like most females who had fears of men, she was used to traveling in packs of them in order to protect herself from other men who might pose a danger. What was weird though, and sort of complimentary, the opposite of what you'd imagine, she did not seem to have any real fear of him.

He could not help but marvel at this, as she sat there just clinging to him. Certainly, she was aware of his mental lapse and strange states when she was in the back seat on the way here. Bi-polar, was what the doctors at the hospital called it the day the cops picked him up, running naked down Ocean Drive, and took him to Jackson downtown for observation.

"Sometimes, it gets so peaceful, you can get too comfortable here," Nakai said, wondering where these words came from when he wasn't even thinking them.

Charlie started to fidget, but she loosened her grip and slowly pulled away from him now, embarrassed at the unexpected closeness with this strange man.

"I think I had a bad dream," she finally said.

Nakai nodded calmly. "Something got to you," he said. "You were bringing down the walls of the old hogan. I had to get you out of there."

"Oh, I thought for awhile there I was captured by aliens and dropped off here," Charlie let out a half-serious laugh.

"Who's the culprit?" Nakai asked, trying to keep his voice level.

Charlie sighed deeply. There was no reason for holding back. "My uncle," she heard herself whispering. "It was a really bad dream.'

"Or a memory," Nakai prodded. "Talk to me. Nobody's going to hear you out here."

Nakai realized that he was probably the first to hear the story that he already knew by the shortness of her breathing.

"I was sleeping or maybe just about ready to nod off. That's when it usually happens, when he starts to strangle me."

Charlie was speaking in a slow deliberate way, making sure that she would not break down crying. Sometimes when she thought about it, she pretended it had happened to someone else and learned that you could remove yourself from the act by doing that.

"So, this uncle," Nakai said, looking straight at a cluster of stars to keep it impersonal, "spent some time raping you, right?"

She looked at him, ready to shake her head in denial, but she knew that was useless. Just his dark round eyes studying her and catching her emotions, was admission enough, she knew. She had traveled out here to learn something about the arrowheads, and now here she was sitting in the black of the desert night having her buttons being pushed by this Indian named Nakai. It was an odd sensation, hard to explain, but there was something being ejected from her onto the sandy earth and deep into the roots of the sagebrush. Yes, she thought, she may have come all the way out here to find out the meaning of two obsidian arrowheads, but it turned out that what she really was finding out about was herself.

24

The sweat poured out of Sander Miller's neck and the sticky, soaking t-shirt reminded him of his high school days playing half-back in the heavy September humidity. Only he was in Broken Bow, Oklahoma, now and not Miami Beach and he sure wasn't playing football here at the Lightning Strike quartz mine. He was just passing some time banging his rock hammer into the wall, trying to figure out why he was headed back out west again, this time to look for Charlie.

Even more pressing was the question of exactly where on the reservation he would find her, since you could find Navajo and Apache types scattered all over New Mexico and Arizona. Then, what could he do if he did find her?

The open pit mine, one of Charlie's favorites, was high in the Quachita Mountains and well hidden by all the pines and hardwood trees in the woodsy area. Since they had missed this spot on their recent trip, Sander had some thoughts that maybe Charlie and the Indian might stop to collect some quartz crystals on the way across to the southwest. He checked out the area for tire tracks, food wrappers, a forgotten item of clothing, or anything that might mean she was up here in the last day or so, but there were no clues.

It was tough to find this mine without a GPS because there were so many forest roads, along with other gravel and dirt roads leading to nowhere in particular, just criss-crossing to more forested areas or cut down lumber or other small mine claims. Charlie was always good at following the north and west points on her hand held Garmin, to reach all the stored waypoints, whereas, he was much better at finding the old mines by remembering certain landmarks, arrows, gravels and natural formations. At any rate, the weather was so unbearably hot, that it was unlikely that Charlie, as bugged as he was by the gorgeous quartz here, would have made the effort to find the mine.

The clear quartz crystals at Lightning Strike were special and somewhat rare because of the chloride inclusions which gave them a stunning dark green color. Sander managed to spot a nearly flawless two inch point in the strong sunlight and quickly put it away for Charlie, before he could change his mind and decide to keep it. He decided that he would also try to find one more for the Indian, if they should happen to meet. He knew that southwestern tribal medicine men often used the crystals in ceremonies and these were really impressive.

The crazy blonde European woman at the farmer's market had told him that this Nakai was a killer but Sander had his doubts. No reason to think he was not worrisome but the fact that the nasty crazy was his girlfriend and she was still alive was telling enough. What Sander really wanted to find out was what this guy wanted with Charlie and why were they traveling together? Did she go with him of her own free will or was she somehow coerced? Then, why was he so concerned about Charlie's welfare anyhow? Was he worried about losing her to this Nakai? Maybe, he was in love with her or something.

Sander swung the rock hammer hard, dismissing the thought. There was a small cluster of crystals embedded deep in a vug type formation about seven inches in, but he would have to carefully break into some hard rock for at least another hour to get in there without bruising them. He wanted the cluster whole, not in five or six separate pieces, but the sun beating down on him, told him it was time to take a break or he was likely to suffer sunstroke, and with nobody here to find him.

The cooler was packed with Diet coke, Mars bars and a jumbo Hersheys, his cousin Doyle's idea of a quick energy fix. Weird how life was, Sander thought, removing a cold can. Just a couple of weeks ago, he and Doyle and Charlie were all together climbing Mt. Antero in the bitter cold wind, joking and carrying on, and now what? Doyle was dead and Charlie could be also for all he knew, and here he was all alone at an open pit mine in the sweltering summer sun of southeastern Oklahoma. He carried the cooler now to an area of the pit that was partially covered by a pine tree and took out the giant chocolate bar. The sky hung over in the gloomy yellow grey kind of pollution known as heat inversion and Sander sat down on a large rock, where he ate the candy and drank his soda. If Charlie were here right now, he thought, she would be singing a song about "a bright golden haze on the meadow. There's a bright golden haze on the meadow..."

"Shit," Sander cursed to himself, throwing a small rock into the pit. "Shit... shit...shit...shit...shit!"

25

The road was bumpy and washed out from snowy winters past, and Shash Benally wished that his son would take it a bit slower with his truck. It was useless trying to talk to Nakai, so instead, Shash looked ahead waiting for the face of Red Mountain to come into sight, the first landmark before they would come upon the medicine man Hastiin Sandoval's hogan.

It was time to do something about his son's split personality or whatever the bilagana doctors called it. One minute, Nakai sounded like a human being and then the next, well, he would fly off the handle about nothing or talk crazy things. Shash had been trying for a long time to convince his son to see the medicine man but Nakai always had something else important to accomplish, leading him to suspect that Nakai was scared. Maybe this was the reason he lived outside and far from the four sacred mountains, all the way in Miami, and hardly came to visit. Last night, though, Shash saw an opportunity in the shape of the blonde lady's nightmares and he decided to act on it fast.

Charlie, sitting in the back seat of Shash's truck, was mesmerized by the beauty of the pink mesas rising up to meet the powder blue early morning sky. Next to her was a sack of Bluebird flour and other provisions that she and Shash had picked up the afternoon before at the large discount supermarket in Gallup. Shash had walked up and down the aisles, with Charlie following, continually filling a large grocery cart with flour, oatmeal, beans, watermelon and other fruits and some loose tobacco, all to present to Hastiin Sandoval as a customary gesture. He had been quiet most of the time on the long drive back to Chilchinbito, but then, stopping at a large monolith that looked like a man's fingers, he asked her a pointed question.

"Tell me, young lady, is there someone in your past, maybe this uncle of yours, who might have put the curse on you?"

Charlie fell silent at the suggestion. She knew that the Navajo often thought like this. It was all about the spirits, both good and bad, and how to balance the two, but as a white woman who was out of that loop, she really had no idea how to answer the man. Then, as if to give her some sort of explanation, Shash took out a photo from his wallet and passed it to her. It was a black and white picture of a woman named Sue who, Shash said, had "put the curse on Nakai" which was why he had this mental sickness. The photo was not complete and had a small character that had been snipped out in a purposeful manner, like a cut-out doll.

"Sue has children," Shash replied, anticipating her question. The children aren't involved so when we get the curse removed, there's no need to harm them."

Charlie felt strong, much better than she had been feeling in a long time. The desert and Shash and Nakai had been good for her and although Shash's question seemed a bit off the wall, who really knew the answers to these things? Maybe she really did have a curse on her. For so many years she had been feeling weak without knowing the cause. The doctors told her she had angina but there was more. If she cut herself while shaving her legs, the bleeding would go on endlessly. She never talked about it though and if anyone questioned why she wore jeans instead of shorts while hiking, even in the hot Mojave in July, she just shrugged it off without answering. The thing was that you never knew when you could trip on a rock or walk into a prickly saguaro. A curse? Well, maybe it could all come down to that.

"Son, stop the car!" Shash ordered. "I want to get out for a minute."

Nakai swerved the old black pickup off the dirt road and into a small sagebrush, causing his father to raise his voice.

"You shouldn't a done that, messing up the plant! Just stop the car, that's all. You know nobody comes up this road!"

Nakai shrugged and laughed out loud, and Shash opened the door and slammed it at him. Charlie noticed his boots with the thick two inch heels. Yesterday, Shash had been wearing sneakers but today he wanted to show respect for the medicine man, even if it made his walk less steady. He made his way toward a tall plant a few feet away and Nakai gave Charlie a small paper bag instructing her to follow him.

"You'll learn something," he smiled. He was not going to give his father the satisfaction of accompanying him after having been scolded, but no reason Charlie should not know about these things.

"This is clozhee," Shash said, putting some long thin green sticks in the bag. You fold those sticks in small bundles and tie them together. I make tea out of it to keep my blood pressure in good numbers."

Charlie nodded. "I've seen that plant before in a couple of Mormon homes."

"Yeah, they figured it out too," Shash smiled. "Now, you see that plant there, the one my son so nicely crashed into?" Shash pointed to the sagebrush, now leaning into his truck. "We call that ts'ah. The bilagana say sage but that means nothing because you have so many different types of sage and each one is medicine for something else. The Dineh have different names for every one of them."

"This looks to be good land for Hastiin Sandoval to practice," Charlie smiled. "He has good medicine all around him."

She watched closely as Shash studied each branch of the plant she had always recognized as "Mormon tea," now called "clozhee." He was very particular, taking only the branches that had the right color and smell. The scene made Nakai somewhat envious, and he decided to get out of the truck to join this somewhat sad, haunted blonde lady, and impart some of the things he felt were worth knowing. His father was always stealing his thunder, but he met Charlie first and he was not about to let it happen here.

Nakai approached Charlie with his arms spread wide, as if embracing the air.

"You are very observant, sister," he said, staring into her eyes. "Yes, there is medicine all around within the four sacred mountains and that is where the medicine man must live and do good for his people. "Of course," Nakai's voice was now getting an angry edge to it, "when the white man decided to steal all our water, much of the medicine couldn't grow anymore."

Charlie shrugged. "It seems to me that most Navajos prefer to go to doctors now just like the white people do," she remarked. "I believe though, as you do, that all the answers are in nature. It's what I write about. I think that if enough

126

voices out there speak up without worrying what the science world thinks, our call will be heard sooner or later."

Nakai was about to say something, but Charlie walked over to Shash now, whose paper bag was overflowing with the thin green sticks.

"Maybe you can get a story going about this tea," Shash said, handing Charlie the brown paper bag. "When you get back to Miami, try it and see if it doesn't make you feel better."

"How do I bundle it?" Charlie asked.

"I'll show you when we get back later," Shash said smiling. He was happy to find the plant looking green and healthy and strong.

Nakai had walked back to the truck now, seeming a bit fidgety and anxious to get going to Hastiin Sandoval, but his father just kept on standing there as if he had all day. He was staring now at the sun rising to prominence above the red of the mesa.

"Hozhoni," he said aloud. "Just beautiful."

Charlie was watching Shash now, as he began to call in the sun by stretching his arms outward and then bringing them back to his chest in a sweeping motion. She tried to imitate him and saw that he was pleased.

"There is a yei. Well, white people would call it a god, I suppose," he said, looking her way, "whose body starts at the foot of Tsoodzil. Well, you call it Mount Taylor. Anyway," he went on, "the yei's body starts there and then curves all the way around on the outside of all the four mountains with the head stopping at Sis Naajini, Blanca Peak in Colorado."

"That sounds like a giant yei," Charlie added, for lack of anything smarter to say.

"Do you know why this is?"

Charlie shook her head.

"This yei is here to give the People, the Dineh, the protection. So, now you see that when a Dineh leaves the boundary like my son Nakai did, they run into all kinds of trouble. There is no balance outside of here, my friend. This was not the plan for us!"

Shash shrugged his shoulders and got back into the pickup where Nakai was leaning impatiently on the wheel. Somewhat annoyed that his father stole his thunder by telling Charlie the story of the four mountains, Nakai pushed down hard on the accelerator, forcing Shash to endure every hard bump of the gravelly road that cut a narrow path through the desert sand.

Soon, Charlie saw two small children, a boy and a girl, no more than ten years old each, playing with a rubber ball, and running barefoot in the awesome panorama of sand, sage and red mesas. They ran past the old gray wooden hogan and past their grandfather's small box shaped white house and up to the face of Red Mountain.

Nakai stopped the pickup short a few yards from the house, and Shash, paying his son no mind, slowly and deliberately stepped out of the vehicle and onto the path that led to Hastiiin Sandoval's home.

26

Hastiin Sandoval and his wife Eunice sat quietly at the kitchen table as Shash Benally carefully laid out the groceries on the red plastic tablecloth in front of them. An imposing silver and black iron stove which had probably been sitting in its corner since the late 1940s, when the Sandovals were first married, caught Charlie's eye.

"We have money too," Shash said, taking out some large bills from a small white envelope, and offering them to Hastiin Sandoval, but the medicine man's eyes were on Charlie and he and his wife were studying her with curiosity. Shash noticed and tried to change the subject by pointing to his son and gesturing with his hands how much Nakai had grown since they last saw him. By Shash's laughter, Charlie realized that the Sandovals probably last saw him when he was a toddler.

"The Sandovals don't speak very much English," Shash told Charlie. "I am going to explain to them about the curse we want removed from our family, from Nakai, and I will be talking in our language. When you talk about your uncle, you can say it in English and that they will understand."

Charlie smiled at Shash in appreciation for his kindness. He was trying to make her comfortable in what was a very new situation for her. She decided that she had nothing to lose by telling them what she remembered. Maybe the Sandovals could find a way to heal her soul. Maybe there would even be another appearance of that Johnny Whitehorse ghost right here in this room.

Eunice Sandoval got up from the table and walked over to a four-foot tall iron stove filled with hot charcoals that sat on the floor in a small room right outside the kitchen. Charlie, watching Hastiin Sandoval leave the table to follow her, understood that this was where the ceremony would take place.

The medicine man was stooped a bit, with white hair, and looked to be about ten years older than his wife. He was probably older than Shash also, maybe in his mid-eighties, Charlie guessed. Mrs. Sandoval still had jet black hair which gave her a more youthful look, and she had a round pleasing looking body. She was probably a foot smaller than her husband, but to Charlie, her face showed that she was the strength of the family.

Shash motioned for Nakai and Charlie to follow him over to the ceremonial area where Eunice was now taking out the charcoals with an iron implement and placing them in a bowl on a small round table. Charlie observed her sprinkling something on the burning charcoals and looked to Shash for an explanation.

"That's the medicine man's special plant, not corn pollen," Shash told her, pointing to a chair around the table where she was to sit. He then took his seat next to her and Nakai took his place on the other side of Shash. Hastiin Sandoval and his wife sat down across from them on raised pillows instead of chairs and Charlie supposed it had nothing to do with ceremony and much to do with a lack of chairs.

Shash began immediately talking across the steam that was shooting up from the coals, as Eunice Sandoval continued to sprinkle them with the same herb. Then, Shash's voice became agitated and Charlie watched him take out the photo of the woman Sue who he was sure put a curse on his son. It was a distinct change from the monotone softness of the Dineh language and it told Charlie just how serious this ceremony was for Shash.

Now, totally engrossed with the charcoals, Eunice began to speak in rapid Dineh as her hand reached out to something red that appeared at the bottom of one of the coals. It looked like a burnt piece of wood that was shaped almost like a bird. She held it up for Shash to observe and Charlie saw Nakai's face light up and then burst into laughter. Shash's face looked content with what this meant and Charlie surmised that the curse that had plagued the Benallys had been lifted.

"That bird was the curse?" Charlie whispered to Shash.

Shash nodded. "Mrs. Sandoval found the curse that Sue used. It was a mournful sounding bird, something like a dove. Now, we are going to pray to remove this."

Hastiin Sandoval started to pray in Dineh and his wife and Shash and Nakai carried on also with the repetitive sounds. She mouthed the prayer along with them, finding it easy enough to do in the somewhat oddly comfortable setting, with her voice trailing off in the smoke around them.

Once the prayer was completed, Hastiin Sandoval drank from a glass of water and then passed it around for all to drink from and participate as one. He then instructed everyone around the table to inhale and exhale the smoke several times. As she continued to inhale the smoke, Shash and Nakai walked outside of the hogan for a minute to call in the sun, and then they returned to the table walking in a clockwise fashion, like the sun, to resume their places. It then hit Charlie all at once that it was going to be her turn to speak, for them to witness her story. Her throat tightened up, in a way that made it difficult to swallow, let alone talk, and then she felt a hand tap her lightly on the shoulder.

The curse having been now removed gave Shash the freedom to smile. "Go ahead, Shéwee. Don't be afraid," he said to Charlie. "It's a good thing, you'll see."

Mrs. Sandoval was once again studying the charcoals and Shash said something to her in Dineh that made her nod and look Charlie's way.

"Why don't you start by telling her about your dream," Shash instructed her.

So Charlie began talking in a hesitating manner, trying to focus on the charcoals instead of on the four people who were seated now, witnessing the strange story told by this bilagana woman.

"I appear to be haunted all the time by someone from my past," she heard herself saying.

Shash was trying to translate for Hastiin Sandoval's sake, but Eunice waved him off in a gesture that was meant to convey that she understood what Charlie was all about.

So Charlie talked about the dream of being strangled, the one she had just revealed to Nakai that bleak night in the desert. Maybe Shash was right about the curse, she thought, and how wonderful it would be if she could leave that bad spirit of Uncle Jake in the charcoals and never think about him again for the rest of her life.

"This uncle keeps returning in my dreams, mostly when I think I am at peace," she said.

Eunice Sandoval said something in Dineh to Shash and he translated for Charlie.

"She tells me that your problems started because your mother ate the bear at the time you were born. You know that the bear is the brother of the human and you don't eat it." Shash saw the confusion on Charlie's face but finished what he was saying anyway. "When your mother ate the bear, it made a lot of bad things happen and so now, it is up to the bear to take the things off you."

Charlie drew a blank. What in the world was this all about? She had said almost nothing and now, Mrs. Sandoval said that she had a conflict with the bear. If she continued on with the story, then maybe things would make more sense.

"My uncle raped me," she said. "It took me a long time to come to grips with it, but now I have."

"Aaoh," Eunice said, which meant "yes" in Dineh.

"Who else lived in your house?" Shash interjected.

"My mother, father and sister. They've all passed on. They are all gone now." Charlie shivered, knowing what Mrs. Sandoval was going to say.

"The bear again."

Charlie was quiet. Even if this reason sounded logical, it could not be because her mother had been kosher. There were enough restrictions on what you could eat. Certain parts of the cow were fine and the lamb also, but there was no way in hell a kosher person would be allowed to eat a bear, unless forced to at gunpoint or if they needed it to survive. And they hadn't lived somewhere in Wyoming near the Tetons, but in New York, for God's sake!

Mrs. Sandoval, seeming like a mind reader, added, "Your mother maybe did not know. Someone who did not like her, maybe even the butcher, may have mixed some bear meat into something. Maybe it happened at the hospital where you were born."

Charlie turned to Shash for further explanation. "How can she know this for sure?" she prodded.

"Because she sees the bear above your head is why. She sees it," Shash said with certainty in his voice.

Charlie was quiet now and in thought. Something that happened back awhile ago was now coming to her. She was at the flea market with Laura from the magazine and there was a psychic there who was doing Kirlian photography. She was taking photos of people's auras for $30 and Laura nagged her into trying it. "C'mon," she said. "What are you, a chicken or something? You can find out a lot about yourself by the colors of your aura."

Charlie still had that photo which showed bright reds and yellows all around her head. The psychic said that it showed some heart stress. Laura's was all happy blues which was supposed to mean contentment and Charlie was kind of taken aback by the differences between the two of them. Then, there were the two small circular images above her head that later that evening Link pointed out to her.

"They resemble bear's ears," he said.

Charlie shivered now, trying to gain some composure. Eunice handed her a glass of water and Charlie took a sip and passed it on to Nakai, who passed it on to his father. They all inhaled the smoke from the charcoals and exhaled, and when that part of the ceremony was complete, Charlie sighed out loud.

"I didn't know that these things happened to people who didn't believe in them," she said softly.

"I don't know about that," Shash said. "The bear is a pretty powerful creature you don't mess with."

Nakai cleared his throat, looking for a way to interject something. He had been quiet, respecting the elders but, after all, it was he who had brought Charlie out here in the first place, and he had a right to offer his opinion.

"I think," he said, speaking in a high pitched voice that sounded almost animal-like, "that Charlie may not have thought she believed in these things, but she was out there searching for some answers."

He paused, looked at Charlie, and then continued in the same high pitch.

"Charlie had a friend who appeared to her to be from another world in many ways. They were writers together and when he passed on, she received two arrowheads out in the desert as an answer to a vision she had that he returned to her."

Nakai now turned to Charlie and pointed to her purse. "Show the Sandovals your arrowheads."

Charlie looked at Shash for his approval and he nodded solemnly. She opened the handbag, took out the small leather pouch and handed it to Mrs. Sandoval. Eunice paused and then opened the leather ties and removed the two shiny obsidian points for inspection. Hastiin Sandoval took one of them from her, glanced at it, and then gave it back to his wife.

Meanwhile, Nakai sat there with his arms folded and chest puffed out. This was a moment where he would shine because he was sure that the Sandovals would know a lot more than his father about those arrowheads. Shash never believed him worth a shit. Just took him for some mental case who did drugs and threw around the dola bichon. Now, he would see that this blonde woman was something supernatural like the spirits. She was getting guidance from those ancient arrowheads and his father had better believe it.

"So, you have a picture of your friend?" Mrs. Sandoval asked Charlie.

Charlie took out the only photo she carried of Link. It was one they took at a show business event at the Convention Center on the beach and there were three people in that photo, Link, Charlie and a television sit com actor.

"He communicated with her in the desert," Nakai repeated.

"That so?" Mrs. Sandoval asked Charlie, while she was studying the photo.

Nakai grimaced, unhappy that the Sandovals seemed to have so little trust in him. It was likely the result of rumors passed by his father and drunk brothers, he surmised.

"Yes," Charlie answered. "He spoke to me in a kind of vision the night before I found those arrowheads."

"You mean the night before those arrowheads found you," Nakai said in that same high-pitched voice.

Mrs. Sandoval put the obsidian points back in the pouch and handed it and the photo back to Charlie. She started to sing softly in Dineh and then motioned to Charlie to go outside to call in the sun. It was a strong summer sun and Charlie stretched her arms out wide to bring it to her, the way Shash and Nakai did. The sun sparkled off the photo of Link she was still holding in her hand and she instinctively made a decision about it. She quickly dug up some desert sand beneath her feet and buried the photo about three inches under. Charlie would remember Link at this place, at this blessed home where he would forever rest in peace on the red mesa.

As Charlie walked back to the house, a soft wind blew towards her. She was sure that she could see a face on that wind, a face that came from the ancients, but she would not tell them about it because she had spoken enough already. Besides, there was a good chance that they would know all about it anyway.

27

It was 9:30 AM when Sander first met the lady at the UFO Museum in downtown Roswell, and now, here she was lying naked in the lone double bed at the Alien Economy Inn.

Strange how these things worked out, Sander mused. He had decided to take a slight detour in his road trip, heading southwest from Amarillo instead of straight across I-40 to Tucumcari. It was on a whim because he started thinking about Link and how he used to come here all the time to talk to the guys at the museum about the notorious alien crash here in Roswell in the 1950s. The museum was chock full of exhibitions and photos and writings about UFO's and abduction cases, and it was possible that Charlie would want that Indian to see the contributions she and Link made to the place. Hell, they even had their names on the brass plaque on the library wall.

The rooms and hallways of the museum were decorated with various configurations of "saucer" pictures that took on various classic shapes, as well as "cigars." They dated back from the early 1948 sightings by pilot Kenneth Arnold, up through recent UFO sightings in the U.S. and European cities.

Sander walked over to a sitting area with a big screen that featured a continuous showing of the alleged Roswell crash and the government cover-up that followed, and that was where he discovered Margie, the raven-haired beauty, playing with a huge oval silver and turquoise barrette, her big brown eyes staring intently at the black and white photos on the screen. At once, Sander knew that he had to have her. The lady was just the medicine he needed to forget about Charlie and her blossoming insanity. So, he sat down a seat away and waited a few minutes for her to turn her head in his direction.

"Pretty heavy stuff we're looking at," Sander began, trying to look as serious as he could for someone who didn't believe any of this malarkey.

"I was out at that rancher's field yesterday, where the crash happened, looking for something like a piece of metal, maybe." She nodded solemnly, her wide eyes looking directly at Sander.

Sander smiled but was determined to not be condescending. Yes, he thought this woman was incredibly stupid, but who cared? That crash had happened almost 60 years ago and even if there had been any evidence then, it would have been scooped away generations ago.

"Ahh," he said, "you beat me to it. I was thinking of going out to that field today. You're welcome to come with me." He laughed lightly. "Maybe as a team we can come up with something major."

She returned his smile but shook her head. "It's a beautiful day out there but today I am going to try to find some of that pink quartz they have out here in the mountains. Do you happen to know anything about that?"

Sander could not believe his good fortune. It was like fate shining down on him.

"You're talking about the Pecos diamonds," he grinned. Yeah, sure I know where to find them."

So he and Margie spent the better part of the afternoon in the hills just north of Bottomless State Park, seeking out the pink and orange quartz points, and he enjoyed Margie's face, looking happy as a clam, thinking he was the greatest thing since whipped cream cheese.

Now, he was caressing her ample breasts as her eyes half-closed on him. She was tired after walking the fields all day and was doing her best to stay awake not only for the lengthy love-making session but for the explanation that came after, about the geography of the Pecos River which Sander said was the origin of those quartz points.

"I'm sort of tired," she said. "I could use a cool shower if it's okay."

"Sure, baby," Sander smiled, trying to sound nonchalant about the whole thing. It was time to think about someone other than Charlie who he didn't have a chance in hell with anyway. God, it had been so long since he'd gotten laid and Margie made him realize just how much he'd been out of the scene. He watched her walk naked to the bathroom and gave an appreciative whistle. It would be fun to just lay back and wait for her to come back for more.

A plaintive voice then called out unexpectedly. "Sander, the light won't go on. We need a light bulb."

It was past midnight and Sander knew there would be no one at the motel desk to help and besides you couldn't substitute a regular bulb because the bathroom light was one of those strange screwy looking fluorescent energy saving things. He moved the desk lamp to the vanity outside the bathroom so he could study the situation.

"Can you fix it?" Margie asked hopefully.

"Well," he said, holding the loose bulb, "the big problem here is that this coiled fucker isn't connecting to the base the way it's supposed to." Sander tried to keep a straight face but he was kind of enjoying the fact that he would be able to impress Margie with some scientific expertise.

"Now, here's the thing," he grinned. "When you can't connect a bulb to the base, even when you screw it tight, you can bridge that gap by putting a simple copper penny in there."

"Wow!" Margie's eyes lit up in grateful admiration.

"So, the penny put in the light socket extends the distance so the bulb doesn't need to be screwed in as far. Copper is a conductor so it allows the current to flow through it," Sander went on.

Margie sat her naked butt back down on the bed to watch the experiment as Sander extracted a penny from some change he had in an ash tray on the night table.

"Everything is simple when you understand the fundamentals of how things work."

He carefully inserted the copper penny in the light socket behind the bulb and flipped the switch. "Voila!" He laughed, watching Margie's expression which was a mix of gratefulness and awe.

Then, suddenly, there was a loud pop that sounded like a big balloon bursting above them. The air-conditioner shut down with eerie silence and the room fell into total darkness.

"Shit!" Sander cursed under his breath, knowing the rest of the night was shot in so many ways by his arrogant stupidity. "I can't believe this! I blew a fucking fuse!"

28

Hastiin Sandoval was sprinkling dark, grainy sand particles onto a long worn looking blanket spread out like a tablecloth on the linoleum floor, as Charlie sat fixated, watching the granules form a small circle. Nakai and Shash Benally were seated on either side of her, patiently waiting for what was to be the second part of the ceremony. Since Hastiin Sandoval was wearing a pair of bedroom slippers, Charlie guessed that this room they were now sitting in was the Sandoval's bedroom. It was hard to know for sure because there was just a small divan on the side and several armchairs.

For the ceremony, Shash had given her a small red throw pillow to sit on so she could observe close up what this medicine was all about and he and Nakai were seated on pillows as well.

"The bear that Hastiin Sandoval talks about," Shash whispered to her, "well, that bear will take all the bad spirits off of you, but you have to help it."

Hastiin Sandoval was now unraveling long leather ties from several small weathered pouches in order to take out the contents. He first removed two opaque white crystals that were terminated on only one side and Charlie, looking at them, was thinking that they were similar to the ones one could find in the mountains of Mount Ida, Arkansas. The old medicine man handed them to his wife Eunice for inspection and she nodded and then placed them both to the north of the sand circle. A grey leather pouch yielded another single terminated crystal which was much fatter than the others and it was placed to stand alone and upright toward the center.

Charlie was trying to hold on to this memory in her mind so she would have the details just right for her note pad later, and the Sandovals were creating an impressive palette for her. Hastiin Sandoval, as if reading her thoughts, now placed a three inch black obsidian triangle-shaped arrowhead on the left, where she was seated. On the opposite side, he put what looked to be an iron bar and then some smaller arrowheads both to the north and to the south. She watched intently, as he finished off the design by sprinkling white sand and corn pollen on the dark grainy sand circle, creating an interesting outline of the four directions.

Charlie realized that she was fighting tears and she knew their source. This beautiful, meaningful ceremony in a matter of just a few short years would be no more. The handful of elder medicine men like Hastiin Sandoval were dying out and there was nobody who had the wisdom and knowledge to take their place. The Dineh oral traditions that had been passed down through the centuries were losing their punch with the teens on Navajo Nation. To be an effective medicine man or hatatli, you needed to know so many prayers for so many different situations: Which verse goes with what illness? Which prayers take away bad spirits that stick to people from curses or by birth? As English, the language some Dineh called "enemy language," was imposed on the Dineh and gradually took hold, the youth moved away from the old ways and there was little impulse for going back. Hastiin Sandoval and his peers were well aware that in the community at large, Beauty Way and Ugly Way and the Shield Song had been overtaken long ago by Western medicine.

Clearing his throat now, Hastiin Sandoval looked Charlie's way. "I'm singing two songs now," he said in halting English. "One, the Earth Song, it puts our problems right into the mother Earth. Then, the Protection Song. You'll sing along and you will understand."

"Thank you," Charlie said, for lack of words.

Nakai tapped softly on her shoulder. "You don't know the words, but mouth them anyway," he said. "Oh, and keep your eyes on that large quartz crystal. It will keep you focused."

Shash nodded at him and Nakai smiled. For once, he did something that got his father's approval.

"Good, Nakai," Shash said, giving Nakai encouragement to go the beauty way, to do the right thing.

Eunice Sandoval sat down beside her husband as he began to sing. The medicine man's voice sounded strong and melodic despite his advancing age. Charlie tried to mouth the words, and by his repetition of the word "hozhoni," she knew he was singing Beauty Way. In a way, it reminded her of the cantorial chants that made her mother cry sometimes during the High Holy Days at the temple when she was a child. The words had a taste to them and it was sweet and healing.

Hastiin Sandoval sang the Beauty Way song for nearly twenty minutes, carefully pausing between verses so he could remember each one, and only stumbling but one time. Then, when he was finished, he passed around the corn pollen for each of the participants to sprinkle in the four directions. He was getting tired now, after the hours-long prayer session, and Charlie could see the strain in his eyes. He turned to Shash and asked if he would sing the Shield Song, and Shash who loved to impress Hastiin Sandoval, was only too glad to oblige.

"It's the story we tell about the strength of the horny toad," Shash explained to Charlie. "In the song, the horny toad is dressed in steel. He and Thunder don't get along because the Thunder wants to steal his song. They fight and fight and the horny toad gets him and wins. He lassoes him in like the rodeo cowboys do. I sing it every morning for protection. And it works," he added, smiling.

Charlie knew the song and the melody by now, because she had been listening to Shash singing early in the morning. Sometimes he sang it even before he got out of bed, but mostly it was when he took his pre-dawn walk up the mountain to greet the sunrise. He would then sing it right after the Sunrise Song.

"Listen to the words," he told Charlie. "Try to feel the Mother Earth and the power of the horny toad."

"I'll do that for sure," Charlie said, bowing her head in a show of respect. Shash began to sing then and Charlie, in a kind of instinctual way, found herself reaching inside her jeans pocket for her leather medicine bag.

"Ben a shanaheh..." Shash sang out, as Charlie's eyes now focused on the large quartz crystal of the sand design while her fingers removed the two arrowheads from the leather pouch. Shash did not look her way to see her unbutton her shirt and almost unconsciously rub the two arrowheads in the space between her breasts. There was, in fact, no reaction from anyone as they all kept on singing.

29

The long flat cliff face of Black Mesa, shadowed by the rows of pines along its upper reaches, contrasted handsomely with the bright red rock of Chilchinbito wash below. In the afternoon sunlight, the glowing warmth of the reservation land shared by the Navajo and Hopi, belied the palpable enmity between the two tribes that shared its sandstone beauty and the precious coal that the land provided.

For Sander Miller, the immense geological presence of Black Mesa was a marvel and its history even more intriguing. The land, once a habitation of tribes going back some 8,000 years ago, was now a point of conflict between the two tribes and the U.S. government and its partner, big business. The sacred mountain had been exploited for all its useful energy sources by the same powers that promoted dissension between the Navajo and Hopi and here at Back Mesa, where jobs competed with the spirits, the old strategy to divide and conquer was very much alive.

Sander had started the day in Indian country by coming by way of Chambers, Arizona to Wide Ruins, a small little village dotted with hogans, outhouses and rusted vehicles. It was the kind of region where a blond woman would have been noticed, especially a knockout like Charlie. After making a few inquiries there and then the day before in Window Rock as well, Sander was feeling discouraged.

The previous day, he was sure he had a good lead, but then he learned something about the Navajo and that was that they could be a pain in the butt to a visiting bilagana. He was at the Window Rock library, which for all intents and purposes could just as well have been the Miami Beach library. There were two elderly Dineh sharing a copy of the Navajo Times at one of the long rectangular wooden tables. They were engaged in some conversation about the song and dance planned for Labor Day at the rodeo arena. They seemed friendly enough, at least to each other, and Sander decide to try his luck.

"Yahteh." He greeted the men, offering his hand.

The taller of the two Dineh took off his glasses to get a better close up view of Sander, and then responded with a soft handshake that Sander knew was typical of the way the Navajo palmed each other. The shorter man had a skeptical look and Sander surmised that he would be harder to fool.

"I'm looking for Nakai," Sander went on. "He left Miami for the song and dance in Window Rock and he forgot his sash and moccasins. He left a message on my phone that it was important but his voice faded out on the machine and I don't know where the hell he's at. I'm about ready to turn around and go home."

"Nakai, huh?" The taller Navajo glanced at his friend, and then they exchanged a few Dineh phrases that Sander could not make out. He could tell though by the expressions on their faces that they knew who he was talking about all right.

"Which Nakai you talking about?" asked the less friendlier of the two.

Sander was stumped. He had no idea what Nakai's surname was or even if he had one. He should have asked that guy Tony at the library before he so impulsively jumped into the Jeep and made his way out here. It's just that the crazy lady Nakai lived with had scared the hell out of him. Well, he decided he would have to just take a chance on something that came to him.

"Listen," he said. "I don't have the time to waste here. I got to go back to work. So, why don't I just get the moccasins and stuff from the car and leave it all with you and you can give it to him."

For a minute, they studied him, and Sander hoped they would not ask to see the goods since he had absolutely nothing in the Jeep to show. It seemed though that they were studying his clothing. A day before this odyssey he stopped on a whim at some thrift store and managed to pick up an old straw panama and some striped shirts and old Levis. "Rez wear," he called it. Out here, his usual get up of khakis or cargo shorts with all the packets for transporting crystals and the faded t-shirts from Reno or Battle Mountain or Laramie just wouldn't work.

"We don't know where he is," the taller man said, "but if it helps you some, I saw him in Gallup with his dad a couple of days ago. It's Benally's son you're looking for, I suppose. Nakai Benally."

Sander quickly nodded in agreement. He had no idea if Benally was the right name but it sounded like the best lead he'd had thus far.

"Yeah," the man went on. "They could be back in Chilchinbito where the old man has some land. He lives in Albuquerque too, so you might check there at the senior center."

Sander fingered his ring, a cheap stabilized turquoise thing he picked up at some trading post along the I-40 close to the Arizona state line. He thought for a moment. If this Nakai was the one he wanted, he would not have dragged Charlie so far from home only to land in Albuquerque. He would want to keep her enthralled with his "Indianness." All those guys liked doing that when they saw a pretty bilagana woman. He decided to try something risky.

"Okay," he said in a more serious tone. "I'll give you the truth of why I'm here. Did you see a blonde woman with him? I think my wife ran off with this Nakai."

Sander watched the men suddenly tighten up on their expressions, motioning each other with their eyes that it was time to leave.

"No," the taller of the two said, avoiding Sander's eyes. "I don't know anyone of that description."

Sander watched the men walk out of the room to the door. They shrugged their shoulders almost in unison and Sander knew he had what he came for. The body movements of the men told him enough. They had seen Charlie all right and they had seen her with Nakai and maybe his old man too and they weren't going to tell this bilagana diddly squat because he meant nothing to them. They would protect Nakai and his father, even if they were kidnapping Charlie. With all that information going through his head, Sander had made the decision to head in the direction of Chilchinbito.

Black Mesa reminded Sander of a giant hand that reached across the Four Corners, as the intersection of the states of Utah, Colorado, New Mexico and Arizona was called. Its fingers were separated by dry washes and three of them, appropriately named First, Second and Third Mesas, were home to the Hopi tribe. Then, there were a series of hilly lowlands at the center, or the palm of the hand, with a small road traveling north from that center that crossed from the Hopi to the Navajo reservation.

It shouldn't be too hard to find Chilchinbito, Sander thought, turning his head sideways toward the colorful checkerboard tribal patterned artwork of a chapter house in this small village called Many Farms. The road, numbered 59, was zig-zaggy and somewhat gravelly, as it churned its way northeast, its main destination Monument Valley and Southern Utah. No, the part of getting there would be okay, he figured. The question was what exactly did he plan on doing once he got there?

What if he did find Charlie with this Nakai Indian guy and she expressed no desire to come back home to Miami with him? Whatever possessed him back there anyway to think that this guy could have kidnapped her? Was he watching some idiot John Wayne cowboys and Indians movie or something? This Nakai was a Navajo, for Pete's sake, not an Aztec from pre-Columbian days. Sander laughed out loud at the whole business he got himself into. Yeah, he thought. It must have been a bad dream from some old B movie with an Italian dressed up in warpaint, playing an Indian who was kidnapping some Christian staid pioneer woman and riding into the hills on a decorated horse.

Sander flipped open the console and took out a John Denver CD. It would be nice to listen to "Wild Montana Skies" while cruising through the gorgeous orange and purple mesas. He was about to insert the CD in the player when he noticed the radio and clock light suddenly die. Without warning, the old trusty Jeep had decided to conk out.

He'd been in his own reverie, not paying attention, and now something was terribly wrong with the Jeep's electrical system. The thing to do, he surmised, was to pull off the road at the end of the curve he was coasting, perhaps in an area where the red sand was more firmly packed so he could check things out. He was slowing up to about 15 miles an hour when he heard the sound he did not want to hear. The engine sputtered for a second or two and then it too groaned to a halt.

"Shit! Shit!" he mumbled under his breath. "It's the fucking alternator!"

There were those warning signs he did not bother to heed on the way out here when the Jeep had a problem starting up. It happened in Broken Bow, Oklahoma, where he detoured a bit to look for quartz crystals, and then again somewhere along the Red River on the Texas border. Sander had attributed it to some battery corrosion then and with some brushing around the terminals, he did manage to get the car started.

Now, he recalled something comical, a tale recounted from a book written by a desert junkie. The guy eventually moved out to the reservation with some Navajo woman, but his firsthand experience in these parts was rankling. His car broke down and he decided to hail down a couple of tribal guys coming through on an old pickup. He was sure they would get him help. After all, it was a given in any outback area, that your fellow man would give a helping hand when needed. It was not to be this time, however. Instead the men decided to harass the bilagana by putting him up in an old empty shack for a week, while they kept on charging him all kinds of money for junk parts that kept the car immobile.

Well, Sander was no sucker for that and he knew something about Jeeps, but when he saw an old pickup come by, he suddenly had a queasy feeling that those two Navajo men would be inside. The truck slowed down and a young boy waved at Sander who was now standing in the middle of the road.

"Hey, mister," the boy called out. Are you in trouble there?"

Sander managed a weak smile. Well, he would get through this anyway. The boy's hair was cropped short and so was his dad's, making them look almost Asian. It was a kind of look that to Sander meant they followed the Roman Catholic stuff or maybe they were converted Mormons. He figured that they believed the old colonialist propaganda that long hair made them behave like savages.

"Hey," the father looked out of the driver's window. "What's going on?"

"My alternator probably, I think. It was good when I left Miami. I wonder what happened."

"Maybe voodoo, "the Navajo grinned. "How are you going to get one?"

Sander shrugged. "I got tools to work things and I can get an alternator in Gallup if I can get there."

"Yeah, it looks that way," he agreed.

Sander took out his cell phone. "I guess I'll try to call AAA," he said, hoping the man would offer to drive him into Gallup but instead he just stood there smiling. "Damn!" he muttered. "No signal out here."

The young boy had opened the passenger door and jumped down, and his father turned his head to watch him hop from one small sandy mound to the next at the side of the road. The man seemed to be in no rush to go anywhere.

"We don't use wireless out here much," the Navajo commented matter of factly." They got a tower in Window Rock for those people though."

His boy started to walk back to the truck, waving to Sander, as he opened the door and hopped back in.

"I need some help out here," Sander tried, looking at the man in earnest.

"Do you have enough water?"

"Well, yeah, of course, I have water," Sander grimaced. This was not the way the rules were played out here and the man was really ragging him.

"You need a blanket. It gets cold here at night. I got an extra one if you want it."

Now, Sander was really pissed and angry at himself besides. He had managed to get himself in the middle of the Navajo versus bilagana game, but nevertheless, he was not about to play the role of the naïve white guy. The man had the door to the driver's side still open and Sander grabbed him by the shirt collar.

"Listen, you dumb shit," he let out. "You mess with my head and I'll beat the crap outta you!"

The Navajo looked Sander squarely in the eyes without changing his expression. Then, with no warning, he spat at him and shoved him to the ground with one hand. He grinned at Sander's astounded expression and turned on the engine.

"Dumb, huh?" he said, starting to laugh. "I'd debate with you who's the dumb shit, mister. I ain't the one stuck out in the desert with no alternator!"

30

Nakai had been brooding for most of the night, mumbling in strange monosyllables and making Charlie uneasy. At first she thought he was talking in his sleep but then she watched him walk in and out of the hogan, carrying something small and brown that looked to be a dead prairie dog.

It was true that Nakai had mental problems. Shash told her early on and repeated it again that morning at sunrise when they were up on the hill doing prayers. Shash was calling in the sun with his hands and motioned for Charlie to do the same. "Follow me, shewee," he said. Charlie knew that was an endearing word for a child and it encouraged her. "Johona'ai shiitra," she called out. Nahaadzan shima."

She had been struggling with her left leg this morning. Poor circulation, she knew, and she caught Shash watching her struggle to climb the hill although he did not offer a hand. As they started to walk back, though, he told her about a little blue plant that would give her strength.

"Just walk with it and say, 'let me walk in beauty' and you'll see how it helps you," he smiled at her.

Charlie looked up at Shash. He was a tall man and his age had not bowed him a bit. She wanted to believe that all that happened at Hastiin Sandoval's would help her to get stronger and seeing Shash so confident gave her the encouragement she needed.

"Thank you, Shash," she said as he finally took her hand.

"What you have to do, young lady," Shash said, focusing his eyes on hers, "is to say to yourself and out loud that you are powerful, and then you leave it to the Creator. Take me," he went on. "I live my life like I'm in the best shape I can be in, like I'm in tip top health. I walk miles every day before I drive the truck. I get up at the sunrise in all kinds of weather. It's the way you think that can keep you sick or get you well."

Charlie nodded. It made sense and she would follow those words.

"Bikeh hozhon," he said out loud and Charlie guessed that it was a prayer for her to walk in beauty.

"So tell me something, shewee," he asked when they reached the top of the hill. "Do you know any songs from your people, the Hebrews?"

Charlie was a bit taken aback but, of course, Shash understood that she had her own spiritual soul even though he was giving her a Dineh education.

"Go ahead," he encouraged, seeing her expression. "Put those songs out there in the desert."

Charlie thought about a song they sang at temple when she was a little girl. It was called Alenu and it was very beautiful and haunting. It was a prayer but like most songs in old Hebrew it was difficult to translate to its full meaning.

"We used to have many bluebirds here on the reservation," Shash said softly. "They would fly real early, before the sunrise and sing out. You don't see them anymore since the bilagana messed up Black Mesa. So, you sing out," he coaxed her, and maybe they will hear you and fly back here."

Charlie sang out and she was surprised that her voice was strong. "Alenu le shabeyach hadon akol...."

There was an echo in the canyon and she could see Shash smiling as she sang. He really believed that she was leaving a song here for all the lost bluebirds and all the desert creatures.

"Why was Nakai carrying a dead prairie dog in the darkness of night, Shash?" Charlie asked. "Was he trying to put the curse on someone?"

"My son is mental," Shash said simply. "It happens when you leave your land and your people and your way of life. Your spirit gets mixed up." Shash looked sad.

"It was a total destruction here," she said, noting a tear in Shash's eye. "Everything was stolen from the tribes and now everyone wants to borrow the ceremonies and the turquoise. It keeps on going."

Shash let out an unexpected laugh. "Honey, you know you aren't stealing anything. I'm giving you an education because I feel like it."

He patted Charlie on the shoulder and they started to walk back to the old hogan.

"As soon as we get home, I'll boil up some sage tea called ahh," Shash said. "You'll take it like I do every morning on an empty stomach when you get back to Miami. It's strong and powerful and doesn't taste too good. It will make you gag, in fact, but it will heal you honey. I'll give it to Nakai too. It's just what the doctor ordered for him to get his head back."

"What's exactly wrong with Nakai's head?" Charlie questioned. "So many tribal people left the reservation and they're not mental." She decided to use Shash's phrase.

"When he was a little boy, he stayed on the reservation with his grandma." Shash scratched his head, conjuring up a vision of what he remembered. "One winter things got so bad that she showed him how to shoot at prairie dogs for food. He's thinking about her now. He misses her."

Charlie did not know what to say. There was so much she did not understand and probably would never understand. Link used to tell her as much when he would show her drawings of aliens from UFOs. The faces were round, pear-shaped and even sometimes squarish, the way the folks who claimed to be "abductees" had seen them. She remembered that they all had one thing in common and that was slanty eyes. The thought came to her as she walked with Shash and studied the silver and turquoise ring he had crafted for his ring finger. The stone was cut into the shape of the sun as the Dineh saw it. It had a mouth shaped like an "0" and slanty eyes.

She was still thinking about that coincidence as they approached the door to the hogan, when Shash suddenly grabbed her hand and gasped. Seated at the open door was Nakai who was laughing hysterically and pointing a shotgun to his head.

"Don't you come near me!" Nakai lashed out as Charlie moved toward him. "Get the fuck away from me or you're a dead woman!"

Charlie backtracked, nearly sliding into Shash's outstretched arms, as the elder Navajo seemed to be transfixed by the sight of his son with the shotgun pointed at his head. Then, almost as if by instinct, he began to sing. It was a prayer that Charlie remembered hearing him sing at the medicine man's home, the one about the protective powers of the horny toad who wore the coat of armor to fight Thunder.

"Ben ah shanah hey eeh eeh eeh ben ah shanah hey eeh eeh eeh eeh...." Shash's voice held steady and strong, belying any fear that Charlie knew he must be feeling. His voice was somehow calming to her also.

At that moment, Charlie vaguely recalled a truism attributed to the Indians about never letting the enemy see you sweat. It was somehow connected to the stoic facial expression that tribal people often put on in front of white people, more often these days to fake them out. White people got annoyed by it which was a big part of the intended goal, but now she was witnessing a new use for it and one with great purpose. It was a literal battle of wits between father and son and she cupped her hands, silently praying that the father would win.

Nakai's face, at first glance, seemed to be devoid of any expression, but Charlie saw by his furrowed brow that he was listening intently to his father's protective healing prayer. She backed away, unnerved by it all, moving herself as surreptitiously as she could to the side of the hogan away from the two men. She decided that if Nakai wanted to kill himself, it was ultimately his own choice that somehow had to do with a conflicted family history of which she knew little. He had issues with his father that went back years and years and they had nothing to do with her desire that his life be saved.

The last few days here in the desert had been an enlightenment of sorts for Charlie, closely observing the interaction of father and son. This one-upmanship between the two must have spanned decades and it was likely, she now realized, that even the attentions given to her came from gamesmanship and family competition. Then again, what did Charlie expect to see? Did she think that the father-son relationship here would be a holy one that was somehow different from non-tribal family angst? Was she hoping for some stereotypical spiritual awakening by watching these two?

Maybe at one time in history, before the Europeans came trampling in, family connections had a deeper meaning and the daily life was more tuned to the medicine ways of someone like Hastiin Sandoval. However, soon, all the men like Hastiin Sandoval would be gone and so would the tie to the land and the life of tribal families living side by side on the reservation. Right now, Shash had more knowledge and more strength than his son because he was still close to his ancestors, but what about Nakai and any future children he might have? Soon the passing of the knowledge of the ancients, all the old stories and songs would be gone if there was no one to keep them going. The sadness of it all, the same way she had felt at the Sandovals' home, had made Charlie forget the turmoil going on just a few yards away.

A sudden blast of the shotgun sounded and Charlie instinctively dropped to the ground. There was a stomping of feet around her and she shivered in terror, but then a peal of laughter caught her unaware. She felt the trickle of urine running down her legs as a sense of relief caused her to sigh loudly. The standoff was finally over with both men the victors. They were embracing each other and Nakai was now smiling joyously. His face had the merriment of someone who had just pulled off a good prank.

"We had you fooled, huh, Charlie?" Nakai laughed.

Shash sighed. "Oh well." He shrugged his shoulders. He and Nakai both knew that it was not a practical joke but the result of a brief manic episode that Shash, by his prayer, managed to break up.

"We're going to boil up some ahh tea," he said flatly, now taking back control. "Then, we'll go into Gallup for some burritos."

Charlie was quiet as she followed Shash back into the hogan. She had been thinking about getting back to Miami, and this incident was now making it more imperative she do so. The only question was how to get back, because at this point, the last thing she wished to do was ride back with Nakai. If she could get them to drive to Albuquerque for some reason, it would be easy to find a reason to split and get a cab to the airport. The nearest city to here was Gallup and this meant catching a Greyhound bus to somewhere, and even at that, it was likely a long wait at the terminal.

Shash took out some dried crushed sagebrush from a brown paper bag and emptied it into the teapot along with two cups of water. The hogan soon took on the scent of the evening desert, and Charlie sat down on an old wicker rocker to take it all in.

"You know, "Shash said turning to her, "When you gather the sagebrush out there, you don't use anything but your hands to break off the branches. No fancy tools, just the tools the Creator gave you."

Shash liked that Charlie seemed to observe everything. "You've also got to remember to thank the plant for giving you the nourishment," he added. "White people say grace and thank God for the food, but you also have to thank the food itself for making you healthy and for keeping you alive."

"Thank you for sharing all these things with me," Charlie said, smiling at Shash. She really liked this man and was grateful that she had the opportunity to meet him.

"And, now you are ready to go back to Miami," Shash smiled back at her.

Charlie was taken aback. How could he read her mind like that? Was she that transparent?

"I hope that Nakai is okay for the trip. I'm kind of worried about him," she blurted out, looking his way. She did not care that Nakai knew how she felt. He did what he did and he should pay the consequences for it.

"He won't hurt you, honey," Shash said, trying to reassure her. "It's time for him to go also. He's having problems with all the ancestors here, the ghosts. When he leaves, he'll be good again."

"Yes, get packing up, Charlie," Nakai called out from the doorway. "My father is right, of course. He's always right."

There was an edge of sarcasm in Nakai's voice but Charlie could also detect the sound of resignation. No, Nakai had not impressed his father on this visit and although Shash enjoyed Charlie's visit, he did not see her as an embodiment of some spiritual being. In fact, Shash's attentions to Charlie were starting to get Nakai envious. If he hung around any longer, Shash might even suggest a sacred sweat lodge for all of them and he would be darned if he allowed any Navajo, let alone his own father, see Charlie naked.

Nakai, ashamed by his thoughts, walked over to the small table to join Shash and Charlie, and together they drank the bitter tea in silence. He was angry at his father for that crack about his upsetting the ancestors and at the same time ashamed of his own nasty thoughts about his father and Charlie. What prompted him to think that Shash would ever ask Charlie to be at a sweat with him? His father followed the old traditions and would never go to a sweat with the opposite sex. Not ever.

After finishing the last drop of tea, Nakai went to retrieve a small suitcase he had put aside at the hogan entrance and called out to Charlie.

"Get your things together. If we leave now, we could be in Page by nightfall."

Charlie picked up some toiletries, a sweater and some t-shirts and packed then snugly in her overnight case. So, they were going to Page, Arizona from here. He would be showing her some of the monuments before they headed home. Well, it was a tourist city in any event and if there was some problem, she would be able to get away and get help over there. She felt the tears well up as she walked over to embrace Shash. She knew that she would probably never see him again and she felt a heavy sadness come over her.

"Hagoonee, Shewee," Shash said softly. "Go in beauty."

Nakai opened the door to the Chevy van and threw his suitcase on the back seat. He had walked out on his father without so much as a handshake, but Shash seemed unconcerned as he watched Charlie sit down in the seat right next to his son. Nakai slammed the door shut and watched the Navajo elder walk slowly back to the hogan, his head unbowed. It was after they were several miles up the main road from Chilchinbito that Charlie noticed the shotgun had come along also. There it was, planted squarely under Nakai's feet.

31

Sander dug into his breakfast tortilla, letting the thick spread of spicy red and green salsa run down the corners of his mouth. It had been a long, hard night hike north to the small town of Kayenta, here at the foot of Monument Valley where the cell phone finally picked up a signal and he convinced AAA at 4 AM to come out and find his Jeep in the northern Arizona desert.

He was lucky that the moon threw out enough light to allow him to make his way up the winding path of route 59. Sander figured that his night vision was sharp as a cat's, something he attributed to an early LSD experience that permanently enhanced his senses. He had walked with heavy steps, to warn rattlers and any other night critters that he was coming their way and in no way was he ever intimidated. Sander loved night hikes and it was no problem taking a nap every so often on an inviting mesa and listening to the sounds of the frogs croaking and the crickets singing. Of course, he would have preferred this hike to be one of choice and not something he had to do to save his ass and his Jeep.

The Triple A guys were not crazy about towing his Jeep from "rezland," Sander mused, while enjoying his breakfast at the Mexican diner in Kayenta. They also did not appreciate having to first locate him at his northwest point on route 59 before heading in to find the Jeep. The protocol was that you were supposed to be standing next to your vehicle, which was something Sander was not able to do without a phone signal back there.

"So, when do you expect to be getting your truck back?" the red-haired waitress asked, smiling as she poured more coffee.

Sander grinned back at her. Yeah, her smile was too broad, a sure sign she was interested and if he had to hang out in this touristy spot for a day or two, he might as well have some good-looking company.

"They took it to some mechanic on I-160 who first has to wait for an alternator to be sent in from Salt Lake."

"He couldn't locate one in Farmington or Page?" she asked.

"My Jeep is ancient," Sander kidded. "Maybe when I get back to Miami, I'll buy a new old Jeep."

She got wide-eyed at the mention of Miami and Sander figured that she had been hanging out at the Anasazi ruins for too long. When you came out to these parts and mentioned you were from anywhere in Florida, people tended to think you were some city slicker.

"It must be a kick walking around all day in your bathing suit and stuff," she commented. "Do you roller blade like those models do? I saw something on the Travel channel about all that and the clubs too."

"Yeah," Sander said breezily, trying to remember when the last time was that he saw the inside of a club. "Yeah, you don't get much sleep. That's for sure."

"Oh, my God, oh my God!" the waitress squealed, suddenly leaving Sander's table and making a dash to the door. He could hear her shouting at the front entrance, "Oh my God, it's really you! I don't believe it!"

Sander turned his head to catch sight of the big-chested Navajo man entering the diner and the eager waitresses all running up to hug and embrace him. He had to admit that the guy was definitely a head turner from his hand-beaded moccasins up to his shoulder length jet hair, tied back with a humongous silver and turquoise butterfly barrette. He was the real deal all right, the classic dream of tourists who came to this part of the world hoping to see a "real Indian." Digital cameras were coming at him now from all directions. The backpacker and SUV crowd who had come to capture the incredible monoliths of Monument Valley were now getting a bonus besides.

The diner's owner, a heavy-set blond white man with fat red cheeks, was standing not too far from the Indian, with a big smile planted on his face. The decorated Indian was good for business, Sander laughed to himself. He could picture these guys going back to Oshkosh or wherever in small town America to brag about the beautiful Navajo man they shook hands with in Kayenta. If a picture was worth a thousand words then this guy was, without question, the "photo op" of the trip.

It was 11 AM and Sander was thinking about checking into a chain motel in the area and renting some kind of car until the old Jeep got running again. Maybe for now, he would walk around and get some sunshine. Motels generally didn't have their rooms ready till the afternoon anyway, so he had some time to kill. Then, when he was checked in somewhere, he could come back for the red-head. He left two bills on the table, paid the cashier and walked out. With all the hoopla the Indian was creating, he could have easily slipped out and stiffed them. But, hell, he wasn't broke. Just a passing thought. That's all.

The 80 degree desert heat was feeling good after the all-night trek, even though he had no protection from the blazing sun. He had left his sunglasses on the passenger seat of the Jeep. He squinted, letting the orange and yellow rays play across his closed eyelids. Then when he opened his eyes fully again, he saw a mirage through the window of a van that strangely resembled Charlie!

Hell! Shock of all shocks, it was Charlie all right! And now, the fancy Navajo was coming out to her with containers of coffee and carrying what looked to be a tray with two platters of huevos rancheros. For a few seconds, he forgot this miracle of actually finding Charlie and instead felt resentment that this man, who was obviously the one named Nakai, had gone into the diner to do Charlie's bidding.

Nakai, for his part, was only too happy to keep Charlie outside of that diner. Who knows how many of those waitresses in there he had slept with? If Charlie thought of him as a holy man, he was going to do his best to maintain that image. He was glad now that he had taken this route through the Four Corners area with its sacred Anasazi spots instead of I-40 with all the billboards advertising the fake tourist "Indian trading posts."

Charlie smiled at Nakai as he came to her side of the van with the steaming platters. She was happy that he was acting normal now and he even let her keep the shotgun on her side of the van. Hopefully, they would make it home without Nakai getting another manic attack. Charlie loved this area of the southwest and she decided she would show him a spot not too far from here where you could locate some beautiful blood jasper.

"What have you got there?" she laughed. "It looks like a wedding platter."

Nakai chuckled. He was feeling warm and glowy inside and the dark period had passed. Charlie hadn't freaked out like his father thought she would and when he got back to Miami, he would call the old man and put Charlie on the phone just to show him that she still believed in him. He wanted Shash's respect, and if he could keep Charlie by his side, that was no small deal.

Sander watched from a distance as Nakai spread a small blanket under a cedar tree a few feet from the back of the diner.

"We're going to eat healthy this morning 'cause we've got a long trip ahead of us."

Nakai placed the extra plastic plates that the red-haired waitress gave him on the blanket. He remembered having a night with that one somewhere awhile ago but he couldn't recall her name. He just prayed that she and the others would stay inside and away from him while he shared this wonderful food with Charlie, because even if his father thought otherwise, he was sure that she was that vision he had seen in the library and nobody could tell him different. Now, always aware of his surroundings, he sensed that there was a guy hanging around not too far from them who was giving him the eye. He was unshaven, with a reddish brown ponytail and he was likely homeless, a drifter. Maybe after they ate, he would offer the guy a lift somewhere. It was a side to his character that Charlie had not seen yet and Nakai knew she would like that about him.

"I love when they make the huevos rancheros spicy like this," Charlie said, digging into the big platter.

"Same with me," Nakai agreed. "They know me here at this place, so they make the stuff extra hot. Try the beans. They got lots of pepper."

"I'm glad you changed your mind about killing yourself back there," Charlie suddenly blurted out.

Nakai turned his head away from hers and put down his fork, his smiled quickly fading.

"It's the place, you know," he said in a serious tone. "It's the old hogan. It can scare the hell out of me like ghosts returning to haunt you, right?"

Charlie nodded. She was learning a lot about ghosts this summer.

"The government, the white man, call it what you want, but they took everything away. My grandmother still had land that was pretty good for grazing, but no more. You got Peabody Coal and that whole mining mess here at Black

Mesa. They siphoned our good water away, probably to Las Vegas. And there my father sits, an old man, an old warrior staring at lost memories."

"I could do a write up about it and at least get it some publicity," Charlie offered. "You never know where these things can go."

Nakai shrugged. "Just eat your food, let the arrowheads find you, and don't worry about this business. You write about things that make people smile and that's good too. You made my father smile and he doesn't do that too often."

"I've seen so much deprivation out here. Old people are without electric or cars or any way to get around. I feel like I should do something about it or at least try."

Nakai laughed sarcastically. "So you think they're deprived, huh? Well, let me tell you something. Some of the elders want to live exactly that way, close to the ground, the sunlight and the sounds of nature. They don't want the noise and pollution of cars and they sure don't want electric bills!"

Nakai enjoyed seeing the surprised look on Charlie's face and decided to keep going with it.

"And, I'll tell you what," he went on. "Being without is a state of mind, that's all, and there are tribal people who can handle things a whole lot better than white people. When white men are hungry, really hungry, they can't help but look like that homeless guy over there with the ponytail."

Nakai pointed to Sander, who had turned away from Nakai's gaze, toward the window of the diner.

Now, following Nakai's finger, Charlie caught herself choking on a mouthful of hot pinto beans. Oh holy shit, she was thinking. The homeless guy sure looked like Sander. Charlie did not have the greatest vision, but damn it, that was Sander all right. What the fuck?! That idiot must have followed her out here and how long had this been going on? She quickly turned her head to look for the familiar Jeep but it was nowhere around.

Nakai, unaware of her discovery, was now walking toward Sander and Charlie watched in amazement as he opened his wallet to offer him a couple of bucks. She heard a few words pass between the men and continued to stare in disbelief. Then her jaw dropped as she observed Sander smilingly pocket the money, thanking Nakai profusely. He was making such a deal over it that Nakai took him by the arm and led him over to the picnic breakfast and Charlie.

"Charlie," Nakai beamed, "I have Sandy here. He says his truck broke down and he's a little down on his luck."

"Ah, Sandy, why don't you join us," she said drily. "Eggs are getting a little cold but the spices are hot enough."

If Sander was going to play some stupid hobo game, she would go along with it. It was better that Nakai did not know that Sander followed them to the west. He would only get royally pissed and who could blame him for that one? It might even provoke Nakai into one of his dangerous manicky states. It would probably be a good idea for Sander to see that gun upfront also, she decided, just in case he had an idea to carry this joke to an obnoxious state as he was wont to do.

"We're going up 191 to look for blood agates, Sandy," Charlie said nonchalantly.

"What's an agate?" Sander deadpanned, picking up a soft tortilla and gulping it down quickly as if he had not eaten in days.

"There's agate rocks and jasper with red spots that look like blood. They're medicine stones," Nakai offered. "You can come with us but we're going to head across I-70 from there so we can't get you back here."

"Oh, I can hitch," Sander grinned. "I'm used to that. "I can't believe you're inviting me! Wow! A real Indian! I was watching you in that diner before with everyone making such a fuss over you."

Sander had a fawning look on his face that was really starting to annoy Charlie but Nakai was clearly enjoying all the attention.

"Hey, where are you from?' he asked, scratching out the remaining eggs from the container for Sander.

"California, I suppose," Sander shrugged. "I was there for the last eight months anyway."

"Let me guess," Nakai smiled. "You were in San Francisco, right?"

Nakai started to gather up all the plastic plates and napkins for the trash dumpster.

"Yup, it was the streets of San Francisco where I left my heart." Sander laughed heartily, trying to catch Charlie's eye each time Nakai bent over to collect trash. Charlie purposely turned away, knowing that he was doing his best to jangle her nerves just to let her know she did something incredibly stupid by coming out here with Nakai.

It was in a way puzzling to Charlie that this surprise intrusion was bothering her at all. After all, it wasn't many hours before that Nakai was ready to end his life with one bullet and she was desperately looking to escape from Chilchilbito. Then, half the time, she could not understand her own emotions, the whys and wherefores, and maybe humans were meant to live these mysteries and not to try to solve them.

"So, Sandy, how come you like to come here to the reservation?" Nakai questioned, while Sander accompanied him to the dumpster.

"It's a good life for me," Sander yawned. "I like sleeping on the mesa."

"Good," Nakai chuckled. "We'll do that tonight. I'll find us the grandest mesa in all Utah and at midnight, we'll call in the stars together!"

32

The otherworldly orange monoliths of southeastern Utah appeared eerier than usual to Charlie. She supposed that it was the purplish clouds of the late summer afternoon that were giving it a fairy tale kind of feeling.

Nakai had decided that he wanted "Sandy" seated next to him and from the comfort point of her back seat, Charlie found it fun to listen to Nakai throwing his weight of knowledge at Sander for a change. By playing it stupid, Sander had unwittingly made himself into a captive audience and when they made the turn north onto 191, Charlie thought about an infamous story that Sander must have been dying to tell Nakai.

She did not remember how far back this went but it involved escaped cop killers called the Texas 7 who were being hunted down by the authorities right around this bend. He and Charlie got caught up in the mess unwittingly because the grey Jeep they were driving at the time just happened to be the same vehicle the convicts had been driving. So, there they were, just out rock hounding and then there they were again with their hands up in the air facing a bunch of State Troopers. She could laugh now thinking about it, but boy, they were scared out of their wits then, especially, when the trooper let them go and said to notify him if they saw a bunch of guys with AK 47's coming through!

Sander turned for a second to look at her and wink and she had to smile. There were so many stories, so many memories they had together of the road. Charlie hoped that Nakai had not caught her reaction to the wink in the rear view mirror, but he seemed to be focused on the strange monolithic planet that is southeastern Utah that was quickly closing in on them.

"That's a fairly ominous cloud overhead," Sander commented. "Once I fell asleep on one of those mesas and I didn't see the storm coming up." Sander pointed to a long flat mesa to his right. "Geez," he grinned, "the rains came down on me so fast and hard I was drenched before I had a second to wake up!"

"If you were asleep, then how is it you knew how long it was raining on you before you woke up?"

Charlie noted the sarcasm creeping into Nakai's tone of voice and guessed that he saw Sander as competition for her attentions. His next comment made her shiver.

"You ought to thank the good Creator that you're still alive," Nakai added. "When you get a storm around these parts, the flash flooding can catch you pretty quick and you get swept away just like the leaves and other debris. People die around here all the time, you know."

Nakai enjoyed throwing around scary propositions and more than once on this trip Charlie had heard the familiar Indian refrain, "It's a good day to die." More crucial was the expression he got, the icy countenance and the vacant look in his eyes whenever he talked about death. It was almost as if it were something he aspired to and she hoped she was wrong about that.

Sander was right about that ominous sky. Those heavy smoky looking clouds up ahead reminded Charlie of those puff balls she had seen in this area and parts of Nevada when forest fires sprang up, blackening out daylight and creating an eerie yellowish color above the mesa line. They could make it up 191 to I-70 okay but if they chose to detour through the dirt roads that zigged and zagged out here to search for blood agates in the canyons, it looked to be a bit hairy. One time awhile back, the Jeep did a 180 degree skid on a slippery dirt road right around these parts and she and Sander almost landed in a ditch that was well hidden behind the thick sagebrush. It was clearly the moment to say something.

"I think it's a good idea to hole up in Blanding for the rest of the day and then get an early start tomorrow. We're in for a storm for sure, Nakai, and this van has no 4 wheel drive. Besides," she added, even if there's no big storm, the gnats will be really fierce out there." She looked to Sander for some support, but instead got typical Sander razzing.

"Hey, Charlie," he laughed. "Where's your sense of adventure? You're too much the worrier, woman."

Charlie shrugged her shoulders, wondering why she did not just give

Sander's "shtick" away. Let Nakai beat the shit out of him and show him a real adventure. She sighed out loud, thinking that it would not be the first time that the gnats and mosquitoes had a meal on her.

The road that turned off into the jasper field would be coming up in about ten miles or so, and once they got on it, she could count on a drive of about 30 miles through mesas, with the dirt road being somewhat passable when dry and mostly worse if it got slick with heavy rain. There were ruts, rocks and boulders to contend with in the more deserted plateau areas far from the main routes and, in other spots, the old washboard affect that tended to make Charlie nauseous. Along the twisted route, an occasional abandoned silver mine with its rusty equipment could surprise you, especially if there were remains of old mining tailings on the hills. In these parts, there were no warnings posted for idiots dumb enough to want to explore the inner workings of an old partially collapsed mine tunnel. In short, part of the adventure Charlie knew was in knowing that once you entered these hinterlands, you were on your own.

The excitement of the unexplored most of the time outweighed the dangers. Between the cactus and the scrub an ancient arrowhead could peek out tantalizingly at you and that kind of discovery, as Charlie well knew, threw shivers of delight up your spine. Sander enjoyed finding the old glass bottles all purpled from laying many years in the sun, and sometimes he found an old toy or even a child's moccasin. However, for Charlie right now, that anticipation was giving way to the fear of danger, of being trapped in this no man's land in a flood situation with an unpredictable variable named Nakai. Sander had no idea what he was about and in such close company she had no way to ask him.

In the vast desert stretches of Arizona and Utah with the long narrow canyons, the flash floods could come up on you so quickly and with such ferocity that Charlie easily understood why the early Anasazi dwellers made their homes up high in the cliffs for their own protection. The clouds were steadily moving closer now and she knew that right at that very moment there was a storm out there somewhere, maybe several miles away that could, without warning, swirl into the canyons and arroyos just east and west of them. The trick was to figure out how to stay on the main road until they reached the I-70 expressway.

"I have an idea that could work," she said, mustering some forcefulness into her voice. "There's a small ranch road just east of Crescent Junction. It's along route 173, I believe, and it goes into Fly Wash and a bunch of other washes around the Green River. What I know is that there's blood agate there for sure."

"Where's Crescent Junction?" Sander asked, feigning ignorance about an area that Charlie knew he wholeheartedly enjoyed visiting.

Here she was trying to save his ass not only from the possibility of a dangerous storm but also from Nakai's unpredictable behavior, and he was acting stupid just to annoy her. But why? He had to know the threat this situation presented.

"The Junction is fairly close to I-70, Sandy," she said grimacing.

"Well, doesn't that sound silly?" Sander laughed heartily. "Why go all the way up to the 'I' when we can turn off here and find those agates so much sooner. Besides, I hate the paved roads."

Nakai grinned, now enjoying the conflict between the two.

"I'm with you, brother," he said, giving the sky above a brief glance. "I've seen a few of these storms in my time, and most of them pass by pretty quick."

Charlie decided that it was going to be a lost cause unless she could come up with something fast, and then, it came to her. Whenever she wanted anything to go her way, she would throw out the magazine trick. If she wanted an entrance to any event, she just dropped the name of one of her publications. Everyone wanted publicity, the fifteen minutes of fame, and if they had any possible shot at it, you could get anything you wanted.

"Hey, Nakai," she said matter-of-factly," did you ever check out the big monolith south of Moab? There's a big hole drilled into what looks like a huge chimney."

"Hole-in-the-Rock," Nakai nodded, glancing back at Charlie. "Yeah, I know it. Impressive white tourist trap."

"I am thinking that it would be great to take your photo in front of the tourist trap for a magazine cover. I do quite a few stories for the travel crowd."

Charlie was careful how she phrased this. She gave no guarantee that she was getting the photo published because in this business, knowing all the editors you had to make your way through, you did not make promises.

"Well then," Nakai shrugged, a small smile shaping the corners of his mouth, "It's decided. We'll do what Charlie wants. I always let the woman win." Then, after that he added, not wanting to disappoint the man he knew as Sandy, "We'll check out that ranch road she talked about and see who gets the best bloody agate."

33

The lightning fired up the walls of the old garage making everything seem to turn a bright orange. Even the old cracked star-patterned linoleum, rolled up on the cold, gray cement floor seemed to be ready for the next boomer that would make it come alive with color for a moment, defying its dismissal from the old house in Queens. Charlie sat on a dusty warped mahogany chest that once contained her grandmother's silverware, and as any scared five-year-old would, she just sat there, fingers in her ears, waiting for it all to blow over.

The lightning and thunder were coming now in frequent shots that caused the side door to creak and whine loudly, and Charlie felt the growing gnawing fear inside that something bad was coming. Just a few minutes ago, she was in the backyard in the dirt in dungarees, playing with worms, even biting one or two of the salty little creatures a couple of times. Then came the clouds, two of them that seemed to rise above the lilac bush. They were heavy and purplish and they banged together suddenly like a lion's roar. Then the rain and wind came up so fast that she could not make it back to the house in time.

"Charlie girl, where the hell are you?"

It was Uncle Jake shouting out there, and cursing too, as the wind kept beating at his umbrella. Just hearing his voice made her eyes dart frantically around the decades of family clutter in search of a hiding place. Old floor mats and rugs rolled up against the sides of the garage were too heavy to move, so she squeezed between two large cardboard boxes, overfilled with pots, pans and dishes that were hauled back inside the house once a year for Passover week.

He was now at the side door, trying to get the creaking thing open while hanging on to his umbrella. It was a stuck door that needed oiling and fixing and she breathed hard, listening to her uncle fighting the wind. Charlie could get in through the door real easy because it always managed to open about ten inches before sticking, just enough for a small five year old to slip in. She prayed the wind would be her friend today and save her from the beating she knew was coming to her, all because she was not strong enough to make it back to the house in time.

Jake's rubber boot was kicking at the door now and each kick carried with it a curse word. Then, Charlie heard a different kind of noise, like a window being opened inside the house. Probably, it was her mother who did a search of the house and sent Jake out to find her.

"There's no answer from the fucking garage!" he shouted back to the window. "You can't get into this damn garage anyway. Someone's got to fix the fucking door!"

Charlie heard Jake's boots now swishing through the puddles, making his way back inside the house. She would wait for the lightning and thunder to let up. It wasn't happening so bad now and she could even ease up on her fingers that had been stuck in her ears for so long that they were in pain from pressing so hard. She was listening for the door to the house to slam shut and then she would squeeze her way out of the garage and make her way to the small slanted shed that opened to the cellar of the house near the damp boiler room. It was always dark down there but darkness was her friend and sometimes she hid there when Jake was alone in the house. Once she got to the boiler room, she would call out to her mother and everything would be okay again.

Memories came at you out of nowhere, it seemed to Charlie, as she let out a small sigh from her back seat of the van. Nakai and Sander would just keep on going with the macho banter and that was okay with her. She was content for the moment to be in her memories, which always seemed to pop up for her at a time they were needed. The message here came from a time she was in trouble without any protection around and she had to figure a way to get to safety without getting hurt. If the two guys had the chutzpah to look forward to fighting a flash flood, well then, she would just have to find an opening, an escape route and go for it. She closed her eyes and was sure that she caught a momentary blue light like the ones Link saw when he needed answers. Link welcomed risks in his life and the danger of the unknown and, right at the moment, she was thinking of one of his cockamamie plans that come to a sudden halt when he died.

Link Davis had a plan all right but he told Charlie that it had to be carried out just right for it to work. A reliable source had told him that somewhere in the deep walls of Mount Archuleta in the northern New Mexico desert, close to the Colorado state line, there were fetuses of alien beings. The source said that it was a documented government project and that the fetuses had been there since the 1970s. Obviously, the mountain and the area around it, including Dulce, New Mexico, were closely monitored by electronic surveillance to keep out the ufonauts and other intruders.

How clever of our government, Link thought, to place these alien fetuses inside a mountain within the confines of the Navajo Reservation, among a group of tribal people who were good at not revealing secrets. Just look at how long the World War II veterans kept quiet about their role as code talkers. But, as always with Link, there was a need to know and if there were indeed fetuses, in glass jars, somewhere in the bowels of Mount Archuleta, then where did they come from? Were they captured from a downed UFO or were they some freakish creation of our own government? If the latter were the case, then why? For what purpose?

For Link, the important thing really was the plan, the how-to. He would work in twos, under the cover of night, to try to thwart government surveillance which was out there discreetly in spots surrounding the mountains. His buddy, a cop from New Jersey named Jerry Sanchez, made the offer to go with him whenever Link felt the time was right, and after many sleepless nights, he had finally come to this conclusion: Jerry would carry the gun and be the lookout, since he was a cop and knew how to handle the weapon, and he, Link, would crawl inside a small opening that led into the mountain where the fetuses were kept. Link had studied several topo maps online as well, as the big section of Mount Archuleta from the National Geological Survey, and he was certain that he could find the entrance.

"You are completely insane!" Charlie had screamed. "If there is something weird going on there, the chamber in there is probably contaminated, and what will you do if you come upon those fetuses? Who will you tell?"

"Even if I can't share it with anyone, I'll know these beings exist and that's what counts!" Link had countered.

But Charlie had insisted that he stay put, even though she knew that once

Link made up his mind about something, her cause was lost. Link laughed at her and got even more preposterous in his thinking.

"Hey," he said, "I'll tell you what. I'll hold the gun and Jerry goes in. Is that better?"

He had pulled Charlie toward him to give her a hug, just before he announced that he was leaving for New Mexico the following Thursday.

"It'll be fine, Charlie," he added, hugging her. "You worry too much."

That Sunday night, when Link started packing his bags, Charlie tried to feel some of the excitement she saw in Link's eyes but she could not. Then again, Link never got to Dulce because the very next morning he had a heart attack and died instead.

It was an improbable situation, Charlie was now thinking, and it was unlikely that Link would have ever found what he was looking for at Mount Archuleta. More likely, he and his friend Jerry would have wound up at some Mexican watering hole in Albuquerque or Roswell after taking some bad guesses as to how to enter the cavity in the mountain where the supposed fetuses were hidden. Why she was thinking right now of Link and that strange ambition of his was anyone's guess. Maybe it had something to do with the predicament she found herself in right now. Maybe there really was no predicament and it would all work out in the end. Why was she always so frightened about losing people she loved or about dying suddenly up on a mountain or in a flash flood or even in the corner of an old garage in a thunderstorm?

The solution to her situation was now coming to her, and at once it seemed obvious. There was a service station at Crescent Junction along I-70 where they would need to fill up. In these parts, there were so few services and they were spread many miles apart, so you took advantage to top off whenever you got the chance. There was likely to be a phone at the station that would not be out of range like cell phones were in this wilderness area, and that phone would be the key. Now, if she could only figure out who to call.

34

Shash Benally had been approaching the Grants exit on I-40 going east when the accident happened. Like an explosion, hundreds of cellophane bags filled with pistachio nuts flew out of a humongous white pickup as it swerved to avoid a speeding tan Ford Explorer, missed the mark, and instead wound up splayed on its side across the black asphalt. The contents of the bags, the pistachios, spilled out in small piles for more than a quarter of a mile, creating havoc. Shash stopped short, in a deafening screech, managing to avert a crash into the car in front of him. He got out of his vehicle at the same time the small Mexican scrambled out of the pickup, surprisingly still alive.

Sometimes, it paid to be a short man, he was thinking. You had the advantage of being able to crawl out of danger in small places. The Mexican's face was red with anger—a shade that Shash had never seen before in a Chicano.

"Que pasa, buddy?" Shash put out his hand. "Esta bien, amigo?"

The Mexican shrugged. "Not good day for me, Indio. I come out here this morning, all the way from the Capitan mountain, from the pistachio farm. Then when I get the delivery to the trading post at the Arizona line, it's closed. So I had to make the trip all the way back. I was tired. I didn't see the crazy man coming at me."

Shash gave the man a light tap on the shoulder and walked past him onto the sandy soil that lined the perimeter of the expressway. He and the Mexican guy both knew that whatever happened, he was still alive and that's what really counted. Now, it would be a slow couple of hours for the tow truck to make its way through all the traffic to get to that truck. He had been hoping to make Albuquerque by noon but that was not going to happen.

Shash understood that these unexpected things happened for reasons we often didn't understand. Sometimes you would find out the reason later on, and sometimes you just never did. For now, it forced Shash into taking a deep breath and thinking about life and things, and as he walked up and down the soft sandy soil, a fuzzy picture of something started to come into focus.

At about one in the morning the night before, the prayer sounds of the night spirits had entered the hogan. It was soft sounding at first, and Shash had listened intently, trying to recognize the song. His hearing was starting to go bad with age, but he knew it was something his mother Shima used to sing. Or, maybe it was his older brother Thomas's song. Now it was bothering him that the song was on the tip of his tongue and yet he couldn't get it. He did recall that it woke him from a rather light sleep. Sure, he'd been tossing around, worried about Nakai and the blonde bilagana and that maybe he should have alerted the tribal police to keep a lookout. Nakai was mental, all right, and earlier on, he might have shot himself and maybe all of them before that. He was not himself when he had those attacks and that lady named Charlie could be in real danger now.

Shash tried to get it out of his mind and go back to sleep but he was feeling uncomfortable, like something was up. Then, when he opened the door just before sunrise to do his prayer, he saw a message laid out all before. There were snake prints all around, telling him that he had better heed that midnight song. Snakes brought messages, and like the coyote and the owl, they were never good. He remembered when his nephew thought he looked so grand wearing a snakeskin belt and Shash just shook his head. The young people just had no hatchin' up. You go and do those things, and trouble will find you.

The old warrior shook his head. He would have to put his plans for Edythe and Chilchinbito on hold. Now, it was more important to make his way up to Sandia tomorrow morning once again, but he would first have to figure out the proper offering for the snake. He had a problem with Nakai, all right, but that snake and those voices were coming from the ancients and they were telling him something important and that was you must never forget who you are and where you come from. No, he would not sell his son out to the tribal police who were no different from the bilagana police. You had to hold your family together no matter what might happen, because in the end, that's all you had if you wanted to feel right about yourself in this jungle they called the United States.

Now, approaching the I-70 junction, Charlie was weighing her options. She could telephone someone at the Crescent Junction coffee shop if it was still around. You never knew from year to year if a business still existed out in the middle of nowhere, just when you needed it the most. The closest city, Grand Junction, was more than a hundred miles away but they would be heading east eventually, and that was a far better place to make her escape. Of course, Sander wouldn't be around by then because he had to retrieve his Jeep. Then again, maybe he had some plan, even in this demented state he was in, to somehow spirit her away with him. Right now, he seemed to be enjoying the camaraderie with Nakai. Charlie shrugged her shoulders. Sometimes it was tough to figure out the male mind.

Sander turned his head around and grinned. "So, young lady, we did the Hole in the Rock and now where are we headed?"

Charlie pointed slightly west, despite the low clouds that were moving slowly their way. She would have to pretend that she was unfazed by the two of them to make any possible plan, she surmised.

"Let's do route 173," she said. "There's some interesting blood agate in the hills."

Nakai turned the van to where she pointed, onto a gravelly road that led to some low hills and a long wash.

"So where do we look, Charlie?" Sander needled her. "Do we go left or right?"

Damn, Charlie shook her head. As if he didn't know where to look. He had been here so many times it was a wonder that he had not raped the field of all the blood agate by now. Once, she remembered, Sander even spent the night sleeping on one of those mesas when he had been too tired to get into Grand Junction for the night.

"I have no idea," she said, keeping her cool. "For all I know, we may find nothing here. I can't even recall the last time I was around these parts."

Sure, she was thinking. The last time we were here was like last month. She would play Sander's stupid game. What better way to let him know what she thought of him?

Nakai glanced to his left, at a small grayish hill that resembled all the other small hills and plateaus they were winding through.

"I got a feeling about that one," he said, pointing to it.

Both Sander and Charlie knew the hill well and Sander looked back at her briefly, nodding his head. The Indian had excellent senses for things, he was thinking. In the past, the two had found some excellent pieces of the red spotted agate and Sander once came upon a gorgeous yellow and black piece of petrified wood over there.

"Nah", Sander grinned. "Those hills are always picked out. Keep on south and just follow the wash."

Incredible, Charlie remarked softly to herself. Sander, in his usual selfishness, was not going to share his rockhounding site with Nakai. Well, she thought, Nakai was not stupid and, in fact, he was now studying Sander out of the corner of his eye and definitely catching on.

"My friend," he said in a voice that was starting to pitch higher, "you sure sound like you know your mineral locations."

Sander's face reddened. I know a little about rocks and minerals since I studied about them in college. Geology is what it was called."

Nakai's expression was unreadable but Charlie could feel his growing anger. He accelerated about ten mph on the sandy, gravelly road that was now becoming sandier and less gravelly. This was never good when you expected a sudden downpour. She watched him swerve onto a higher road cut that twisted narrowly between two elongated but roundish gray hills. That was when she felt the sudden spray of gray sand sting her face through the open back window of the van. A large raindrop now fell like an anguished tear on the windshield.

Sander studied the dark clouds that seemed to be rushing their way and realized that those were the same clouds that had been playing tricks on them the whole ride up. They had been there all along, just lurking behind the huge orange monoliths. He had surmised, when he hadn't seen them anymore, that they had disappeared somewhere to the south of them, but now they were coming at them so rapidly that it would be difficult to get the van out, let alone to try to outrun the fast approaching storm.

With an expression as if nothing of importance was going on, Nakai opened his door and walked out into the swirling sand. He stared in silence at the sky and then began the climb up the smaller of the two hills. For a moment, he looked back at the two of them and Charlie took that as a signal for them to follow. Now, she understood why he revved up the engine to get them to this uphill point. Of course, he'd spotted the storm coming, maybe sensed it before they did. This was his land and he understood it far better than they.

"Leave your handbag and any other junk you're carrying inside the van," Sander said, turning his head to avoid her glance. He was shutting all the windows and pointing up the hill to Nakai.

"We'd better trail him if we want to get the hell out of here alive!"

It made no sense to argue with Sander under these circumstances. Charlie took one last look at the van, as she began the trudge up the hill, hoping it would still be above water and still running once the storm passed through. Fortunately, it was the old fashioned kind of vehicle with windows that opened with the twist of the handle and not by electrical power. If it were not, they would have a real problem recovering their stuff later when the flood subsided.

Splashes of mud came hurtling at Charlie, in a horizontal direction, making it hard to breathe, let alone climb a hill. Sander was already several yards ahead, having made the climb easily and Nakai was nowhere in sight. The rain and wind seemed to be pounding at her now and she wondered just how long she would be able to keep up with all the forces accosting her. She could see the cascades of water pushing through the steep canyon walls just to the north and feared that the bottom of the dry wash, now about ten feet below her, would soon become a swirling eddy. Already, there were remnants of tree branches floating through the wash in the surge of water. She would have to keep on climbing and fast or she would soon be thigh deep in it. She could see patches of mud and some dead plants that had settled down on the ridges from previous storms.

Sometimes in danger, she thought, you could think of the oddest things. At times, she would find a small yet beautiful piece of petrified wood on a small hill all by itself in the middle of some desert. It had never occurred to her that it was there because some swirling dust devil or storm could land it there. She smiled for the moment, but then another recent memory rose up to disturb her thoughts.

It was a news story about a flash flood, somewhere in Arizona, where walls of water, maybe 30 feet high, rolled through the deep canyons, catching some surprised and horrified hikers, and sweeping them along in the onrushing torrent to their deaths. She was, in a way, thankful that they were in an area where you could at least climb up the mesas, and not at an area like Green River where the monoliths were so steep and forbidding that you would just have to prepare to meet your maker.

Charlie could see Nakai's van now in the distance and it was in at least three feet of water. She prayed that the vehicle was airtight.

"Hey!" A voice came at her from a few yards away. It was Nakai and he was laughing, almost like he did not give a damn. She was at this point thrilled to see his face.

"Can you follow me?" He put his hand out to Charlie. "We can watch the van disappear better from up there."

After crawling up to his level, Charlie thankfully grabbed Nakai's wrist. The mesa was steeper here and would take her out of any immediate danger.

"Where's Sander?" she asked, looking in all directions.

"Oh, that's his name. Sandy for Sander."

She realized her slip of the tongue, but decided not to backtrack from it. By now, the rain had subsided and it was just a question of how high the water was going to rise.

"He's a guy I know from Miami," she said.

"So, why did he come all the way out here looking for you?" Nakai questioned, easing her up the craggy hill. He had a grin on his face which kind of surprised Charlie.

"He was looking for you, you know."

"Probably," she nodded. "Or as the Aussies like to say, I reckon that's true."

Nakai burst out laughing. He once heard that expression from some silly white hillbilly somewhere. Right now, he was enjoying the comfort of Charlie's hand in his and felt no jealousy. He surmised by the look on her face, that any romantic interest came solely from this guy Sander's direction and not hers.

"Your friend is a good tracker."

"He's good at giving out free knowledge," Charlie countered. "He's even better at letting you know that he knows so much more than you do."

Her breathing was getting more labored now with each step. She was looking around for Sander now and Nakai could see she seemed worried.

"He's up there," he said quickly. "Just that tan jacket of his blends into the scenery so good. He's like a lizard that changes color."

Nakai pointed to a small hill off to the right. "You see the dark stripes on the shirt? That's him up there."

Charlie felt relieved that he was all right, that they were all okay.

"The only real problem we got is my van," Nakai said, suddenly changing the focus of his interest.

"There wasn't much we could do about it but it's done its disappearing act and all we can do now is wait until it emerges."

Nakai stared blankly into the wash, trying to figure out exactly where it was but the whole area just looked like a sea of sameness. Charlie squeezed his hand to let him know they were all in this together. It was already late in the day and she knew that nothing was going to change until morning. She also knew that Sander was the only one who thought about taking a backpack up and that backpack would have water and some supplies like granola bars to make their lives more bearable. It was the main reason she traveled with him. He was a confident son of a bitch, but he always seemed to know what he was doing.

35

The desert took on a surreal appearance as the deep blue sky and late afternoon sun pierced through the clouds, lifting them and creating puff balls of dark grey and orange over the eerie looking, storm-created lake of water. Nakai stared expressionless, with his arms spread wide, like a bird in flight, perhaps an eagle drifting on the wind so it could soar above it all.

Nakai had seen this a few times, enough times to know that the deluge would evaporate slowly and he likely wouldn't see the silver top of his van until sunrise. The van might be useless, however, he thought, and that would mean that they would have to trek all the way to the expressway to get help. It would be rough for Charlie, he knew, but she was tough enough mentally to do it if she had to. For now, there was little to do but concentrate on the beauty of the mesas, now turning pink in the late afternoon sun. His senses took in the aromas of the drenched desert, and at least for that moment, he felt free.

Charlie watched Nakai and then instinctively took out her camera to snap him in his element. She smiled for a moment, forgetting the situation, and thought instead about what happened earlier in the day. Nakai had stood there smiling, right in front of the bright orange chimney-like monolith called Hole-in-the-Rock. That tourist favorite would likely be the only part of this trip that would appeal to the readers of the magazine she worked for.

This southeastern part of Utah, with its otherworldly orange and red formations set against a turquoise sky, was hauntingly gorgeous, but when the 100 plus degree days came in late June, it was definitely not your primo tourist attraction. Sure, her magazine featured the unusual and the road less traveled, but that road came risk free to the readers. They would never see the poverty of the real southwest, of Indian reservations like Chilchinbito, with its old railroad tie hogans and outhouses, lest the readers might feel guilty about their "Native Americans."

Sander had climbed higher than Nakai and Charlie and he could see them now about forty feet below and to the west of him. Charlie was kneeling, but she seemed okay and even looked kind of calm, with the breeze tossing around her blond hair. He was happy for the wind because it would keep away the mosquitoes and gnats that always made this area uncomfortable for her.

It was a mistake to climb all the way to this mesa, but it seemed to be flat enough to rest on and besides, he had to shamefully admit to himself that he had done it mostly to show off his hiking abilities. So, now here he was, observing Charlie photographing that strange Indian, the one who kept a shotgun on the passenger side of his van. He was not able to see what happened to the van from where he was but since Nakai was just standing there, waving his hands and doing Indian things, he guessed that the van was history. That was the one thing about Indians. They always seemed to just accept disaster with calmness, he thought. They would just shrug it off and keep on going, where white guys like him would go nuts over it.

Sander scratched his head, pondering his choices. He could pick his ass up, retrace his steps and get with the two of them. Since they would all be spending the night together here at the Floy Wash, they may as well hang out together and eat some of his supplies. Sure, the Indian would likely be pissed at him for not helping Charlie up the hill. He had that kind of God complex about him and there again was that shotgun in the van. Sure, he could be a selfish bastard but at least he wasn't nuts or half dangerous like Nakai.

What the hell did Charlie see in him to schlep all the way out here with this Geronimo? And what did he want with her anyway? The guy wasn't bad looking, good bones and not a fatso like so many of the Navajos you saw around these parts. They all liked the fast food junk and then blamed their obesity on whitey as if they were force fed. But this Nakai, hell he could find someone half Charlie's age, white or Indian, in the blink of an eye like he did back at that diner. Was Charlie that big a deal? Sometimes she seemed to him like a Jewish princess, only one with visions of arrowheads and UFO's. Sander grimaced. He was convinced that neither Charlie nor this Indian had the corner on spirituality. In fact, when it came to Nakai, his family probably lived around these parts for centuries and yet he didn't even know there was blood agate around.

The question now was whether to just observe them from his vantage point or make a move to get down there. Nakai was flapping his arms like an eagle, and who knew how crazy he was? Maybe he would decide to swoop down and carry Charlie to his nest! Sander was tired now and he knew that nothing was going to happen to Charlie. In fact, she seemed to be deep in concentration. She was kneeling on a small rock and then, possibly aware that he was staring at her, looked up at him for a split second. Then suddenly, she seemed to lose her bearing.

Sander, stunned, watched her slide, at first slowly, then rapidly with momentum, down the hill and into the deep standing water.

36

An overcast gloomy horizon accompanied Shash Benally the whole way up on his steep climb of Sandia Mountain.

Nothing had gone right for him this morning. He was sure that he had taken the purple coneflower in a small paper bag. It was a bit dried out but still good and he had planned to walk with it, and pray with it, saying "Let me walk in beauty" in both the Dineh and English languages. Then, when he fished around in his pocket, he realized he had taken the wrong bag with him.

On a walk the day before, he had come upon a plant he hadn't seen in a while, but one that was on his mind. The plant called sohajahee was a diet plant that could help really fat people lose the weight. He had some of it with him and he was planning to decide what to do with it. Shash felt sorry for some of these people he saw on the television talk shows who weighed 400 or 500 pounds and had miserable lives. They were bilaganas though and this is why he hesitated. But, soon he would not be around anymore to help anyone. The Dineh were overweight with diabetes but nobody on the reservation seemed to want to take the sohajahee and someone should know about it. It was a quandary. Well, he was thinking that if he had the opportunity, he would help the bilagana too. It was a terrible thing to go around looking like that.

Shash felt that he could almost touch the grey clouds here at 8000 feet. They gave out a cold dampness that seemed like a kind of warning, much like that snake gave, and maybe it had something to do with Nakai and the blond woman. Yep, he really could have used that coneflower this morning to help him.

Now why in the world did he ever allow that woman to travel with Nakai? She was a bilagana, but one with a good heart and he should have helped her. You've got to help everyone, he thought, because if you didn't then the whole world would come apart. That hate was a very bad thing.

Shash was now sitting under his favorite cedar tree, holding the leather pouch he always carried with him in his jeans pocket. The heavy air was affecting his breathing and there was a harsh wind beating down on his chest making him cough some. He checked his other pocket for the cough drops but he had forgotten them also. Lately, his mind seemed to be failing him when he least expected it. Most hikers took along water but Shash didn't like the plastic container weighing him down. He would have to think of something or the cough would get worse and worse.

A wet breeze slapped his face, forcing him to turn his head toward the rocky cliff that looked down on the city of Albuquerque, and that is when he spotted the precious osha root. He had forgotten all the other times he had come here in late summer just to gather the osha or bear root, and here it showed up just in the nick of time for him to chew on. Shash smiled, knowing how the Creator always took care when you needed it. The root would open his chest and allow him to breathe easier. He pulled on the root and the pungent yet sweet odor filled his senses, shooing away any bad omens he had before.

The plant had brittle dark brown tiny twigs and Shash broke off a piece and placed it between his teeth, sucking in the taste. Yes, white men called it bear root and knew how to use it but what they did not know was that this root could scare away all the bad spirits which accounted for so many of your problems. Shash would see them shopping at the flea markets and powwows, buying up the small brown paper bags filled with herbs that some Navajo seller told them were good for this or that, but they had no idea why some root or sagebrush could heal.

Now feeling better, Shash decided to stay right where he was at the edge of the cliff. Maybe he would even get closer to the edge just like he did when he was 14 and full of piss and vinegar. He would sing out Beauty Way across the canyons, even across the city of Albuquerque down in the haze of pollution below. The old Navajo unwrapped the laces of the medicine pouch slowly and took out a two inch long perfectly clear quartz crystal point. Holding it tightly in his right palm, he thought about the words to the Hozhoni, the Beauty Way prayer. He needed to say this to keep away the snakes and all the other bad omens. Enough was enough. He would make sure he remembered all the words before singing out to Johona'ai, the sun, now starting to peek through the early morning damp grayness.

If he sang out loud and strong, that sun would break out of the clouds, brighten the skies and make everything work again in a good way.

37

"Please stop it already! Please!"

The screeching was deafening and Charlie kept shouting back, begging for that noise to stop. Then, in a split second she listened and understood that the voice screaming at her was her own echo.

A nurse came into the room to quiet her and then Charlie could feel a tightening of her wrists. Her eyes, slits through the head bandage, tried to focus on the white gauze ties that the nurse was fastening from each arm to the adjacent side of the hospital bed. The five foot two petite black woman, who looked to be in her early thirties, had a concerned yet sympathetic demeanor.

"Ma'am, you've been fussing and crying and the staff is afraid you'll fall from the bed and cause more injuries to yourself. When you get a bit calmer from the medicine, we'll remove them."

Charlie closed her eyes, fighting back the tears that were welling up. She'd gotten the report this morning from a heavy-set doctor who reminded her of the activist Michael Moore. She fell down a mountain, he said, which she vaguely remembered doing, and there were broken ribs and a mild concussion. This is what they found so far. There were cat scans waiting and MRIs and all that medical stuff that Charlie tried to avoid all her life. How long had she been here and what day of the week was it anyhow? A depressing kind of weakness had consumed her body, coupled with a dull pain that no doubt would be unbearable without the sedatives.

What had happened out there in canyon country anyway? Charlie recalled that she had felt lightheaded, almost weightless. There was Nakai, lifting his arms to the sky, making like an eagle, pretending like he didn't have a care that his van was buried under ten feet of water. Then, there was that moment where she felt like she was rolling down the craggy hill, though feeling no pain. But then the memories of her life came flooding, just like she'd heard others talk about, when they were drowning.

She saw her uncle Jake coming at her, then pushing her down the staircase. She was suddenly a young child again, maybe four years old and he was mad about something as he always was. Then she saw herself in the wheelchair with a broken leg, the way it happened back then, when the neighborhood kids took turns wheeling her though the playground. So, she was rolling down the mountain, like it was that staircase, but then it was all over and a splash of grayish water came lapping over her. She heard heavy footsteps coming down the mountain right at her now, maybe her uncle, and he was coming fast now. It got quiet as the water seemed to suck her into its abyss, into the arms of Link Davis who was waiting, arms outstretched to embrace her. It felt good, almost exhilarating for a second or two, but then Link seemed to move away, back, way back and the man with the footsteps, Nakai, grabbed her, and pulled her, doggedly out of the flood water.

The pillow under Charlie's bandaged head felt damp from the tears and sweat that accompanied her screaming. Now, she could hear bells or gongs from some TV game show the nurse had put on to try to distract her. Television, Charlie, thought. Something she used to watch once in a while before the internet came around. It was a dumb pastime then and was probably even dumber now with these reality shows and even sillier game shows. A nurse's aide peeked into the room and gave a light rap on the wall.

"You have company, dear," she said cheerily. Charlie squinted enough to see that it was Sander Miller, carrying a bouquet of purple flowers and a small package wrapped in reddish paper. She knew that this was not his first visit because the nurse had him scrawl messages, which he left on the bed table. She had been asleep, and he was told that it was the sedatives and probably not wise to disturb her. The last note from him read, "Your rock buddy says hey."

Sander glared at the nurse's aide whose smiling demeanor was about to crumble. He pointed his finger at her and shook his head in exaggerated disbelief.

"Hey, if you don't get those fucking restraints off of her, I'll personally hang you with them!"

"They're for her own protection," she snapped back. "You remove them and you're responsible, not the hospital!"

She turned her back to him and left the room, leaving Sander to take up her challenge.

"Bastards," he growled almost under his breath. "I wonder if we get even more of this under the healthcare package all the pols are fighting about."

Charlie smiled and was about to laugh even, until she remembered her broken ribs. Sander put his hand in his jeans pocket and pulled out the old Swiss Army knife that came in so handy up in the mountains and he used it to cut carefully the gauzy strips that bound Charlie's wrists to the bedrails.

Underneath the gauze were two large arm bandages which covered the bruises she had sustained in the fall. Miraculously, her arms had survived with just some minor sprains.

"Shit!" he grinned. "Some rock trips just aren't worth it!"

Sander combed his fingers through his reddish-brown mane that he had forgotten to tuck back into a ponytail and Charlie took note of the dark circles under his eyes. He had been up worrying, about her, no doubt.

"What happened to the van?" she asked.

"It's a part of history now. Maybe it'll become a rusted coral reef in the desert sea," he laughed. "The Indian made it out though and got us help on I-70. He returned to the scene with a cop and a couple of troopers. He surprised me."

"I don't remember very much," Charlie said softly.

"That's because you were out, kid. Out cold. They airlifted you here."

"Where is here?" Charlie asked, realizing she had no idea where she was.

"You're favorite town, GJ. Grand Junction, Coloradda."

Charlie smiled. She always enjoyed it when Sander made fun of the western lingo, especially when he'd shake his head and say, "I'll be darned!"

"So, what's in the package?"

Sander looked at the small box that he had put down on the bed, while he was cutting the gauze strips.

"Oh that," he grinned. "It's just something from the Mesa Mall."

He handed her the box but she pushed it back toward him.

"You open it. These fingers don't work too well just yet."

Sander unraveled the red paper and opened the box.

"Oh yeah," he said, remembering. "Your friend Nakai, he took the

186

Greyhound back to Miami. He told me that the witch he lived with was going to kill him when she found out about the van. So, I gave him one of these also for good luck."

Sander was rubbing something between the palms of his hands and had a mischievous look on his face. He placed a perfect piece of white stone with bright red stripings in Charlie's hand.

"I made sure to get them just as we were getting the hell out of there," he laughed. There they were, where they always are on the first mesa of Floyd Wash. Blood agate. Just wanted to make sure we got what we came for!"

38

"Slidell, Loosiana," the Greyhound driver announced to the bedraggled two dozen passengers, who were making their way slowly across the country from west to southeast.

Nakai, paused outside of the bathroom stall as the bus took a sudden swerve to the right and onto Interstate 10 that would take them from Slidell all the way to Lake City, Florida. The floor of the bathroom had been strewn with toilet paper, cigarette butts and spilled urine and had that stench of the homeless and dirt poor who had no idea exactly where they were headed or what they would do when they got there. Nakai shrugged and commented to no one, "Yup, these are the great United States of America, folks."

He fell into his window seat in the back of the bus next to nobody, which was fine and dandy with him. Soon night would fall and he would have some room to spread his worn out legs across the long row of seats and take a nap. He was tired, bone tired, as they called it and it was no wonder. It had been that kind of a day where so much was squeezed into it, that it seemed like a hundred hours instead of twenty-four. First there had been the trip back to Salt Lake, courtesy of the Utah state trooper who drove him there, once they got Charlie on the helicopter to the hospital in Grand Junction. Then came the lengthy Greyhound trip to Albuquerque, where he had the idea of getting his brothers together to regale them with heroic tales of flash floods and bilaganas, maybe smoke some weed, and then figure out what to do next.

When he got to Albuquerque, all that greeted him was disappointment and sadness. Sure, Pop was back at the old house, but nobody was visiting. He should have guessed it because nobody ever came to see Pop, himself included, but somehow he hoped this time would be different. The two of them sat on the sofa, which was and always had been covered with bath towels, facing the old fireplace that hadn't seen a fire in the last twenty years, and the stale odors that lingered from cigarettes and moldy walls depressed Nakai. It was painful to think about those times when his mother would be proudly carrying trays of frybread, tortillas and mutton stew to the dining room table, enough to feed a dozen or so of her children and relations. It was no wonder that Shash wanted to abandon this house for the reservation. It looked like chicken shit. The whole neighborhood looked and smelled like chicken shit.

"I prayed for you," was all Shash said. "You did the right thing saving that woman's life, and you were right about her," he added. "She lives in our world."

That coming from his father, totally took Nakai by surprise and even more so now that Nakai had started to have his doubts about her. He had watched Charlie rolling down the hill, plummeting to an almost certain death, and her face had been solemn, no fear or doubt there. Nakai knew then that she was traveling somewhere familiar and it was not to Chilchinbito.

"What I want now, "Shash said, focusing his eyes directly on his son, "is to build a medium size hogan out there on the reservation. There's a woman with money but she has her own home so I don't yet know."

Nakai looked back at his father with anger now in his eyes.

"We don't need any woman, Pop. I'll help you build that hogan. I've got a plan for that."

Shash turned his head away, so his son would not see his displeased expression. He had heard it all from Nakai a thousand times in this lifetime and he was tired of the dola bichon. Maybe the hogan would never get built but he always walked with hope, and he could never give up that hope, because if he did he would not be a Dineh warrior anymore. You never snatched hope and prayer away from a Dineh.

Nakai walked to the desk in the hallway and picked up the phone. "Still has a dial tone," he shouted out surprised. "They haven't disconnected it yet, huh?"

Shash got up and walked to the front door and opened it wide. He knew Nakai would be calling that woman with the mouth of a rattlesnake, and he did not want to hang around for the hollering and cursing that was sure to follow.

With his head now pressed into the silvery gray quilted back of his aisle seat, Nakai observed the half dozen passengers as they disembarked at the

Slidell terminal. It was 7:30 AM and he figured that if they weren't ordered to change buses anymore, he had a good shot at being back in Miami by midnight. The apartment would be empty with Hannelore gone by now, he mused. She'd freaked as was expected when he told her about the van, and then, he decided to throw in that he had sex with Charlie. He laughed to himself over that one. As Pop would have said, a bunch of dola bichon.

It was also a bunch of dola bichon that she would be gone, Nakai grimaced, knowing that she would be there, waiting to take a punch if he did not think of something fast. Just now, he was feeling both dizzy and hungry and it was hard to think. The last meal he had was somewhere in Mississippi, a couple of buses ago, last night at some snack bar with junk food. He had bacon and those precooked eggs on a muffin that you threw in the microwave. It tasted like shit but it was food at least and if he had that now he'd be happy. Most of the stops the Greyhound made were just for ten minutes, to get in a smoke or take a piss or get a bag of chips and a coke. Of course, most of the people who were on this bus had no money to spend anyway.

"Hey, dude! Are you a real Injun?"

The tall lanky ranch hand plopped down on the aisle seat next to Nakai, quickly offering him some jerky.

Nakai bit his lip, holding back his usual remarks to this question. He could smell the gin on the cowboy's breath and figured it was useless to start a fight at this time. They would both just get thrown off the bus. He took the jerky and just put on a good stoic Indian face.

"Hey, buddy, sorry. I just couldn't help noticing that cool necklace. Reminds me of a picture of my dad from the seventies."

Nakai touched the silver claw resting on his chest and then moved his fingers upward along some turquoise beads and small silver "squash blossoms." It was a good thing he had not fallen asleep while wearing this, he thought. It could draw thieves to you like sharks to blood.

"So where are you headed?" Nakai asked the man whose long scraggly blond hair reminded him of the pictures he'd seen of the summer of love in San Francisco.

"Looks like Miami, I guess," he grinned, showing a set of fast rotting teeth.

Nakai figured he was 27 or 28 years and fading fast.

"I'm divorced," he announced. "We split everything fifty-fifty and I got my fifty percent right here with me on this Greyhound bus!"

The cowboy started to laugh in a drunken sort of way that Nakai knew well, from his nights at the Indian bars. It was a long trip and the company was fun in a way, but the gin breath was a bit more than he could take.

"So what kind of Injun are you?" he asked. "One of them Nava-joes, I bet."

"Dineh tribe," Nakai muttered, shutting his eyes, trying to close out the conversation. He had to try to concentrate on the urgent matter at hand.

For a good long time it was fun having a rich white bitch to jerk around. In fact, lots of times it had stopped him from going to some bar just to punch someone out when he got the urge, when the rage got to him so bad. She was like having damage control right under your hands. Then, standing up on that mesa in Utah and feeling the balance, he realized just how much he wanted it, the balance, that is, and sitting on this bus for so many hours gave him the time to think about that rage and how it was eating into him and destroying that balance. Seeing her, would only start it up again and why would he want to go back to that?

"Hey, you know what, cowboy?" Nakai stirred in his seat, now, his eyes fixed on his drunken seatmate. He gave him a light poke in the ribs, and then laughed at the man's startled expression.

"I'm going to do exactly what you did, my friend," Nakai explained. "I figure if the woman's still there and I don't have it in me to knock her dead, then I'll just sneak out, carrying my 50 percent in a backpack. Maybe," he winked, "I'll just grab her jewelry and call it 80 percent!"

"So, you got a babe back home, huh?"

"More like a barracuda, I would say!" Nakai shook his head. "She came here from Germany and like you she was impressed by a real live Indian."

"Hey, buddy," the cowboy looked somewhat annoyed, "I didn't mean that as an offense."

"I know," Nakai said, studying his expression. "You're just drunk. That's all."

The lanky man decided to keep his silence for awhile. These Injuns could get touchy, he'd heard.

"She's got a wealthy father," Nakai went on. "Aristocracy or some kind of dola bichon bullshit, but she likes being beaten up by an Indian. Maybe it's that white guilt." Nakai laughed sardonically. "Anyway, it was a good game while it lasted."

"So, you must have a fancy set-up in Miami?" The cowboy looked interested. A lot of Indians had to do with casinos these days, even if they rode the Greyhound, he figured.

"Yeah," Nakai nodded. "Fancy china, Italian design this and that, French perfume. It's a regular United Nations of expensive junk. Like I said, I'll take my 80 percent."

"So, when do you tell her you're splittin'?"

"I told her to be the hell out of there by the time I got back. I even told her that I totaled the van just for effect," Nakai lied. "Then I told her that I have another woman."

"You know what I think, buddy?" The cowboy leaned back in his seat, closing his eyes tightly. "I think that when you get back home, you'll find her gone and all the stuff gone with her. No 80 percent. No nothin'!"

The remark came unexpectedly for Nakai. To his quick thinking it was totally uncalled for and woke him from his friendly talkative state back to the reality of things. This dude needed a lesson fast, and Nakai decided that somewhere along the road, he'd invite him to have a few beers with him. Then he would punch the living shit out of him.

39

It felt so good to be back in Miami Beach, resting in her own bed and staring at the swaying palms outside the window. Another warm day was just starting and maybe the ocean would be calm enough to bathe in and help her sore ribs heal.

There was a point in all of this, Charlie mused. As crazy as the last three months were, she knew that the healing had begun. What she experienced out there defied any notion of scientific hypothesis, any physician's approach to medicine. She had truly communed with the spirits who could be seen, they were the ghosts in her photos, and she had heard their voices coming from time past. The gift of the arrowheads that came her way had transported her back to the ancient footsteps, to a time when prayer could work miracles on tortured souls.

A psychotherapist might call her delusional but Charlie knew her experiences were real. Yes, they were real all right and she would always own them. They were nothing she could ever write about in any journal because they could not be believed without the benefit of personal experience. A writer attempting to describe a paranormal experience can come close but could never get all the words down without seeming to embellish on the truth. Link had that problem all the time, especially with mainstream readers whom the editors did not want to "freak out" too much. Charlie remembered that when he wrote about UFO's, he always used the word "alleged" and never told the readers what he really thought about the phenomenon, which was that aliens were not cute little E.T. characters but that they posed a real threat to the world.

There was a telephone number written on a small slip of yellow paper, tucked in halfway under the phone on Charlie's night table. It was Shash's exchange in Albuquerque and she kept it there so that she would be sure to call him. He had put the paper in her palm when she had said her goodbyes to him in Chilchinbito and she found it amazing that it was still readable after all it had been through. While deep within her jeans pocket, that slip of paper had made its way into the flood, the washing machine at the Denver convenience store where Sander drove by on their way to the airport, and all the way back to her bedroom, without a smudge. Charlie glanced at the small digital atomic clock next to the phone. It had already reset for Eastern Time which was 8:15 AM. For Shash in New Mexico, it was 6:15 and sunrise. She took a deep breath and dialed.

"Ya' aah' teeh," came a faraway but familiar voice.

"Ya'aah' teeh, Shizhee Shash!" Charlie blurted out, unsure of how he would respond.

There was a short period of hesitation and then Charlie gratefully heard the warm laughter.

"Well, it's so good to hear your voice, honey. Did you make it back home to Florida all right?"

"Yes, I did, Shash, but it took a little while."

Charlie was not sure just how much Shash knew or even if Nakai had told him any of it. After all, Nakai was supposed to take care of her on the trip, not half kill her in a flash flood!

"I kinda know about it," Shash said, his voice taking on a more serious, softer tone. "My son was by here and he had tales of a big storm that carried all of you away."

"Nakai saved my life," Charlie said.

Shash paused for a moment and then, because he had been so used to his son screwing up, had to ask. "Are you sure Nakai didn't push you down into the water?"

Charlie had to chuckle. "No, Shash, it was my dumb suggestion to go looking for rocks over there. Nakai was a hero. He got me up the mesa away from the water. I just got dizzy, lost my balance and fell right back into it. Then, he had the task of pulling me out!"

"You got to take care of yourself, She'wee'."

"It was a learning experience, Shash," Charlie laughed. "I think next time the adventure presents itself, I'll pass."

Shash was quiet. It was the Dineh way to wait for more from the other person and he somehow knew intuitively that Charlie had called to ask him something and not just to hear the sound of his voice.

She seemed to move into his thoughts, "I was thinking of putting it all down in words like the thoughts I keep in my journal. I want to write about it, Shash, but how and where, I don't know."

Shash brightened at her politeness and honesty. She was a smart bilagana all right. He still kept his silence, waiting for her to go on.

"You see, part of it is my experiences with you and Nakai out there in Chilchinbito, and well, I need your permission for that." Charlie shuddered, thinking about Nakai with the gun to his head but then she heard laughter from the other end.

"You have my permission, young lady. Of course you do." Shash was smiling to himself now, and could not help adding, "Just be sure to tell everyone how good-looking your Dineh dad is!"

Charlie beamed. It was an unexpected response from Shash. After all, he hardly knew her.

"You want to know what I think?" Shash continued. "I think it's time you stopped writing all those things in that little notebook you carry, and started thinking about a big book!"

"A book," Charlie repeated. "Yes, that does make more sense than some stories for a magazine."

"Just promise me," Shash laughed, "that when you get it sold and make some money, you'll buy Nakai a one-way plane ticket here and give your Dineh dad some cash to build me a hogan!"

"I'll help build it too," Charlie agreed.

There was a pause again on the phone and Shash's voice took on a more serious tone.

"You know that his lady friend cleaned out the apartment and split for Germany. And, oh yeah," he remembered. "She left him a butcher knife on the kitchen counter and a note telling him what he could do with it."

Charlie felt a tug at her heart. There had been no communication from Nakai since that day of the flood. She knew he was a troubled soul but had prayed for better things for him.

Another silence on the phone and then in a low voice Shash said his goodbyes. "Hagoonee, She'wee. Walk in beauty."

She held the phone to her ear, long after Shash had hung up. A book, she was thinking. A book, to record it all. You could even throw in the rockhounding. Had anyone ever fictionalized those ambitious, hardy folk who spent days banking hard rock in search of fire opal, or climbing to the top of a fourteener mountain on the slim chance of finding a clear blue aquamarine? Then, there was the central storyline of that writer who excitedly picks up two arrowheads that change her life.

You could say anything you wanted in a book because it was yours alone to give to the reader, and if you could get a publisher to believe in it and put up all the money, that was the big time. With the book labeled fiction, you could change all the names and ages and faces and really get all your emotions into it. What fun it would be to write about a "Sander" character and to follow his development as you had seen it!

Charlie got out of bed and headed for the shower. She would take a fast swim in the ocean and then head for the library, where she would sit for a long time and concentrate on the story about to unfold.

40

Nakai never cared much for the humidity that lingered in Miami Beach in late September, and it was even less enjoyable when the thunderstorms hit without warning while you were trying to sleep on the rooftop of a forty story high rise.

All things were relative. It had never been a big deal to sleep tent-less in the desert, unless you forgot the netting to keep away the gnats, but here you had other things to contend with too. There were the homeless, the drifters, panhandlers and dealers who walked the beaches night and day, looking for you or someone just like you. No way could you sleep on the beautiful soft sand or take a chance even napping there. Once he had watched two hustlers near the grassy area, talking it up big and trying to look young and pretty and tough at the same time as they vied for the same territory. "Hey, asshole, work your own bench!" one of them shouted out to the other. Nakai snickered now, remembering how he cracked up hearing that. He'd had a home then.

There were 25 bucks left in his pocket, the remaining cash he had been carefully guarding since the trip back from Albuquerque. If he had had any hatching up, he would have asked his father for some money. Hell, the rest of them did for things like brandy or crack or weed or other real important shit. The truth, though, was that he was hoping his father would ask him to stay, but he hadn't. So, he wound up taking the long, arduous bus ride home, seated next to a bunch of creeps, only to get back to the Beach to find Hannelore and all his stuff long gone.

The security guard told him he found out from a good source that she was selling his silver rings and bracelets on Lincoln Road for pennies on the dollar, a fact that was verified when he spotted Tony at the library wearing one of his $400 prizes. He asked and Tony put up ten fingers. Ten bucks for a $400 piece of silver was her way of getting even good, making his stuff as worthless as a cheap piece of costume jewelry. Nakai kicked the soft sand and then heard himself laughing out loud. That bitch got me good, all right, he was thinking, and he had to give her credit, even admire her for that.

It was going to rain again, and you could smell the dampness in the air, but Nakai knew he would be at the library in less than ten minutes. Despite being temporarily homeless, things could be a lot worse, he figured. At least you could never freeze to death in this hot box, and besides, he knew enough people in this town to get by. Last night, the security guard let him do his laundry in the washroom, free of charge, and he even took a fairly good shower at the public facility on Fourteenth Street beach. At 92 degrees, you didn't have to worry that the outside shower would be too cold.

Nakai kicked off one of his flip-flops and cursed to himself, remembering how he had ruined his beaded sandals while climbing the mesas. It was a dumb thing to wear Birkenstocks if you were hiking, but then he never expected to be out there in Nowheresville, Utah, in a flash flood no less. As soon as he got it all back together, the first thing on the to do list would be the sandals and he would have to dream up a whole new beaded design, since the last one got the car and Charlie all messed up. For now, he thought, these cheap shit kickers would have to do.

It was always amazing, the things that came to you just when you needed them. Like those flip-flops were left right at the shore, probably by some tourist who picked them up for the beach at Walgreen's and then had no more use for them. It was the same when he needed to call pop and found the $5 phone card with half the time remaining. He figured pop was calling his cell phone and where that wound up was anyone's guess. He tried to be upbeat with pop, laughing and lying about how he sent Hannelore packing, and he never hinted, even once, that he was now homeless and walking the beach. If pop guessed that he might be alone and without cash, he did not ask, nor did he ask him to come home.

Nakai felt a few drops fall on his cheeks and looked at the sky. Still gray but no rain yet. Yeah, they were his tears all right, but no big deal, he thought, walking now at an even faster clip. No point in waiting for the first lightning strike. It always happened the same way here on the beach. First the lightning hit, then came the wind in your face, and then the sheets of rain, and they would come in so suddenly, so fast and hard, that you found it hard to breathe. It reminded him, yet again, that he had no real shelter.

When he opened the big glass door to the library, sure enough, there was Tony, bullshitting with another librarian Jennifer. Tony glanced over, gave him a wide smile and rolled up his sleeve to show Jennifer his brand new shiny silver and turquoise bracelet that had once been the property of Nakai. For his part, Nakai ignored both of them, walking at a swift pace past the computers to the reference desk. He picked up an available copy of the Wall Street Journal, and was looking to find a seat when he spotted Charlie walking up the steps to the library.

Her walk was reserved and guarded, and to Nakai, that meant she had some kind of rib cage damage. He knew the troopers were supposed to have taken her to the hospital in Grand Junction but he had not stayed around to see what was what. Besides, one service aide had offered to get him a ride back to Gallup and he said yes right away because he knew then that he no longer had any means of transportation. The van was history, all flooded through and through. At least in Gallup, he would have the opportunity to hitch a ride or two to get back to pop in Albuquerque.

Nakai began to walk her way, something he had not been accustomed to doing. After all, he was always the center of attention in these parts. However, he figured that she might be pissed at him for leaving the scene back there in Utah, even after he had safely dragged her out of the water. Yeah, it was he who trudged the five miles up the road to get help and not her pony-tailed friend who liked to show off what a great hiker he was. Of course, if truth be told, Nakai preferred to take that detour because he had fears that Charlie would not make it and he really did not want to be around to watch her die.

Charlie saw Nakai coming her way and he was relieved to see her face break into the broadest smile he had ever seen.

"Hey, you!" he shouted, as she opened her arms wide to embrace him.

He wrapped his arms around her in a light bear hug so he would not do any damage to her ribs and he would purposely hold her that way for at least a couple of minutes knowing that Tony and his ten dollar bracelet would be staring the whole time. Maybe Tony would think they were a couple, Nakai laughed to himself. No, he was under no illusions about Charlie's feelings but, hey, if Tony was jealous as hell, that was just as good.

"Hey, let's get a place to sit down or you're going to slip in that puddle," Nakai suggested. Charlie's soaked umbrella was starting to make a small pool underneath their feet.

"So, how the hell are you doing anyway?" he asked jokingly.

"No worse for the wear," Charlie laughed, "but what about you? Your shorts are all wrinkled."

"I'm joining the homeless ranks right here on the beach," Nakai answered, his face turning serious. He held out a seat for her at an empty table near one of the front windows.

Charlie noticed how drawn he looked, which was no doubt a combination of traveling buses and scrambling for food and shelter. She had been thinking about Nakai and wondering how he was faring from all of this, and after speaking to Shash, she knew what she would do if she ran into him. There was no point in wasting time and she took out her checkbook.

"I spoke to your father just this morning,"

Nakai looked up at her, surprised. "You're communicating with Pop?"

"I wanted to see how he was doing. I wanted to know about you." She sighed. "He's a very tough man who seems to deal well with adversity."

Nakai laughed loudly, shaking a long lock of thick black hair as he watched Charlie hold the pen over the checkbook. White people were funny, so funny. You save their life and they need to write you a check for it. She seemed to sense what he was thinking and for a second gave him a serious, determined stare he had never seen before from her.

"My dear Nakai," she said in a voice that matched the stare, "I have no idea where I am going in my life but I'm planning to write a book about all that has just happened to me and maybe I can figure things out."

"What about your friend with the ponytail whose got the dibs on all the answers?" Nakai deadpanned. "I bet he can figure it out for you."

Charlie smiled, remembering Sander's worried look back at the hospital. It seemed that he had all the answers except the one to explain why he had such a hard time expressing his emotions.

200

"Some of us have real knowledge," Nakai added.

Charlie nodded, and handed him the check. It was made out to Shash Benally and Nakai Benally, and her hope was that neither could cash it without the other. Nakai stared at both names and then at the $5000 figure that was written clear as day on the small line right after. He tried to hide his surprise, by clearing his throat a few times, but it was hard to conceal. After all, Charlie was not made out of money and this had to be a big deal for her.

"You know that Shash needs you to be with him," she went on.

"How do you know that?" he challenged her.

"Because he said as much."

"He said that?" Nakai asked, brushing back his hair in disbelief. Yet, he knew Pop had to have said that because Charlie wasn't the kind to lie.

She nodded, understanding the conflict that Nakai and Shash had with each other. They were so different and yet the common thing was that damn stubbornness. Neither would reveal to the other what was in his heart, so instead, they had to keep on one-upping and challenging each other to the very end. Here, they longed to be together out there, building that hogan, but they could not admit it because they were both too proud and unyielding. But Charlie had seen Shash's pure love for his son, she had seen him singing, praying for Nakai with the medicine man, fixing him tea that had been gathered with blessings. So she nodded. She could not say out loud, that Shash had asked her to get Nakai a plane ticket back when she sold her book, but Charlie knew that if she waited that long, Shash might not be around to see it. There was no time like the present, as the saying went.

"You do want to be out there with him, don't you?" Charlie asked. "You do want to help him build a better home, maybe one with a cedar bed for me when I visit."

"Why are you doing this?" Nakai studied her face, curious about her motives.

Charlie shrugged. "I don't know. Maybe I want to be rid of you. Maybe I have a desire to empty my bank account and start fresh. Maybe because..." She hesitated, feeling a tear roll down her cheek. "Maybe I miss having a family," she added softly.

Nakai took her hand and held it gently, this time not caring if anyone was observing them.

"So, what's next for us, sister?" Nakai asked, not really expecting any answers.

She looked at him, and found herself staring into his dark eyes. They were mysterious, filled with so many emotions at once. There was laughter, surprise, longing, sadness, terror, rage and fear. Nakai's world would never be her world, she knew. It was a world you could visit and even stay awhile, and you could even be in love with it, but it was a world that you could not live in if you were not born into it.

The sun was now starting to peek out from the clouds and a white ibis, that was making its way along the grassy swale in front of the library, suddenly made a turn toward the glass door of the library and stood there squawking.

"I think the little guy is telling us something," Charlie laughed, happy to break the emotional tension she had been feeling. "He sounds a lot like Sander!"

"So, what's he saying?" Nakai prodded. "This should be a good one!"

"He's saying that he's going to ante up for drinks and dinner tonight, Nakai," Charlie grinned. "He says he still owes you for that breakfast back in Kayenta!"

Link Davis

It was a week ago to the day that Link Davis went to see his old friend, the psychiatrist and noted psychic, Dr. Burt Roessler, at his beach house in Melbourne. They talked about the many patients who had come to Burt during his 40 years of practice, claiming to have witnessed UFOs, and Burt had treated Link to a great lunch of baked yellowtail and rice at a fancy local spot with an ocean view. Link took it all in, Burt's kind blue eyes, the smell of the sea breeze and the stories that spanned many years.

When he and Charlie were writing an article about any notable person who claimed to have extraordinary powers, they would travel north on I-95 to verify the claim with Burt because he was the expert, the Harvard graduate, and one of the few in this field who was respected by his peers. Today, Link traveled alone, leaving Charlie behind. He told her that he and Burt had old business to discuss, but, in fact, that was a lie. The truth was that Link wanted something verified by Burt about himself. Burt would not hesitate because he could not lie to his old friend.

Link suspected that he was dying, because the vague pains that radiated from his chest in the past couple of weeks had become more pronounced with each passing day. His heart was finally giving out and short of a heart transplant, which he definitely could not afford, he seemed destined to leave this earth fairly soon.

It really wasn't that big a deal, he thought. And, in fact, he almost seemed to enjoy observing the pain, where and how it traveled. In a way, he was surprised, given the circumstances of his health, even from the outset, that the Creator had given him so much time on this earth. The only thing he did worry about was Charlie and how she would fare after he was gone. He was her family, her only family for more than a decade and he knew that although she had a hard time expressing her emotions, she loved him deeply. Then again, Charlie loved exploring the deserts and mountains for quartz and jasper and maybe that would be her way of finding herself for her remaining years without him. Link figured that her heart, weak as it was, would soon give out as well and then he would be waiting, his arms wide open, for her to join him.

From his partially opened closet, Link stared at the old beige raincoat he had bought in New York City about 15 years ago, before he met Charlie. He laughed to himself remembering Charlie's happy face, one time when he was riding down the escalator in the Port Authority to meet her. She told him that in the crowds of people at the station, she could spot him by that raincoat. It was his good luck raincoat and, in all the years they spent together, Charlie never knew of the treasure he kept hidden in his left inside pocket, the little leather pouch that contained two arrowheads. An old Navajo he had met a long time ago had sold them to him, saying that he had no idea where they came from but that they were part of his own father's collection. What was it that he had said? It was something about how they connected you to the ancients who came before but also to your future.

He was sure that when Charlie sorted out his things, she would hold onto the raincoat for good memories and maybe she would search the inside pockets and come upon the arrowheads. Link smiled at the thought of her uncovering that secret treasure he had carried with him for so long, and hoped it would not take her too long to find it. Maybe, he would give it a couple of months and if she still hadn't made the discovery he would find a way to get them to her. He could envision her holding the arrowheads together in her hand and then closing her palm tightly. If she concentrated long enough she would know it was a gift for her, and a gentle reminder to think of him every now and then.

Burt Roessler had seen the worried look on Link's face. He suspected that had less to do with Link's own impending death than it had to do with the woman he was leaving behind. Link would pass to the spirit world within the next week and Burt would be writing his condolences to Charlie. He already knew what to say and, although Link was worried, Burt knew that he needn't be. From his desk drawer, he opened his box of assorted cards, found the appropriate one and wrote the following:

Dear Charlie, Link was indeed a gifted gentleman, always seeking answers and never afraid to probe wherever the information might lead. Please accept my sharing your loss. His memory is imperishable and who knows where things lead and what developments lie ahead for you? With love, Burt

Burt Roessler closed the card that he would mail at the appropriate time and stared at its cover wistfully. Sometimes in life, you never dreamed of all the possibilities. On the cover of the card was a beautiful red sunset, that impossibly gorgeous crimson that can only be seen in the southwest, and an eagle flying right into that sunset, with the orange clouds billowing around it. The image was of Monument Valley in Arizona, and there was the Indian, in full regalia, his left arm raised toward the eagle, holding a feather.

Burt put the card away and thought about its romanticized design for a minute. It was of a way of life that had ceased to exist and maybe never had existed in such perfection. He stared out of the window of his office into the distance, his distance of palmettos and periwinkles and a fiery ball of orange setting over a man-made lake. He stared until his cataracts created haloes and his vision dimmed, and then he got up and closed the blinds.

CPSIA information can be obtained at www.ICGtesting.com
Printed in the USA
BVOW04s1021150415

396212BV00002B/63/P